DEATH IN THE DECCAN

Celebrating
30 Years of Publishing
in India

ALSO BY ADITYA SINHA

Kashmir: The Vajpayee Years
(co-author)

The Spy Chronicles: RAW, ISI and the Illusion of Peace
(co-author)

DEATH IN THE DECCAN

ADITYA SINHA

HarperCollins *Publishers* India

First published in India by HarperCollins *Publishers* 2023
4th Floor, Tower A, Building No. 10, DLF Cyber City,
DLF Phase II, Gurugram, Haryana – 122002
www.harpercollins.co.in

2 4 6 8 10 9 7 5 3 1

P-ISBN: 978-93-5699-535-2
E-ISBN: 978-93-5699-536-9

This is a work of fiction and all characters and incidents described in this book are the product of the author's imagination. Any resemblance to actual persons, living or dead, is entirely coincidental.

Typeset in 11.5/15 Minion Pro at
Manipal Technologies Limited, Manipal

Printed and bound at
Replika Press Pvt. Ltd.

FSC www.fsc.org MIX Paper from responsible sources FSC® C016779

This book is produced from independently certified FSC® paper to ensure responsible forest management.

For Mrinalini
Magical Mystery Girl

1

Four men were dead in the same office—their hearts gave up at the same time. They were Vuvuzula Sankatram Reddy, a bankrupt media magnate; his brother, Velveti Rompy Reddy; his son, BJ Reddy; and the media house's human resources head, Sainath Rao.

'Sainath was apparently found with his, er, how should I say this … his little fellow inside a tin of paayasam,' said G.P. Shrivastava, director general (DG) of the Sardar Vallabhbhai Patel (SVP) National Police Academy.

'Little fellow?' Assistant Commissioner of Police (ACP) Mona Ramteke asked. 'Oh!' she added hastily when she realized what the DG meant.

'Yes.'

Mona's stomach rumbled mildly in protest. She had been on her way to the canteen for lunch when she was intercepted by summons to the DG's office. She now stood at attention in his office, facing a desk that was cluttered with police pennants.

DG Shrivastava, leaning back in his chair, peered at her through his bushy salt-and-pepper eyebrows and his oversized tortoiseshell glasses. What he saw was a small and wiry woman with a boy's haircut. Her complexion was a shade darker than wheatish. He scoffed. *She is a Dalit*, he thought, *probably in the force through reservation*.

'Simultaneous fatal heart attacks,' DG Shrivastava said. 'Mrs Sharmila Rao, the chief minister's daughter, wants you to look into it.'

'Of course, sir,' Mona said. 'But why me?'

Mona was curious because this was Hyderabad, not Mumbai where she had spent most of her career. She was in the city for a six-week training, after which her recent promotion from inspector to ACP would be formalized. She knew little about Hyderabad and had never met the chief minister or his daughter. In fact, she knew barely anything about the state police and was yet to meet the city's police commissioner.

'How do I know?' DG Shrivastava said, taking off his glasses. 'The Reddys are an influential lot. Or *were*, I guess. Their newspaper, *Deccan Testament*, is a big deal here. Highest print run in the state and the families are influential. Their deaths will rattle the elite.'

'Sir.'

'You're a high-profile investigator back home, but here, in Hyderabad, you are an outsider. That might count for something, for the powers that be at least. You are probably perfect for the job, whatever it might be. I'm sure I don't need to know. It's a complicated mess, but I am confident that you'll figure it out as you go along.'

'Understood, sir.'

'You will not be officially associated with the investigation, but you will assist it. Or be an advisor, or a consultant, whatever you want to call it. A sub-inspector will assist you.'

'Sir.'

'You will report to the local ACP, Chittla Srinivas Kumar, who in turn reports to DCP Chittla Suresh Kumar. They're brothers. Messy.'

'Sir.'

'Off you go now. No time for lunch. Try to get to the *Deccan Testament* office before the bodies are taken away for post-mortem examinations. Now.'

'Sir.'

Mona saluted and departed, still wondering why Sharmila Rao, the chief minister's daughter, had asked for her. *Shouldn't the minister himself make the request?*

She left the DG's office and was soon in the parking area, where she mounted her Royal Enfield and rode out of the lush campus. She turned on to the Hyderabad–Bengaluru highway and headed to Secunderabad, about forty minutes away depending on the traffic. *Why hadn't the request come from the chief minister's son or his nephew, who are both important state ministers*?

Perhaps it was because Sharmila Rao knew Srividya Suryawanshi, whose father was a powerful politician in

Maharashtra. Sharmila and Srividya had both sat in the previous Parliament and were friends. Sharmila was now in the state assembly as a member of the legislative council. Srividya had probably advised her to rope Mona into the probe.

Mona focused on the unruly traffic as she passed Hussain Sagar Lake. The drivers here were worse than Mumbai or Pune, or even Aurangabad. It was complete chaos, as if all the crazy motorcyclists were on the road. She turned right at the Clock Tower and reached the opaque black gates of the *Deccan Testament* office. She honked her way past the frazzled watchmen and stopped at the two-wheeler parking area.

Mona took off her helmet and was immediately hit by an acrid smell emanating from a nearby drain. She quickly wore a mask that had become a permanent fixture thanks to the COVID-19 pandemic.

A tall and strapping dark-skinned woman in a khaki uniform and peaked cap approached her. Her name tag read Pavani Reddy. She, too, wore a mask.

'Jai Hind, ACP Ma'am. Welcome to Secunderabad,' Sub-Inspector Pavani said, standing at attention and saluting.

'Jai Hind, SI Pavani. Thank you, and at ease.'

Pavani leaned forward and whispered, 'A lot of the sirs are annoyed with you for taking over the investigation, but they dare not say anything.'

'Is that so?' Mona asked.

'They're afraid the chief minister's family will send them on a long deputation to the Indo-Tibetan Border Police.'

What else is new, Mona mused.

ACP Mona and SI Pavani climbed the steps to enter a four-storeyed, old-world, off-white building. They passed a defunct Linotype machine on display behind a glass screen, as if was in a museum, and crossed the foyer. To their left was the entrance to the Classifieds department, where she detected barely any activity. They marched straight to the reception where a lady sat with her head wrapped in a black dupatta, leaving just her sparkling eyes visible. She stood up and gaily sang, 'Good morning, ma'am.' A watchman sprayed sanitiser on Mona's hands, but when he tried to scan her temperature she clicked her tongue sharply, making him step back towards the wall.

Pavani handed Mona a pair of surgical gloves as they entered, turned left and walked past a narrow staircase and an old lift towards a row of glass cabins behind a wall of glazed glass bricks. The office felt strange. The usual hustle-bustle was missing—it was eerily silent. Perhaps it was because of the pandemic-induced low attendance, but even then the unearthly silence dominated the cream walls and the grey linoleum.

They spotted half a dozen staffers crowding around the last cabin. 'Hey, move aside,' Pavani said, using her baton to part the herd so that the two of them could walk through.

Inside, a forensic team was at work. A woman examined the body of a roughly fifty-year-old man sitting on his chair, his chin resting on his immobile chest, his perfectly oiled and combed grey hair shining in the cabin's bright ceiling lights, his grey safari top uncreased. He was surprisingly fair-skinned and looked like he had lived a privileged life.

The black frame of his glasses was gleaming over his unblinking, startled bug eyes. Though his face was at an angle, it was apparent that he wore a light-blue triple-layered surgical mask. As ACP Mona and SI Pavani stepped closer, they saw that behind his desk his pants and underwear were pulled down to his thighs. His shrivelled penis was submerged in a tin of pinkish rice pudding.

'What happened?' Mona asked, pulling on gloves though she had no intention of touching anything.

The lead forensic expert addressed them in Telugu until Pavani uttered the magic phrase: 'English, please.'

'ACP Ma'am,' said SI Padmaja Rao, saluting, 'the victim was masturbating into a tin of paayasam. It was procured from a sacred place of pilgrimage in Kerala.'

'Blasphemous,' Pavani said.

'No wonder his eyes are wide open,' Mona remarked. 'Must have realized that Lord Shiva had a—'

'ACP Ma'am, no one masturbates to death,' Pavani noted.

'Not unless he had a bag over his head or a belt around his neck to induce autoerotic asphyxiation,' SI Padmaja said. 'To heighten his orgasm.'

'Get to the point,' Mona said. 'Cause of death?'

'Ma'am, prima facie evidence shows that it is coronary failure,' she said. 'The post-mortem will surely confirm it.'

'Surely? So, no murder? Natural death? Let's see the other bodies. Were they also found like this?'

'No, ACP Ma'am.'

Mona followed Pavani through the same gawking crowd, a couple of whom Pavani whacked with her baton for good measure. 'Why aren't you idiots wearing masks?' she asked. The crowd evaporated.

They stepped into the lift and Pavani pressed the button for level three. 'Ma'am,' she said to Mona, 'third floor is finance and administration. First floor is marketing and circulation. Second floor is editorial.'

'And the ground floor is for masturbating savarnas.'

Pavani giggled.

The lift opened to a warren of cubicles and workstations. Pavani, however, turned left and walked through a deeply tinted glass double door into a quiet corridor where a constable guarded a heavy wooden door not far down on the right. He clicked his heels to attention as the police officers entered the room.

Behind a well-appointed desk, in front of a bookshelf that occupied the entire wall but was itself filled with fluffy reading, a light-skinned man in his early thirties sat in a swivel chair, his chin immobile on his chest and a fly exploring his woolly hair. He wore a pale green dress shirt and steel grey slacks. There was no mask. Drool had left a trail from the left corner of his slightly agape mouth down to his chin. A forensic team was brushing the tabletop for fingerprints.

Mona lifted the victim's weak chin with a forefinger. His eyes did not look back at her, or anywhere at all.

'Ma'am, his nostrils look raw,' Pavani said. 'Do you think he snorted cocaine early in the morning?'

'The toxicology report will tell us, no doubt,' Mona answered.

'It would account for the coronary failure, ma'am,' Pavani said. 'But that's not all.'

'Of course. Show me.'

They climbed the stairs to the top floor. To the left of the lift were two forbidding and intricately carved teak doors that a constable opened for them. As they stepped inside, Mona felt as if she was stepping on to the set of a Telugu blockbuster involving celestial battles and scantily clad fair damsels. The walls were covered with such opulent paintings and ornate wood carvings. The long corridor had three doors—the one on the left was a double glass door that led to a conference room; further to the right was a narrow teak door that was slightly ajar; and straight ahead, at the end of the corridor, was another imposing carved teak door.

'Ma'am, end of the corridor first.'

'First?'

The teak door led them into a vast wood-panelled room divided into two sections—the one closer was like Aladdin's cave, full of old cameras, books and framed photos, all of which featured a man with a walrus moustache and dyed long black hair slicked back, posing mostly with politicians. The unchanging expression on his fair-skinned face was midway between superciliousness and ennui.

The second section of the room, partitioned by a shelf of objets d'art, was dominated by a desk almost as large as one that might be used by the authoritarian head. The supercilious walrus sat behind it, his prickly chin resting on his chest. He wore a purple dress shirt and his white trousers were still on, but the face mask was nowhere to be seen. Behind him was a tinted window that muffled the sounds of invisible traffic, and to his sides were display shelves of generic idols and dubious trophies. The day's newspaper was on the desk in front of him.

Mona went around the desk to lift his chin and examine his face. He bore an uncanny resemblance to someone she had seen before.

'Mahishasura,' Pavani said.

Yes, that was it! Mahishasura was a demon speared in the heart by Goddess Durga at every puja pandal Mona had visited in her childhood. The victim's eyes had the same look of surrender.

'Heart failure?' Mona asked.

Pavani nodded.

From the victim's chair, Mona looked across the room towards a narrow hall? that held up a large-screen TV. Deeper into the room were bookshelves. On the back wall was the victim's photo. A forensic team was wiping down the frame.

'And the last dead body?'

Pavani nodded and turned to lead her out.

They went back out into the corridor and through the teak door. This room was similar to the third-floor room that they had visited, but with subdued lighting from the false ceiling. A man in an azure dress shirt and thick, spiky greying hair sat behind the desk, dead like the others.

Mona lifted his maskless and lifeless face by the chin and nearly dropped it after seeing the venal look frozen on it.

'He looks like he was plotting someone's murder.'

'Or plotting to rob someone.'

Mona gently placed the victim's head back on his chest.

'Can you tell me who each of these dead men are?'

'Ma'am,' Pavani said, drawing a deep breath, 'the first one, on the ground floor, was the HR manager, Vaniti Sainath Vulvapuram Rao, fifty-three years old. Mr Sai, for short. The other three were from the Reddy family that used to own this newspaper.'

'Used to? What were they doing here then?'

'Ma'am, it's a complex legal story whose details I've not totally grasped.'

'We'll figure it out soon enough. Tell me about these family members.'

'The patriarch, the one in the largest room, is Vuvuzula Sankatram Reddy, sixty years old. This is his brother, Velveti Rompy Reddy, fifty-eight years old. On the floor below is Sankatram's only son, Babloo Jubilee Reddy, or BJ Reddy, thirty-three years old.'

Mona paused. 'No more men left in the family?'

'Sankatram has a wife and a married daughter in Delhi. Rompy has a daughter, but no grandchildren. BJ is childless.'

'And they no longer own this newspaper?'

'Yet they are rich … their wealth is secretly stashed abroad,' Pavani said. 'How strange that they all had heart attacks and died, along with the HR manager, on the same day.'

'Four people in the same office don't die of simultaneous heart attacks by coincidence. There is no such thing. It has to be planned. It has to be murder.'

'Whoever did it must be devious.'

'No doubt.'

'How will we ever find out who it is?'

Mona's phone buzzed just then. She looked at the screen, but it was not a number she recognized. Truecaller was of no help either. She declined it, but before she could return her phone to the pocket, it buzzed again.

'Yes?'

'This is Sharmila Rao, MLC.'

Right. The chief minister's daughter, and the reason she was here right now. 'Yes, ma'am,' Mona said.

'How does it look?'

'It's a …' Mona looked at Pavani. 'It's a puzzle, ma'am.'

'A puzzle?'

'At the moment, ma'am.' Mona paused for further instructions.

'Well, whatever you do, and whatever you find, I merely ask one thing of you.'

'Yes, ma'am?'

'Let me know before you tell my brother.'

2

The next call that Mona received almost immediately after Sharmila's was from another unlisted number. 'Hello?'

'ACP Mona, is it?' the caller said. 'C.N.T. Rao here.'

Chandramohan Nageswara Tommy Rao was Sharmila's brother, the Urban Business and Information Technology (UBIT) minister in Hyderabad. At the academy, UBIT was called 'Urban Blight and Indifferent Technology'. Being the son of Chief Minister Chandrababu Ramalingam Rao, CNT was de facto the second most powerful man in the state. After all, his father had taken a backseat to allow him to use the wealthy state as his ATM.

'Yes, of course, sir.'

'Tommy.'

Mona said nothing, waiting for him to get to the point.

'What have you got?'

Mona steeled herself. 'Four dead bodies, three of which are Reddys. All apparent heart attacks, Minister Sahib.'

'Yes, yes, I know. Three Reddys and one Rao. No foul play?'

'Not as yet, Minister Sahib,' Mona said, deciding not to reveal her suspicions at this moment.

CNT paused. 'Whatever turns up, please inform me before anyone else. Even before my father,' he said and hung up.

Mona turned to Pavani.

'The corpses are being taken to Gandhi Medical College and Hospital for post-mortem,' Pavani said.

Mona's phone rang again. The screen told her it was Commissioner Chandravardhan, chief of the Hyderabad City Police.

'Jai Hind, sir,' she greeted.

'Yes, yes, Jai Hind,' he stammered. 'ACP Ramteke, I'm extremely happy and completely relieved that you're handling the case.'

Mona's face brightened. 'Why thank you, CP Sir.'

'But don't tell anyone I said so. If you do, I'll face a revolt from all the Velamas and Reddys.'

'Okay, CP Sir.'

'If you need anything, just let me know. Anything.'

'Thank you, CP Sir.'

'Just keep it quiet. Don't tell anyone that I have offered you help. And don't tell anyone that I asked you not to tell anyone.'

'Yes, CP Sir.'

Commissioner Chandravardhan put the phone down.

Mona turned to Pavani, who was gawking at her. 'Anything on the CCTVs?'

'Nothing, ma'am. There are cameras in every corridor of the building, but there is no footage. Not from the gate, not from the lifts and not from Sankatram Reddy's room.'

'How is that possible? Did someone erase the tapes? Dastardly.'

'No, ma'am. Due to the company's cost-cutting measures, the cameras were kept switched off,' Pavani said. 'The only time they were turned on was for the union's general body meetings on the premises. The management would then use the CCTV footage to punish the organizers.'

'Cell phones? Computers?'

'Yes, ma'am. The cybercrime unit has taken away two cell phones from each of the victims, the hard drives from each of their desktops, and also BJ Reddy's personal computer. They will go through all the call records and emails.'

Mona's phone rang again. 'Ma,' she said. 'Not now. I'm on a case. Yes, in Hyderabad. Okay, okay. Later.'

Pavani smiled. 'Is your Amma pestering you to get married?'

'No, she gave up long back, when I crossed thirty,' Mona said, putting her phone on silent mode. 'She wanted to know what I had for breakfast.'

'Sighing loudly, Mona asked, Do we have a timeline, or do we have to wait for the autopsies?'

'Ma'am, the Reddys came to office around 11 a.m. Rao came half an hour before that. The bodies were discovered one after the other, during lunch, around 1 p.m. First Rao's and then the Reddys' who usually left for home, or for lunch, by 1 p.m. When they did not exit their rooms by 1.10, the attendant went in to each room and found them dead.'

'Between 11 a.m. and 1.10 p.m.,' Mona noted. 'Well, even the medical examiner won't be able to narrow the timeline more than that.'

'Yes, ma'am.'

'Have someone talk to the receptionist and get me a list of all the outsiders who entered and left the building after 10 a.m. Let's also have a list of people in the building this morning. Doesn't look like much, but it might help to narrow down our suspects.'

'Yes, ma'am.'

'Also, let's begin questioning people. We can have a set-up in Sankatram's room to interview the employees in attendance. I don't know how many of them have ever been in that room, but whoever has must have found it intimidating. That should give us a minor advantage.'

'Yes, ma'am," Pavani said with a grin. 'They could do with a bit more trauma.'

Mona chose a spot deep inside Sankatram's room. She ordered a constable to take down his portrait. She had the constable position it against the wall.

A plush chair was dragged from behind Sankatram's desk for her. Mindful of social distancing, another chair was placed a little away for Pavani, but there was none for those to be questioned.

'Shall we start from the top?' Mona asked.

'That would be L.S.D. Gopalaiah,' Pavani said, checking her notes.

'Sounds promising.'

A frail man, resembling a skeleton, walked in but looked as if he was on the verge of collapsing. He peered through his tinted glasses in a metal frame. His pencil moustache and hair were pitch black from an industrial-strength dye. He looked around before asking, 'Can I take one chair?'

Pavani gave him a resounding slap on the head. He stumbled on to a nearby bookshelf and in steadying himself pulled down a few books about the 1948 Hyderabad police action.

'Pavani.'

'Don't worry, ma'am,' Pavani said. 'I have enough hand sanitizer.'

'You can't give me the third degree,' Gopalaiah said. 'I'm L.S.D. Gopalaiah, the company's deputy CEO.'

'Lickspittle Gopalaiah? Where's your mask?'

'Right here,' Gopalaiah reached into his pocket and pulled out a surgical mask before stuffing it back in. Noticing the two police officials' expressions, he quickly pulled it back out and wore it.

'How would you like some paayasam stuffed up your deputy CEO backside?' Pavani said.

'Really, Pavani?' Mona stepped in. 'Stand up straight, Mr Deputy CEO.'

She stared at his face for a long, quiet moment.

'How long have you been with the company?'

'From the start of my career. I began as a cashier in Rajahmundry. Worked my way to the top.'

'A regular Tenali Rama,' Pavani smirked.

'What is the Reddys' history with this newspaper?' Mona asked.

'They were the owners.'

'Still?'

'No, not any more. In 2017, they filed for bankruptcy under the Insolvency and Bankruptcy Code and their case went to the National Company Law Tribunal (NCLT). Then in 2019, the NCLT handed the company over to an investment firm called Shrek Fund.'

'The city's number one newspaper went bankrupt? How is that possible?'

'Oh, these people … they ran amok. Now they're dead. They were no less than Ravana, Kumbhakarna and Meghnad.' Gopalaiah looked at Sankatram Reddy's portrait and lowered his voice to a whisper. 'Basically, Sankatram Reddy wanted to be like Vijay Mallya—a fugitive billionaire living a good life.'

'A discount-rate version of the billionaire? With the exclusive bikini calendars?'

'Yes. In fact, someone had suggested the Reddys bring out their own calendar … of bikini-clad women,' Gopalaiah said, seemingly searching his memory. 'They started a cricket team, too, for the Twenty-20 league. They also had a chain of bookshops.'

'They were literary-minded?' Mona was curious.

'No, no. Who reads books? It was a loss-making business meant solely for laundering money, especially the cash transactions at the newspaper.'

'Cash transactions?'

'Yes. The Reddys wanted to start an airline and call it "Deccan Turbulence". They bought real estate all over the country to hide their black money.'

'What went wrong?'

'The timing. The Reddys were awash in easy money till 2011. Like many others, they were borrowing more than they could return. They fell behind on interest payments. They became reckless about juggling different creditors. They were borrowing from one bank to pay off another. And you know the corruption in public sector banks. Officials would approve loans without due diligence. They all fed at the same trough.'

'And you didn't?' Pavani remarked.

'I am just a dedicated employee trying to provide his children higher education, which is not an easy thing. I have never indulged in easy money,' Gopalaiah said. 'The Reddys, well, now they're dead. They might have continued to juggle all their debts and liabilities had it not been for a streak of bad luck.'

'Such as?' Mona said.

'They had placed an order with the Aviation Industry Corporation of China, but the deal fell through due to the government of India not granting approval. The civil aviation minister had endless demands. Then the cricket team was suspended because of complaints about online gambling. All their ventures fell apart. Liquidity became a problem.'

'Bad luck, indeed.'

'Also, they made lots of enemies. Everyone was out for them. When everyone is against you, bad luck finds its way to your door much quicker.'

'How much did they owe?'

'The banks say about ₹8,000 crore, but much of that is unnecessary interest. It should be ₹3,000 crore, if you ask me. If we are unable to pay now, it is wrong to keep tacking on interest. Anyway, it's notional money. Bad practices by selfish banks.'

'Why did the newspaper have to repay the other companies' bad loans?'

'The newspaper was the holding company, which is why it was saddled with the bad loans. The one guaranteed money-making venture, *Deccan Testament*, which had been showing profits for seventy-five years, was burdened with the debt and then handed over to Shrek Fund in 2019.'

'Then why were the Reddys on the premises? Where are the Shrek people?'

There is an ongoing legal case over the "Deccan Testament" title. One bank claimed it and appealed at the tribunal. Shrek Fund's promoters don't want to move in till the legal dispute is cleared. So, the Reddys were still in control even though they had no money for salaries or newsprint. And newsprint costs have gone up in the last decade. It's not cheap to print a newspaper.'

'So, the case isn't over?'

'Surely the police are familiar with the slow wheels of justice,' Gopalaiah said.

Mona considered this.

'Anyway, what a tragedy! With the Reddys out of the picture now, maybe Shrek Fund can come in and take over, infuse cash and make the paper profitable.'

'I'd say these four deaths were most profitable for Shrek Fund,' Mona noted.

'If they weren't heart attacks, you might think Shrek had them murdered,' Gopalaiah said, laughing. 'But well, they were just heart attacks. Too much of a coincidence though. BJ Reddy was too young to have a heart attack.'

Mona decided to drop a bomb on the deputy CEO.

'What if they *were* murdered?'

Gopalaiah's eyes widened and his whole demeanour changed. 'Murdered?' he stammered.

'We don't know yet. The post-mortem report is pending. But if it is just simultaneous heart attacks, then it is bad luck for the Reddys.'

'And for Sai,' Gopalaiah added.

'And for Sainath Rao.'

'Tell me, Mr Deputy CEO, did you meet any of the four victims this morning?'

'Of course, of course. First I met Sai at the parking lot and he gave me a small container of homemade paayasam. Not the one from Kerala. Now I don't know what to do with it. How can I eat it or give it to my wife, or even thank God for it?'

'At the time of his death, Sai was holding paayasam, but it was not homemade,' Pavani said.

'Still, just the thought of it,' Gopalaiah said, lost in his thoughts. Mona could not tell if he was visualizing Sainath going at it, or just the paayasam itself. 'I can't,' he muttered.

'After that, you did not meet him?'

'I did ... We had a meeting with the chief financial officer, Bhoolchuk Maaf, in Mr Rompy Reddy's room. We discussed how to delay the salary payments by another two weeks. I went back to my room after that.'

'You saw nothing unusual?'

'No, ma'am.'

'You met nobody else?'

'I had a meeting with BJ,' Gopalaiah said. 'He had hired a newspaper designer, on the advice of our former editor-in-chief. But the designer had not been paid for several months, so the work had stopped. We had to figure out the bare minimum amount to pay him to get the work restarted.'

'And he was not showing any signs of heart attack while you were in his room?'

'No, ma'am.'

'How did you hear about the deaths?'

'First, Ms Sadhana, who worked under Sai in HR, called me. She was crying and talking incoherently. So, I went to her and found Sai's body. I thought we should remove the tin, but the receptionist had already called the police, so I thought it better not to touch anything.'

'Smart move.'

'Just then, Ms Rajkumari, the Reddys' secretary, called up screaming that the chairman, I mean, Mr S.R. Reddy, was dead. My first thought was if he too had any paayasam on his lap. Then she called up again, screaming about Rompy. I went up to the fourth floor and was relieved to see that both men had their pants on. Then she called a third time about BJ.'

'And then?'

'And then my mobile battery died.'

'No, I mean, what did you do after that?'

'I had to disburse some funds for the payment of salaries in Vijayawada and Vizag, so I got busy with that,' Gopalaiah said. 'What to do? There is such an unrelenting pressure when it comes to salaries. Union people get aggressive sometimes. Staffers, too, write so many emails.'

'You didn't go and check on the dead people?'

'I was going to, but then I thought that if Shrek Fund was coming in, I should present the company in the best light. The dead are anyway gone, and because of coronavirus I'm not going near any cremation or funeral.'

'That's cold.'

'What to do? There's no threat of the Reddys sacking me now,' Gopalaiah said philosophically. 'If anything, I should worry about Shrek Fund. No doubt I will be the first person they will want to sack.'

'Why?'

'Shrek Fund thinks I'm a stumbling block. But I'm not even the promoter. They think I fudge figures and withhold details, and that I don't discuss company plans. But how could I when the Reddys had instructed me to do so?'

'The Reddys did not allow you to share information with the new owners?'

'The Reddys kept referring to Shrek Fund as "investors", not as the "new owners",' Gopalaiah said. 'They planned to stick on forever. Whatever their plan was, I had to follow instructions. I know that as deputy CEO, I'm the number one target for Shrek Fund.'

'So, by not going to the cremation, you plan to distance yourself from the Reddys,' Mona said. 'Do you think Shrek Fund will buy it?'

'Of course not, but I have to try.'

'In any case, Shrek Fund had the most to profit from the Reddy deaths, no?'

'Yes, ma'am.'

'Okay. You can go, but don't leave the office just yet. We may still need you.'

As Gopalaiah left, Mona mused that she now had a suspect, or suspects, and a motive of corporate murder. All she was missing was the confirmation that it murder, and not just a horrible coincidence. And if it was in fact murder, she was missing a murder weapon.

3

The medical examiner, Dr Dharma Irukulla, phoned Mona and told her that though the victims had died between 11 a.m. and 1 p.m., they had not died simultaneously because rigor mortis had started to appear on just one of the faces—S.R. Reddy.

'Also,' Dr Dharma said, 'prima facie, none of them appeared to have suffered a heart attack due to natural causes. Rompy Reddy was possibly en route to one, given the level of plaque in his left coronary artery, but it hadn't reached the stage of blocking the vessel entirely and causing an arrythmia.'

'So, the heart attacks were sudden but not natural?'

'Yes. I found no clots, no cholesterol, no fatty deposits, no calcium and no fibrin that usually triggers an attack in someone suffering from a heart disease. In Babloo Jubilee's case, a toxicology report will tell us how much cocaine he had in his system. But there was no tear in his aorta, no unusual atherosclerosis, and it doesn't look like the heart walls had thickened. I don't think he had a heart attack because of a cocaine overdose.'

'I suppose he would have had residue in his nostrils.'

'True, but that can be from the night before.'

'How will the toxicology report help?'

'Maybe there are metabolites that will give us a clue. Something is not right about these four deaths. The same office, and two on the same floor. Though an autopsy can't ascertain the exact time, something tells me their deaths were staggered. Perhaps by twenty minutes or so.'

'But you can't be certain?'

'I can't be sure. Twenty minutes is an average. It could be half an hour between the first two deaths and only five minutes between the next two. It is difficult to pinpoint.'

'It might be a stretch, Dr Dharma, but could the heart attacks have been induced one after the other by someone with a criminal intent?'

'A deeper examination is necessary to be sure. Perhaps they were injected with a reactive agent. If so, the agent would have metabolized into chemicals we would find in the toxicology report. It would help confirm that these were murders and how they were committed.'

'Did you find syringe punctures?'

'Not yet, but we're looking. We have a chemical that can phosphoresce in special lighting. The chemical reacts with the reactive agent, and it gives off electrons that we can see in the special lighting.'

'Artificially inducing heart attacks sounds very dramatic.'

'The Nazis used phenol injections at Auschwitz. The Russians, under Stalin, induced vascular embolisms by injecting syringes of air into veins. Maybe modern spy agencies still use them, though the Russians sure seem happy to openly poison dissidents.'

'Are you saying the Government of India could have killed these four people?'

'No, no, of course not. Bharat Mata ki jai! It is possible that one person alone did this.'

'A terrorist?'

'No, no, ACP. Just a deranged individual or criminal.'

'How so?'

'Calcium gluconate and potassium phosphate, or both, can induce a heart attack, but they would have to be administered separately. These chemicals raise potassium levels in the body and appear as routine metabolites in a toxicology report. There's also succinylcholine, used by anaesthesiologists, that breaks down into metabolites routinely found in the body's own chemistry. And then there's potassium chloride, which would also show up in a toxicology report as high level of potassium that the body releases during a heart attack.'

'Sounds like the murderer has medical background,' Mona said.

'Or a pharmacist.'

'How long before we have something definitive?'

'I'll try for the earliest. If you submit a written request, we'll open up their hearts to visually inspect the walls and valves and let you know. But I can confidently say that murder must not be ruled out.'

Mona hung up. Pavani stood waiting with a list of the people who were in the building during the critical two hours and ten minutes.

'Ma'am, since the lockdown, the administration and other staff have been coming to the office in rotation, which is every alternate day. So, only half of the admin staff was present. The marketing department works out of office mostly, and the editorial department arrives late in the afternoon as they work till after midnight. However, some editorial staff was here at the time: ex-editor Sukhi Puri, recently terminated editor Rocky Borkataki and current resident editor Canning Sairam.'

Mona brightened at the mention of Rocky Borkataki. They had met during the investigation of Bastard Das's murder in Mumbai some years back. 'Is Rocky still in the office?'

'No, ma'am, but we can summon him.'

'Any other visitors?'

'Several, ma'am,' Pavani said, 'including two Tollywood producers. Rowdy Panja Naidu met Sankatram Reddy, while Raghupathi Pullaiah met Rompy. Maximillian Reddy, an industrialist, and Swami Bonanand, also came to meet Sankatram. A realtor named Bharathi Rao came for Rompy.'

'Anyone for the others?'

'A starlet, Gurleen Kaur, met BJ. A former player from their cricket team, Richard Lessness, also met him. A minor functionary of the Sanskriti Suraksha Sangh (SSS), Nageshwar Rao, came to meet Canning Sairam. Dr Kiran Mulukutla, a cardiologist, dropped in to meet the features editor, Mrs Magnolia Reddy, who is Sankatram Reddy's wife … widow. She was wailing and slapping people, so they let Sukhi Puri take her home.'

'No worries. We can interview the two of them together,' Mona said. 'Where does Magnolia stay?'

'Jubilee Hills. Posh area.'

'I take it that none of the other visitors are in the building at the moment?'

'No, ma'am.'

'Okay, so we have a number of away-from-crime-scene interviews to conduct.'

'Yes, ma'am.'

Mona's phone rang just then. 'Yes, ma'am?'

'Please, call me Sharmila.'

'Of course, ma'am.'

'Can you talk?'

'Yes, ma'am. But there isn't much to report at the moment.'

'Four heart attacks! The TV channels are going to town with speculations. I can hardly believe it to be a coincidence.'

'Yes, ma'am, but we have no conclusive evidence suggesting otherwise,' Mona said. 'At least not yet.'

'Keep me posted.'

As soon as Sharmila Rao ended the call, Commissioner Chandravardhan rang Mona.

'Sir.'

'Ramteke, the TV channels are asking me about some conspiracy theory about the four heart attacks.'

'Sir, I think Hyderabad witnesses more than four heart attacks each day. But maybe not on the same premises.'

'True, true. What do I tell these bastards?'

Tell them to fuck off, a voice inside Mona's head commanded. Out loud, she said, 'Sir, please tell them that the investigation is on and we don't have any answers for them yet. Till then it would be helpful if they don't concoct any theories from there end.

The commissioner had barely cut the call when Mona's phone rang again. This time, her face lit up. 'Hello, boss,' she said, her voice sounding chirpy.

'You sound chirpy.'

It was Sandesh Solvekar, an ACP but still posted in Gadchiroli, far away from Mumbai, presumably combatting non-urban 'urban naxals'.

'You sound low, sir.'

'Arre, Ramteke, please don't call me "sir". We are the same rank. "Boss", though it sounds filmy, is better.'

'Okay, boss.'

'What to do, Ramteke? You know what's worse than a lockdown in the city? A lockdown in the forest.'

'How many cops does it take to impose a lockdown in the forest?'

'Is that a trick question? I would have ignored the lockdown order if the district collector wasn't living in the next bungalow. She comes over all the time to nag me.'

'Who is the collector?'

'Pushpa Purandare. Do you know her?'

'I've seen her,' Mona said. 'She's a fox. And she's got a big bum.'

'You know, she sends reports to the chief minister saying that I'm not enforcing the law. Nobody here wears a mask, not even for thirty seconds. Even those with a cheap mask leave it hanging on the chin. How many youngsters can we slap around? Perhaps she will be impressed if people wear masks in the district headquarters at least.'

'What a bitch.'

'That's not the worst. The isolation, the loneliness, the waiting and the arguments over the phone really get to you.'

Mona said nothing. *Poor Boss*, she thought. He was too good a person. She thought of telling him to spank the collector; it would probably end the nagging and the complaints, but she refrained from doling out unsolicited advice.

'The TV channels are reporting the four deaths due to heart attacks in a newspaper office,' Solvekar said.

'Boss,' Mona said and then paused. 'It may be more than a coincidence.'

'What?' Solvekar went quiet for a moment. 'Sounds like an interesting case. How I would have loved to come and help you. After all, I'm only a nine-hour drive from Hyderabad. But I'm sure the chief minister's people are already sitting on your head. It doesn't sound enticing at all.'

Mona thought for another second. 'I will call you and pick your brain at some point.'

'Anytime, Ramteke.'

Mona hung up and put her phone on silent again.

'Ma'am, shall we start with Sadhana who worked closely with Sainath Rao?'

'How closely?'

'Ma'am, if it were that close, he wouldn't have put his dick into the paayasam.'

Good point, Mona thought and nodded.

Pavani looked out of the glass door and gestured for a short, plump lady in a lemon polyester sari, a pink blouse and an oily plait to come in. She was dry-eyed and, though she wore a cheap surgical mask, her eyes conveyed a business-like attitude.

'Sadhana, tell us about Sainath Rao.'

'Ma'am,' Sadhana said and then the words abruptly gushed out of her. 'Mr Sai was an efficient man. He didn't have many original ideas, but he was good at following orders. He was lucky, I think. He followed office timings. He had a big car, and was always spic-and-span. He was God-fearing. And he always brought me paayasam from a famous pilgrimage in Kerala. Thinking of it now makes me want to vomit.'

'The facts, please,' Mona said. 'Why do you say he was lucky?'

'Ma'am, he was promoted as HR manager by default when the company declared bankruptcy three years ago.

The previous manager was sacked for embezzling funds. So, Mr Sai, who had joined from Indus Tin Ltd. eighteen years ago as a clerk, was promoted. By default.'

'That means you too could, by default, become the next HR manager?'

Sadhana's face lit up and then fell. 'Doubtful,' she said. 'Shrek Fund will bring in its own HR manager.'

'How can you be so certain?'

'Last winter, Shrek Fund sent a gentleman from Kolkata. He spent a week interviewing people in each department. A lot of forms were filled out. He noted that the place was run poorly and that no professional HR practices were in place. He will probably take Mr Sai's place when Shrek Fund takes over. I am sure they are happy that Mr Sai masturbated to death.'

'So, Sai wasn't a good manager?'

'Not at all, ma'am. He made me draft all the termination letters this past year when editions were shut. Dozens of those who were sacked wrote to him again and again for final settlements. But because the company had no money, he never replied to their emails. And now this heart attack. So sad! Who will look after his mentally retarded son now?'

'That's not the correct term.'

'Sorry, ma'am. He doted on his son who has Down's syndrome, I think. The boy is twenty years old, but mentally he is only five. Mr Sai even took him to that pilgrimage in Kerala this year. The boy could only travel by car; travelling by train was not convenient. But this time Mr Sai decided to splurge and bought airline tickets to Kochi. Poor boy.'

'Did Mr Sai act differently of late?'

'Not at all, ma'am,' Sadhana was quick to answer. 'We came in to work every other day due to the pandemic, unlike the marketing staff that worked from home. We worked for an hour or so and then left. The thumb scanner has not been used since Covid began, so attendance was not electronically monitored. We could come and go as per our own convenience. Nobody in administration worked from home; we attended to all official matters from the office only. Mr Sai had been complaining loudly that no journalists came to work, and what kind of a newspaper office was it.'

'But the paper came out every day?'

'Yes, ma'am.'

Mona paused. 'Would anyone have any reason to kill Mr Sai?'

'Well, maybe the staffers who were terminated or are still waiting for their November 2019 salaries. But even if they wanted to, they are late. A heart attack has proved to be faster than an assassin's knife.'

'What assassin?'

Sadhana drew a blank. 'I don't know, ma'am, I was just saying.'

'So, he had no enemies?'

'Can't say, ma'am. He was one of those people who smiled at everyone while twisting the knife in their backs.'

'A typical Telugu Brahmin,' Pavani observed.

'Or a Brahmin from anywhere,' Mona said.

'Ma'am, I can't say such things or I'll be sacked,' Sadhana remarked.

'Nobody in the office was his enemy?'

'Maybe in editorial. I think Sukhi Puri used to summon him and make him stand outside her cabin just to scream at him. The former editor-in-chief seemed friendly enough, but he was a north Indian so Mr Sai didn't trust him.'

'I thought Rocky was from the Northeast?' Mona said.

'Yes, ma'am, same thing. He didn't trust Canning Sairam Sir either. Called him "Cunning Sairam". Rocky Sir came up with that name.'

'Why didn't he trust Canning Sairam?'

'Sairam Sir was a fellow Brahmin, but he was a Brahmin from Vizag.'

A paranoiac with his penis in paayasam, Mona mused. 'Okay then.'

Sadhana was dismissed.

'What do you think?' Pavani said.

'Too early to say anything.'

Pavani pointed to another short, dumpy woman in a purple sari and lavender blouse and waved her in. Ms Rajkumari, secretary to all the three Reddys said that she had not noticed any unusual activity lately.

'Ma'am, they came in occasionally for an hour or so, sometimes even half an hour, due to Covid,' she said. 'But they made us sit for the whole day.'

'Did any of them seem disturbed or tense lately?'

'Well, ma'am. There was definitely tension because the ongoing case at the National Company Law Tribunal was nearing a conclusion. Shrek Fund was expected to play a bigger role after that. Maybe it would have taken over. Also, the Reddys were trying to scrounge up money to pay salaries. They didn't even have money to pay the pending corporate phone bill, much less the current dues.'

'Aside from business matters,' Mona asked, 'anything on the personal front?'

'Rompy Sir looked a bit tense. The union had threatened to strike because they hadn't been paid their May wages, and the last time they were paid was half of the wages in April, two months ago. With the holiday season coming, they put pressure on Rompy Sir. The union's general secretary, Ghattu Katcha, even met Rompy Sir this morning, but he came out of the room looking furious.'

'What about the patriarch?'

'Sankatram Sir? I can't say, ma'am. His face was always clouded behind cigar smoke.'

'And the son?'

'Yes, ma'am. BJ Sir was feeling very stressed ever since the former editor-in-chief called him an illiterate eunuch.'

'What!' Mona was taken aback. 'Rocky called him that to his face?'

'No, ma'am. Borkataki Sir had messaged his then second-in-command, Canning Sairam Sir, on an app. Sairam Sir took a screenshot and forwarded it to BJ Sir who had Borkataki Sir sacked. Now Sairam Sir is in charge in Hyderabad.'

'He sacked Borkataki for calling him an "illiterate eunuch" in a private message on an encrypted app?'

'No, ma'am. Mr Sai sent a termination notice citing a differet reason. It said that when Borkataki Sir joined fourteen months back, the paper had sixteen editions, which had come down to just four. Also, advertising revenue had dried up due to the economic slowdown and pandemic restrictions. Cost-cutting was also citied as a reason.'

'Poor Rocky.'

'BJ Sir was so upset at being called an illiterate eunuch that I thought he would have a heart attack,' Rajkumari said. 'Maybe that is what it was, but who can say for sure? I know for a fact that he once telephoned an actual eunuch to ask if he looked like an illiterate eunuch, or even a literate one. Rocky Sir was a disrespectful man.'

'Who was this eunuch?'

'Someone called Manjula.'

'If he was so tense, why did he call a starlet in for a meeting this morning?'

'Ma'am,' Rajkumari said. 'Miss Gurleen could only come at this time before her shooting.'

'What shooting?' Pavani interrupted. 'There are no film shoots happening because of the pandemic.'

Rajkumari shrugged.

'Where is the shoot?' Mona asked.

Rajkumari began to tremble. 'Ma'am, I have no idea. I just fix the meetings.'

'Anyway, she wouldn't have come to office just to suck his dick,' Pavani said.

Rajkumari stuck her tongue out in horror.

'Why were the two film producers here? And why did they meet different brothers?'

'I don't know, ma'am,' Ms Rajkumari said. 'But they all appeared cheerful, the producers as well as the Reddys.'

'And the swami?'

'Chairman Sir always called Swami Bonanand to find out what will happen in the next tribunal hearing.'

'Who's Chairman Sir?' Pavani asked.

'Ma'am, Sankatram Reddy Sir.'

'I thought the company was no longer his.'

'Ma'am, it's true that he had no legal standing, but he was the chairman for so many years that it has become a habit.'

'The swami can predict judicial adjournments, postponements, reserved judgments and other creaking of the wheels of justice?'

'I don't know. Swami Bonanand advised the company to declare a holiday on Ganesh Chaturthi six years back,' Rajkumari said. 'Also, he said to keep the Ganapati yantram at the entrance of the office. He also said that the generator house in the southeast corner needed to be demolished and that the car parking had to be filled with mud. Nothing seemed to work though.'

'What a surprise!' Pavani scoffed.

'What about the industrialist, Maximillian Reddy, who was also here?' Mona asked.

'Ma'am, he was a good friend of Chairman Sir, though sometimes they fought and the newspaper printed front-page stories against him. When the company was angry, the headlines called him "Maxi" Reddy, like the long dress. Otherwise he was referred to as "Maximum" Reddy.'

'Currently they were buddies, I take it?'

Rajkumari shrugged.

'Who will know more about the dealings the Reddys had with these producers and industrialists?'

Again, Rajkumari shrugged.

Mona sized her up. 'Okay, get out,' she said. 'But don't leave the office yet. We may need to talk to you again.'

Rajkumari scurried out of the room.

Mona's phone vibrated. It was C.N.T. Rao.

'Yes, Minister Sahib?'

'Ramteke, I'm told that you are working on the theory that these four deaths are homicides.'

Mona inhaled sharply. 'Minister Sahib, I am still interviewing people. I don't have any theories as of now.'

'And yet, word at the Gandhi Hospital's forensics department is that at least one of the deaths is a murder.'

4

Mona was annoyed. Either Dr Dharma, or someone working under her, had blabbed to the minister, as a result of which he had given Mona an earful. When he ended the call, Mona telephoned Dr Dharma.

'Why?' she asked, exasperated.

By the end of their conversation, it became clear to Mona that Dr Dharma had not called C.N.T. Rao. However, the doctor had no control over her deputies and clerical staff, and many of them were beholden to the government.

'Many of them nearly flunked in the private medical colleges that charged lakhs as capitation fees, and after scraping through college they paid lakhs to be recruited for this government job,' Dr Dharma told Mona. 'They will never withhold information from this, or any, government.'

True, Mona mused. The minister, after all, was the heir apparent to the chief minister. He was going to loom large in Hyderabad for the foreseeable future.

'But that aside, it is definitive that Sankatram Reddy was murdered,' Dr Dharma added. 'A vascular air embolism. Someone injected perhaps 160 or 180 mm of air into his artery.'

'You found the injection mark?'

'Yes, but it wasn't easy. We did an x-ray of the pulmonary arteries and confirmed it with a transoesophageal echocardiogram,' Dr Dharma said. 'So, we searched for an entry point for the air and found it camouflaged by an old burn injury on his neck. Who knows how he got burnt there! I can tell you one thing though. Whoever killed him knew the injury existed. The killer probably knew the victim intimately.'

'Thank you,' Mona said. 'Now the grind begins.'

'Yes, unfortunately none of the others died of a vascular air embolism. We need to determine a cause of death for them. After the Sankatram Reddy finding, I'm presuming they were also killed.'

After Dr Dharma hung up, Mona called up Sharmila Rao and informed her of the development.

'This will be music to my father's and brother's ears,' Sharmila said. 'They passionately hated Sankatram Reddy. Haughty fellow, they said.'

'Is it, ma'am?'

'Thanks, and keep me posted. My brother no doubt is keeping a close tab as well. Don't let him cow you down. Ultimately, he has to rely on you for the truth.'

'Yes, ma'am.'

The MLC disconnected.

'I need to get out of the office and clear my head,' Mona said to her.

'Ma'am, we've located the starlet and one of the producers, Rowdy Panja Naidu, 'Pavani said. 'They are at a film shoot, at Ikea.'

'Ikea? That furniture store?'

'Yes, ma'am. It's gigantic. I went once. It's out in Hitech city and takes an hour to reach. It'll get late; it's already 4 p.m.'

'So what? Film shoots go on till late.'

'Yes, ma'am. It's just that the chief financial officer has been here all day and requested to be the next interview. Also, the resident editor says he will get busy by six, and he may not have time after that for an interview. And Mr Rocky has returned.'

'Oh, him first. The others can wait.'

Rocky entered, waving a hello at Mona. He hadn't changed much since she saw him in Mumbai eight years ago, other than the greying hair and thicker waist. He still walked with a distracted air. Today, he was wearing red-framed glasses and a red mask.

'You're an ACP now?' he said by way of greeting. 'May I have some hand sanitiser?'

'Rocky Sir,' Mona smiled. 'What are you doing here today? I'm told you've parted ways with the *Deccan Testament*.'

'Deccan Testicle!' Rocky corrected her. 'True, true. I was sacked. A blessing in disguise.'

'You have another job?'

'No, no. I'm trying to manage my health. High blood pressure, for the first time in my life. Imagine that! Thank you, Deccan Testicle. Thank you, City of Nizams. And thank you to the Nizam's biggest testicle, Sankatram Reddy. A pretend-Nizam. Like the Raja of Marh in *A Suitable Boy*. Have you seen it yet?'

'No, but I had read the novel in my teens.'

'Aah, yes! A languid read, the first Indian-English aspiring heir to Jane Austen. Far from *Anna Karenina* in any case.'

'What are you planning to do other than managing your health?'

'Oh, I'm in touch with another former journalist,' Rocky said. 'He's developing a web series. Wants me in his writer's room. Perhaps you've heard of him? Aditya Sinha?'

'Vaguely,' Mona said, though she had no idea who Rocky was talking about. 'So, are you scriptwriting serials now? No wonder getting sacked is a blessing in disguise.'

'Yes, yes. Too much tension, too much stress.'

'Did you feel overworked?'

'Are you kidding? Work is a piece of cake. My third stint as an editor-in-chief and I could do the job with my eyes close. Come to think of it, at times I actually did that.'

'What was it then?'

'The other stuff. Company's finance are a mess.'

'But that's not your job?'

'True. But editorial colleagues from Kanyakumari to Kashmir would call and text and email all the time about their salaries. Day and night. Many hadn't been paid in nearly a year. Only Hyderabad was pampered; colleagues here were just two or three months behind on their salaries.'

'Because DT is number one in Hyderabad?'

'Yes, this is where the ad revenue came from. A day's strike here meant lakhs, or even ₹1 crore, of revenue loss. As it is, DT isn't breaking even month-on-month due to the economic downturn and the pandemic, which only shrank circulation and collections.'

'The staff could have written to the administration.'

'The Reddys and their admin puppets are feudal,' he said. 'Never bothered to answer calls, emails or text messages. Sankatram himself said he never opened WhatsApp messages unless it was something he wanted to see. Callous. I couldn't let my journalists down. I answered each phone call, each message, each email. And such sob stories! Somebody needed to hospitalize an elderly parent, someone had to pay an EMI on their flat, somebody had to pay their kid's school fees, someone just needed to pay rent. But, you know, the salaries were not the Reddys' obligation; they were the staffers' due. Their right.'

'So, they turned to their editor-in-chief?'

'I tried to push Gopaliah and Sai as much as I could to pay even half a month's pending salary. It was difficult. Even though I was based in Hyderabad, I still haven't got my full March salary. It's nearly festival time.'

'That couldn't be why they sacked you?'

Rocky shook his head. 'The night before the lockdown, I took the last flight home. In the nick of time. I live alone here and had no desire to spend the next three weeks or months, or whatever it was going to be, alone in a ghost town, driving through empty streets, sitting in an empty office. I wanted to be at home with my wife, in a pleasant space. But it upset the Reddys.'

'What was their problem?'

'I told you, they were feudal. That people could work remotely bothered them immensely. When I returned, Babloo Jubilee insisted that I summon the entire editorial staff back to office. I refused. I couldn't compel anyone to come while the pandemic still raged. People lived with elderly parents and small children, and I did not want them to risk taking Covid home.'

'True, true,' Mona acknowledged. 'They were correct to be afraid. The Mumbai Police lost so many personnel to Covid. I knew several of them, from my station postings.'

'Babloo Jubilee said the other departments were coming to office. What an argument! He forgot that the other departments come in every other day, but the editorial produces the newspaper each and every day. It is the core of the company,' Rocky said. 'And trust me, working from home is no joke. Zoom meetings are a pain, especially with squabbling colleagues. My laptop was on all the time, so I couldn't wander about or watch TV. Quite unlike the admin babus who did meaningless paperwork every other day for just an hour or two.'

'Didn't the Reddys realize the work editorial put in?'

'Sankatram knew the business inside out. He had been running the paper since the '80s; he was involved in every nitty-gritty. Lately, though, with bankruptcy and the airline crashing before take-off and his high life drying up, he left the paper's managing to Babloo Jubilee, who knew zilch.'

'He is the fellow you called an "illiterate eunuch"?'

'The same, the same. Lord Cunning whispered to me about how Babloo Jubilee was a cokehead, a playboy living the good life when the family owned a cricket team, partying with Shah Rukh Khan and Sid Mallya and other VIPs. That life folded up with the cricket team going down. Lord Cunning claims that, after bankruptcy, Babloo Jubilee had to make do with discount whores at his uncle's farmhouse.'

'Canning Sairam? The fellow who backstabbed you?'

'The same, the same. A fake journalist! Began on the DT desk twenty years ago. Left journalism almost immediately and became a PR person for convicted scamster Ramalingam Raju. In 2008, he returned to journalism when I roped him in for a column in the *New Indian Success*. Then, in 2014, when a friend working for the *New York Times* needed a writer from Hyderabad, I suggested Cunning Sairam. Of course, Lord Cunning will claim that he already knew my friend, but I want to see him try to say this publicly.'

'Seems untrustworthy. Characterless.'

'Yes, but it's my fault. I shouldn't have trusted him so much even if he was my deputy. Never should have messaged him calling Babloo Jubilee an illiterate eunuch. I also accused Babloo Jubilee of choking on CNT's dick.'

Pavani giggled.

'In my last conversation with Lord Cunning, I asked him why he had shown my messages to the illiterate eunuch. He mumbled something about the prisoner's dilemma.'

'Some excuse,' Mona said.

'Some number two. He's more like a piece of the other number two.'

'Reckless Rocky!'

'True, true. But the Reddys started it. Sankatram began to abuse me on the phone in June. He accused me of warming my ass at home. Warming my ass! He also accused me of plotting with the people from Shrek Fund.'

'Were you?'

'Of course not. I did occasionally get a call from Manish Manaktala over there, but that conversation never got anywhere. Manish wanted me to sack lots of people and reduce the staff strength to bring down the salary bill so that the newspaper, when Shrek Fund finally took charge, was no longer loss-making. He wanted almost everyone sacked. Irrational redundance.'

'Irrational redundance?'

'Yes, you know, like Alan Greenspan's irrational exuberance. Anyway, once Sankatram started abusing me, I realized my time here was up. I also began to abuse them back, privately though. Lord Cunning also abused Sankatram, calling him "Bahadur Shah Zafar II", rolling around drunkenly on his carpet while his empire crumbled. Raja of Marh, I guess.'

'Leaving DT to Babloo Jubilee ...'

'At the start of the lockdown, Babloo Jubilee closed the paper for a day. Then it was just an e-paper for a week. When we began printing again, hawkers did not want to distribute the paper. Readers were also afraid that touching the newspaper would spread Covid. Circulation plummeted. Today, the newspaper has recovered to 92,000 copies per day, whereas pre-pandemic it printed 2,64,000 copies. India's largest circulating paper, the *News of India* is at 37,000 per day in Hyderabad. Its readers, the young techies, have deserted it. Such readers will likely never touch a newspaper again.'

'Tell me about why you were angry with the Reddys?'

'It wasn't just about the salaries. It was always "carry this story but not that". They were shit-scared of criticizing the government. If a critical story slipped through, Sankatram would call and abuse. It made no sense because the state never gave us ads anyway. The chief minister and his son made it a point, on a former prime minister's birth anniversary, to give a full-page ad on the front page of every newspaper in town except ours. And we were number one. I say, there's no point in kowtowing to thugs, they only understand the language of power. I prefer to be on the offense, printing lots of negative stories till the government comes crawling.'

'Why did the Reddys want to curry favour with the chief minister and his son?'

'The government owed about ₹30 crore for advertisements. The Reddys wanted this money before handing the company over to Shrek Fund. They were salting away mountains of cash. Taking cash for classifieds. Just the obits would come to ₹80,000 a day. Every evening, the cash box would be handed over to the Reddys, no questions asked. No accounting. The books also showed full-page ads as discounted ads, even though payments were received in full, in cash. It was all to support a fancy lifestyle, Sankatram's cigars and Babloo Jubilee's cocaine. Once in a blue moon, some change was spared for staff salaries.'

'Why did the chief minister and his son hate them?'

'Oh, a complicated yet simple matter, like politics always is,' Rocky said. 'Sankatram was a supporter of the Congress party. He nearly became a Rajya Sabha member back in the 2000s. Now, Sankatram was arrogant that he understood politics better than anyone else. He never gave the current chief minister the time of day when he was in the opposition, even back when he agitated for a separate state. Lo and behold! The Congress leadership in Delhi bifurcated the state to cut to size the local leaders who had grown too powerful. They even had the then chief minister bumped off, if rumours are to be believed.'

'What?'

'Yes. And after the state split and the agitationist became the chief minister, his family saw the Reddys as interlopers from the old state. Now the chief minister doesn't give Sankatram the time of day. After all, if Sankatram is feudal then, as Lord Cunning put it, the chief minister is the biggest feudal of them all.'

This was a lot to process for Mona. She caught Pavani staring at Rocky in awe. It was time to change tack.

'Why did you come to the office today?' Mona asked.

'To kill the Reddys,' Rocky said.

'What?'

'Yes, my plan was to induce their heart attacks, though rushing from room to room with Ravi, the peon, watching me was a bit of a giveaway.'

'Why shouldn't I arrest you?'

Rocky paused. 'Because,' he said, 'I don't want to be executed near the airport like those four guys who raped and killed the veterinarian last year.'

'I don't believe you murdered anyone,' Mona said. 'But I am interested in knowing how you know these were murders.'

'Why else are you here, questioning all of us?'

'A fair deduction. But tell me why you are here. Today.'

'Believe me, I would avoid being here if I could. But it's an asinine administration led by the illiterate eunuch … withholding six months of salary, not facilitating the return of my phone number from the corporate account to my personal account and withholding documents,' Rocky said. 'Sai even told his staff to ignore my requests. I wanted to raise a ruckus with Gopalaiah before I left town.'

'Don't leave just yet,' Mona said. 'Not till we sort this out.'

'Oh fuck. I already shipped my bed.'

'Just a couple of days.'

Rocky stood up. 'But you must tell me the whole story,' he said. 'I'll novelize it.'

'What happened to the one you were writing before?'

'Don't ask.'

Rocky left.

Mona asked Pavani who was next.

'Ravi, the peon, ma'am. Then the chief financial officer. Then Canning Sairam.'

'I feel like having a snack,' Mona said. 'Can't we step out for a bite?'

'Maybe we can order, ma'am. We can even ask Ravi once he's done.'

'Good idea.'

A thin and small-built fellow with a shock of oiled and uncut hair and twitching eyes stumbled in. He smiled dazzlingly, but a glare from Pavani inverted his expression. He wore a white shirt and black pants, presumably the support staff's uniform.

'*Yahaan khaane ko kuch milega?*' Mona asked him.

'Ma'am, lots of places,' Ravi said, speaking in Dakhni that was more degraded than Mumbaiyya Hindi. 'Dosa? Parallel road has many eateries with takeaway. Dosa Express, Dosa Heaven, Dosa Forever, Dosa Palace, Dosa Anand, Dosa Love, Dozens of Dosa …'

'What about something non-vegetarian?'

'Near Paradise circle. Paradise Biryani you must be knowing. Opposite that is Nizam's Biryani, and next to that is Biryani Heaven. Then there's Biryani Banao Pulao Khao, Biryani Bomb, Biden ka Biryani and—'

'Stop, stop. What about a simple plate of kebab?'

'For that, go to Tolichowki, ma'am,' Pavani interjected.

'Tolichowki has Irani kebab,' Ravi said. 'Also, Afghani kebab, Lucknowi kebab, Kolkata kebab, Kashmiri kebab ...'

'What did you do, feed the Reddys to death?'

'No, ma'am, I didn't kill anyone.'

'How do you know they were killed?'

'Ma'am, that's all everyone is saying,' Ravi said. 'The health reporter found out from the Gandhi hospital that Sankatram Sir was killed, and she told Cunning Sir, I mean Canning Sir, who told his assistant, Mr Sachya, who told the librarian, who told his peon, who then told me. Also, it's on Telugu TV news.'

Mona sighed. 'Do you know how he was killed?'

'With nothing, ma'am.'

'Really?'

'Yes, ma'am. They said he was injected with nothing.'

Mona scrutinized Ravi's face. 'Are you anxious? Worried about something?'

'Ma'am, everyone has been smiling at me. It means they will target me next. They are angry about their delayed salaries. Because I'm the office boy for the Reddys, they think I was their right-hand man. In fact, I, too, haven't got my salary for seven months. The other peon, also called Sai, left this job to drive an auto-rickshaw after the lockdown lifted. He could not keep working without a salary. I had no choice.'

'Who did you see coming and going from the Reddys' rooms on the fourth floor this morning?' Mona asked.

'Four VIPs came. Also, Swami Bonanand.'

'From inside the office?'

'Rocky Saheb tried to go, but Sankatram Sir refused to see him. Ghattu Sir, our union leader, went to meet Rompy Reddy Sir. Canning Sir then met Sankatram Sir briefly. Then Srilatha Madam met all the three Reddys, as she did every morning.'

'Who is Srilatha?'

'She is the lady placed here by Shrek Fund.'

Mona chewed over this bit of information. 'Did you kill the Reddys?' she spoke suddenly.

'No, ma'am, not even one. Never.'

Mona was assessing Ravi's expression when her phone rang.

'Jai Hind, ma'am. SI Anantamula Ananth this side,' the caller said. 'From the Secunderabad cyber cell.'

'Jai Hind.'

'Ma'am, I thought you would not want to wait for the complete analysis to hear that one of the victims had received multiple death threats over email.'

'Over email?' Mona asked. 'Who?'

'Sainath Rao, ma'am.'

5

'How many death threats? And who sent them?' Mona asked SI Ananth impatiently.

'Ma'am, there were two threats, each from an anonymous handle created solely for the purpose of sending the email,' SI Ananth said. 'The handles are deccandacoits@tormail.com and starvingstaffers@protonmail.com. We can't identify who they belong to, or where they originated. From the servers, it appears that the first one came from Kyrgyzstan while the other seems to have come from a government office. Obviously, it didn't.'

'What do these emails say?'

'Ma'am, I'll forward you screenshots of the emails, not the emails themselves. Protocol.'

'Why would anyone send the HR manager a death threat?'

'Many emails are from staffers begging for salaries, demanding to know when their statutory dues will be cleared, threatening to go to court over unpaid salaries even after they left the organization. There are emails from general handles not linked to a specific person but from the entire staff at centres like Mumbai or Bengaluru, demanding salaries and threatening to go on a strike. There's a pattern of angry and despairing emails, of which the anonymous emails would merely appear to be extreme examples.'

'Send me samples of the emails you've gone through,' Mona said. 'As screenshots. What about the Reddys' emails?'

'The Reddys never said much over email, though they too received similar pleas from distressed staff members,' SI Ananth said. 'There are many commercial propositions, too. Vuvuzula Sankatram got emails from politicians wanting their op-eds published. Mostly national party members and also the junior home minister. Velveti Rompy got emails that the others did not, from vendors demanding payments and also from Shrek Fund.'

'How did the Reddys reply?'

'None of the Reddys said much besides "fine" or "okay" or "no"', SI Ananth said.

Mona had a hunch. 'Can you go through the email exchanges between Velveti Rompy and Shrek Fund?'

'Yes, ma'am. Jai Hind,' he said and ended the call.

'Should I call the chief financial officer in, ma'am?' Pavani asked Mona.

'Damn him,' Mona replied. 'Let him wait. Let's look at the emails. How can we both see them on my phone?'

'Shall I turn on the TV?'

Mona nodded and proceeded to sync her phone with the TV. The screenshots from SI Ananth had begun arriving. The first one read:

> Dear Mr Sai,
>
> This is to inform you that I have not received my salary for six months. We are all going through tough times (COVID-19 for the past three months), but I hope you understand my predicament, too. I have had to go through four COVID-19 lockdowns without any salary. Hence, I humbly request you to acknowledge my email and pay my pending salary at the earliest.
>
> Regards,
> Raghunathan

The next one read:

> Dear Sai,
>
> I wanted to know about the status of my pending salary, still I am unable to understand. I've been told that I'll be getting my dues, but not a single penny credited to my account.
>
> Despite sending you repeated emails, you haven't sent the salary slip of July month yet. There is neither any communication on these pending salaries nor any clear statement. I'm going through a tough phase,

I am staying in transit, and my savings are getting exhaust.

Please credit my pending salaries on sooner the better policies, and provident funds, too. I am in need of it. My salary is so less, then too you guys are not crediting. I know the company is in tough patch, but then too our boss made us work, and we have been working. Now it's getting too difficult to manage. I don't have money to recharge my mobile, if you need evidence will share a screen shot.

It makes me feel demotivated towards the work. Imagine you aren't paid for year and asked to work, will you be able to contribute?

Sai ji, there is a severe financial crunch which I am having right how. Please release my pending salary. Not crediting provident fund is also a crime, but still I haven't complaint or raised voice against about it. I hoping there would sigh of relief soon.

Hoping for an optimist reply.

Yours, Pratibha

Mona grimaced. *What kind of journalist makes so many grammatical and language errors?* she wondered.

'Just imagine if they hired only English literature graduates,' Pavani sniggered.

Mona glared at her.

'Sorry, ma'am, I didn't mean that,' Pavani said, alarmed. 'Please forgive me.'

'Here, look at this,' Mona said. 'Here's an email from payussalary@gmail.com, a group email, from the DT journalists to the Supervisory Committee, copied to Rao.'

It read:

> We, the employees of *Deccan Testament*'s Editorial, are collectively writing this letter to you to apprise you of our concerns and to seek clarifications.
>
> At the outset, we would like to draw your attention to certain observations made by the courts and several government orders, which are relevant to the current situation at DT.

Mona skimmed through a list of judgments and National Company Law Tribunal orders that followed, until she came to a part of the email that made her gasp.

> The management has not paid us salaries for the last three to four months. Employees in some centres/ units have not received salaries for the last six to seven months. The provident fund amount is being deducted from employees' salaries but has not been deposited for the last three years.

Mona decided to call SI Ananth.

'Yes, Jai Hind,' Mona said. 'You must have seen many email complaints about the non-payment of provident fund. Please copy them for a criminal case against the company's deputy CEO and the CFO. File an FIR. Have someone take a statement from the Provident Fund Commissioner.'

She hung up and turned to Pavani.

'SI Pavani, please place both Gopalaiah and the CFO … what's his name?'

'Mr Bhoolchuk Maaf.'

'Yes, well throw Maaf's ass in a lock-up along with Gopalaiah's.'

'Yes, ma'am,' Pavani said and went out.

She was back in a few minutes.

'Ma'am, they've been taken to West Marredpally station lock-up.'

'Why?'

'Maaf was muttering that we should arrest Shrek Fund.'

'Let him tell the judge that,' Mona said. 'Three years of no provident fund? The judge will double his police custody and lodge him in the central prison, where hopefully someone defamed by DT will take care of him.'

Mona went back to the email.

> DT's financial situation has become worse because of the lockdown imposed by the government to stop the spread of coronavirus. The management paid us a paltry sum of ₹10,000 each last month even though the company received advertisements for all but seven days in March 2023.
>
> The payment of ₹10,000 is not enough. If the management continues to pay this amount, there will be a steady exit of employees, which will lead to the

> implosion of the company. It would cause further loss to the creditors ...
>
> ... there cannot be any leadership action without effective communication between the leader and those he leads. But the management has never conveyed its decisions to the employees, who are important stakeholders of any company as emphasized by the Supreme Court ...

The email went on in this vein for a while, until it ended, signed by the 'Employees of *Deccan Testament*'s Editorial'.

'If the government did not pay my salary for six months, I would go on strike,' Pavani said.

'You can't. The police are an essential service.'

'I know, but when the lockdown began, didn't the government call the press an essential service? They were exempt from the lockdown.'

'True, true,' Mona said and scrolled through some other screenshots. All of them were similarly worded: some plaintive, some curt, some angry and some demanding the Form 16.

'Form 16? For tax deducted at source? The company hadn't deposited the employees' income tax either?' Pavani asked.

Mona called SI Ananth again. She asked him to have someone send all the emails with complaints about not receiving Form 16 to the Income Tax Commissioner in Hyderabad.

'Let's look at those threats now,' Mona said to Pavani after the call.

The first one read:

Sai,

Enough of your silence. My salary is my right. The management has not only lost my loyalty, but also its right to live.

Respectfully,
A starving staffer

'That was straight to the point,' Mona mumbled.

The second read:

Sai,

The company has closed several centres and terminated many colleagues. Many innocent heads have rolled. It is now time for the guilty heads to roll. The management is nothing but a gang of dacoits.

Yours, The victims of Deccan Dacoits.

'"Deccan Dacoits" sound like a Twenty-20 cricket team,' Mona noted.

'Ma'am, these could only have been written by journalists.'

'Also, neither of the emails threatened Sai specifically,' Mona said. 'Perhaps we ought to talk to the trade union fellow.'

Just then, Mona's phone rang.

'Have you cracked the case yet?' a man barked from the other end. 'ACP Chittla Srinivas Kumar here.'

'Jai Hind, sir,' Mona said. She knew that if he hadn't been her senior, he wouldn't have used that tone. 'No, sir. Long haul ahead.'

'Report to my office when you're done for the day,' ACP Kumar said and disconnected the phone.

'Shall I call in K. Ghattu now?' Pavani asked.

Mona's phone rang again.

'Namaste ACP Ramteke,' a silky voice said. 'DCP Chittla Suresh Kumar this side.'

'Jai Hind, sir.'

'Jai Hind, Jai Hind,' the silky voice continued. 'I wonder if you've been able to make any headway?'

'Not yet, sir. Too many things to consider.'

'I know, I can imagine. The rich and the powerful would never have a simple case. The TV channels have gone berserk. When you wrap up for the day, I am sure you have been summoned by the ACP for a briefing.'

'Yes, sir.'

'After that, do drop by and brief me as well, if it's not too much of a bother. Good evening.'

The call ended. *Was it evening already?* Mona looked out the window, but she couldn't tell because the glass was tinted. She checked the time on her phone. *Not yet, not yet.* She would wind up here after this interview and go to meet the ACP. She nodded to Pavani.

The sub-inspector led a hefty man in. He looked to be in his forties, his hair was darker than the salt-and-pepper beard peeping out of his surgical mask, and he wore a checked synthetic shirt and dark trousers with well-worn sandals. His eyes were close-set and his wide smile stretched his nostrils over his mask's edge.

'*Tum yahan union leader ho?*' Mona asked if he headed the union.

'Yes, madam,' he replied in Dakhni.

'What do you do besides blackmailing the management?'

'Madam, the management blackmails the workers, so it's only fair, no?' Ghattu's smile never wavered. 'I work in the phototypesetting department. Not much work, technology has come a long way.'

'Must be a strong union at the state's number one newspaper?'

'Used to be, madam. Past tense.'

'And now?'

'Now, the company has no money. Shrek Fund hasn't taken over, so what's the point of threatening to go on a strike? We can put down our tools, but if the paper isn't published then no ads will appear, which means less money earned, which means that our salaries are further delayed. We're trapped.'

'You seem sympathetic to the management's troubles.'

'Madam, twenty-seven years I have put in. Many have put in over thirty. We have nowhere else to go. As Rompy Reddy Anna said, we are like a family at DT.'

'Well, he, Sankatram and Babloo Jubilee were certainly family.'

'Don't forget Magnolia Madam and their daughter, Deepthi Madam, who married and left, though she understood the paper best. The chairman and his son, they were almost carbon copies. But the chairman also knew politics.'

'Did they ever call you "family"?' Mona asked.

'No, madam. Only Rompy Reddy Anna called us workers "family", even if it was just once.'

'You mean Mr Rompy invited you to his farmhouse to screw cheap whores?' Pavani suddenly asked. 'He gave you free tickets to Twenty-20 matches?'

'No, no, not like that,' Ghattu said. 'Though, you know, Rompy Anna's farmhouse is not far from the printing press on the outskirts of the city. I have heard many stories of his parties.'

'Like what?'

'Babloo Jubilee and he had a twisted chacha–bhatija (uncle–nephew) relationship. The boy once danced topless with two naked ladies during a loud and late party. He took a drug, too. "Cooking", it's called, I think.'

'Cocaine,' Pavani corrected him.

'Yes, yes, cooking, cooking,' Ghattu said, his eyes half-closed, as if he had just inhaled some cocaine himself.

Pavani rolled her eyes.

'You were close to Velveti Rompy?' Mona asked.

'He is the one who interacted with the union always. The chairman spoke mainly to the journalists, and also the politicians. Such was his stature that we dared not approach him. Ever. Babloo Jubilee was too young and hot-headed. Also, he was inexperienced.'

'The former editor-in-chief called him an "illiterate eunuch".'

'Is it?' Ghattu said. 'Chief Editor Sahib is a good man. Best journalist. Kind, always wished us. No airs. He is unlike Gopalaiah and Sai, who always act as if they are also nawabs, simply by association with the Reddys.'

'Is it?'

'Editor Sahib even attended a union meeting once. We put him on the dais. He sat for an hour even though we all spoke in Telugu. I never expected such patience from a north Indian.'

'I don't think he's from the north,' Mona remarked.

'True, he did not even have samosas after the union meeting. How can that be? He he, illiterate eunuch. Good name for Babloo Jubilee. Poor late illiterate eunuch. Om shanti.'

'Would anyone have reason to kill Sainath Rao?' Pavani asked.

'Everyone,' Ghattu said cheerfully.

Pavani gave him a slap on the head. She then whipped out her sanitiser and cleaned her hands for twenty seconds.

'Pavani,' Mona sighed.

'That was not a helpful answer,' Pavani replied.

'But it's true,' Ghattu said, his smile no longer visible. 'Salaries were not only delayed but also reduced. Everyone blamed him for the reduction in salaries. Maybe twenty per cent reduction was due to the economic slowdown after the lockdown. Thirty per cent reduction in the Andhra centres. Fifty per cent in centres outside the Telugu-speaking states. Everyone blamed Sai for the non-stop bad news. Yes, everyone also blamed Gopalaiah for the delay in salaries, but they mainly held Sai accountable.'

'What did you think of him?'

'Typical Brahmin ready to stick a knife in your back.'

'I know, I know,' Mona said. 'But that's no reason to be casteist.'

'Pardon, madam,' Ghattu said, looking warily at Pavani lest she hit him again. But no, her hand sanitiser was safely back in her trouser pocket. 'I don't think any journalist would kill Sai, because Sai is already dead.'

'What kind of a union leader are you?' Pavani asked. 'Haven't you heard the rumours circulating in your own office?'

Ghattu blinked repeatedly. 'Madam, I don't think any journalist can kill anyone. They are all soft,' he said. 'Timid.'

'Is it?'

'Madam, believe me, I know what is tough. Years ago, we had many tough men in the union ... men at the printing press who stopped putting in hours because they hung around outside the building, in front of the time-office at the main gate. They were the muscle.'

'The muscle?'

'Yes. To enforce strikes. To keep out troublemakers, like the government. There was once a time, in the 1990s, when the newspaper wrote about a local politician in Siddipet being a gangster—T. Raghunath Rao. He was enraged. He called up the then editor, Sukhi Puri Madam, and threatened to bring his supporters and burn down the office. So our Mani Rao, big man and big muscles, stood at the gate and waited for them. When the crowd approached, shouting slogans, Mani Rao told T. Raghunath Rao that he dare not step inside the gate unless he wanted to be thrashed in public. He also told T. Raghunath Rao that he would never win another election. T. Raghunath Rao considered this and then led his procession towards the police headquarters instead.'

'You're saying the union is tougher than the police?' Pavani asked.

'No, no, SI Madam. Different time. DT was a powerful institution then. Now everyone knows that the Reddys are con artists in deep trouble with both the banks and the central government.'

'You don't believe any journalist could be a murderer?'

'Canning Sairam could probably be a cheat or a pickpocket, or even a forger. But a killer? No.'

'Who would be happiest with the deaths today?'

'We all would,' Ghattu said. 'The staff of the *Deccan Testament*. All centres. Across India.'

'Because ...'

'Because it would mean that Shrek Fund can finally take over the office and pay us our salaries and provident fund.

Many retired union members are waiting to collect their gratuities. Lakhs of rupees.'

'But the newspaper has no money.'

'Yes, but the paper was handed over to Shrek Fund by the National Company Law Tribunal last year after it won the auction. It promised to inject ₹500 crore to revive the newspaper. The Shrek Fund people told the union that their first priority was to clear the dues and salaries. So, why shouldn't we want them to come? But the Reddys didn't want to let go. They just delayed and delayed the handover.'

'How?'

'With nonsensical legal cases. Proxy legal cases. One by a public sector bank, for the 'Deccan Testament' masthead. Knowing that Shrek Fund wouldn't want any legal case hanging over its head, the Reddys planned one delay tactic after another. If the Reddys remained alive, the handing over would have taken years, if not forever. We would be years behind in our salaries, not just months.'

'Why didn't you just leave?' Pavani asked.

'And go where? Who will hire me?' Ghattu responded, the smile returning to his face. 'Many of us have never seen the world outside this company's walls. We have limited skills. We're unionized. And we are unemployable. We have no choice but to stay here.'

'You want to end up like those cloth mill workers in Mumbai, or those sugar mill workers in UP, who have not been paid for decades?'

'What to do? We are hostages of DT. Of the Reddys.'

'That explains the Stockholm syndrome,' Mona mused aloud.

'But did the Reddys care? No, madam. They were ingrates. Feudal lords who believed that they were entitled to everything they had, and more, without a care for the staff. They even treated journalists like personal maids and butlers. Their ingratitude was at the core of their vileness.'

'The Reddys and Rao were murdered,' Mona said. 'Did you kill them?'

'Madam, the union had nothing to do with their deaths.'

'The union didn't kill them, the journalists couldn't kill them,' Pavani said. 'Then who did? Who else benefitted from their deaths?'

Ghattu looked back and forth between ACP Mona and SI Pavani. 'Shrek Fund,' he finally said.

6

Mona parked her Royal Enfield in front of the DCP's office inside the civil court complex, which also housed the ACP's office. Though it was barely five minutes away from the DT office, Mona had to cross the busy SP Road and Parade Ground flyover, which would usually be clogged with traffic jams.

She was ushered into the ACP's room. ACP Chittla Srinivas Kumar looked around her age, maybe even a year or two younger. He had bulging eyes, scanty eyebrows, a narrow nose and thin lips. He was neither wearing a mask nor did he seem inclined to do so. The steel letters 'IPS' sparkled over the shoulders of his khaki uniform. He kept signing piles of files one after the other, tossing each on to the floor behind him. Hearing someone enter, he brusquely gestured for her to sit.

'You're at the police academy's induction training course, is it?' he asked. 'Hoping to be promoted from the state police service to the Indian Police Service.'

'Not hoping but preparing.'

'You might have solved a few high-profile cases in Mumbai, but you will never be an IPS officer even if you qualify technically.'

'The political leadership has trusted me with this investigation,' Mona responded and then spoke after a pause. 'Sir.'

ACP Kumar leaned back in his chair. 'An officer is only as corrupt as the political leadership,' he said. 'I'm sure even the saints in the Mumbai Police occasionally find their hands tied behind their backs.'

Mona immediately thought of Solvekar Sahib posted in Gadchiroli for the second time, as punishment. She said nothing.

'Anyway, what's the status of the investigation?'

'One homicide has been confirmed by the medical examiner. We're interviewing everyone who was on the premises at the time of the deaths. Overlapping motives are emerging. But no suspects yet.'

'Motives?'

'The victims were all managing a newspaper whose staff had not been paid for months. Many staffers were on the brink of desperation.'

'That's the motive? Disgruntled employees?' ACP Kumar said and looked at his computer screen. His hand was busy scrolling with the mouse.

'Possibly corporate rivalry and competition. As I said, they were murdered just this morning. Let's see what tomorrow's investigation coughs up.'

'That means no progress? I'll have to report this to the commissioner.'

'By all means,' Mona said and stood up to leave.

'This case should have gone to the Crime Investigation Department and not to some outsider. It feels like someone is trying to manipulate the case remotely.'

'I can assure you that no one will manipulate the case so long as I'm on it.'

'No reason to have called in the Mumbai Police,' the ACP muttered. 'Do you know Jammikunta Police Station, formerly under my charge, was adjudged as one of the top ten police stations of the country? By a panel comprising DGPs and IGPs? Not a single thana from Maharashtra was on that list.'

'We're too busy solving crimes to continually sweep and paint our police stations. Good evening.'

'Where's your salute?' ACP Kumar said, staring hard at her.

'Go fuck yourself,' Mona said as she saluted him. 'Sir.'

'You should be careful,' he said and stood up. He was almost as small and wiry as she. He took two menacing steps around the table.

'Or what?' Mona also moved towards him. 'You'll complain?'

ACP Kumar stopped in his tracks.

'I'll do more than having an insubordinate attitude,' she said. 'If the brass has such little confidence in you, then I have nothing to lose even if I hang you upside-down from the top of the flagpole outside.'

With that, Mona left the room and headed to the DCP's office.

'Hello, hello,' DCP Chittla Suresh Kumar said, standing up from his chair. He wore a mask, which did little to conceal his wide smile. His eyes smiled so brightly. Mona realized that the ACP and the DCP were not just brothers but twins.

'Yes, yes, we're twins,' DCP Kumar said, laughing.

'But you're his boss, sir,' Mona said. 'Jai Hind, sir.'

'Ah yes, Jai Hind. Who says twins have to be the same rank? Srinivas may have emerged from our mother first, but he passed the UPSC exam five years after I did. So I'm his senior officer. It's probably what makes him sullen.'

'He's not sullen.'

'Really? You came in here looking flushed. Obviously there was a run-in. You must be careful, however. The police force is a divided lot. There's always one group with whom he stays aligned. He can make life difficult for you if pushed too hard.'

'Thank you, sir,' Mona said and then paused. 'Sir, do twins have telepathy?'

'No, no, we're just highly empathetic. Or else I'd be solving his cases and he would be blackmailing my contacts.'

'If you don't mind me asking, sir, what about your wives? Are they twins too?'

'Srinivas is married. To a beautiful woman. As for me, I'm a confirmed bachelor.'

'As am I, sir,' Mona said, warming up to the DCP instantly.

'My brother and I used to be very close. We had a good time in college, switching places and fooling lecturers who never bothered about students. We even fooled a girl once.'

'Like in Marquez's *A Hundred Years of Solitude*?'

'Exactly. Things soured when I qualified for the UPSC in the first try. Everyone fussed over me, which drove Srinivas away. Each year he failed that was another quantum jump away. By the time he eventually passed, I couldn't recognize him even though he is my twin. It was like looking in a funhouse mirror.'

'Or like Dorian Gray looking at his portrait.'

'Or like Einstein's twin paradox.'

They laughed.

'Sir, how is it that both of you ended up in the same cadre? That's a rarity.'

'I was with the Andhra Pradesh cadre before the bifurcation and opted for the new state when it was formed. Simultaneously, Srinivas entered the IPS and opted for the Telangana cadre. Neither of us knew what the other was doing until we were both in it.'

'And the same district posting?'

'I think the IG (Administration) was being ironic. But I take care not to order Srinivas around, though he has no choice but to salute me in front of the rank and file.'

'Sir, how come you're sharing so much with me? Are you always this forthcoming?'

'No, but when you walked in I saw that you probably had a turbulent meeting with my brother. Don't worry about it. His complaints have to pass through me. Just don't push him to precipitate matters beyond my control. For my sake.'

'Yes, sir. Of course.'

'I hear that you're at the academy, preparing to move from the state police service to the IPS. Great news. Quite an accomplishment. I hear that some police officials pay good money to make that climb. But you, you deserve it. I wish you all the best.'

'Thank you, sir. Could you tell me what's the police commissioner like?'

'Him? You should go and meet him as soon as possible. He's probably still in the office. Nice enough. No supercop though. Terrified of the groupism in the force, which has only worsened divisions. He's happiest doing the chief minister's bidding. Also, I hear he's the go-between the chief minister and the head of the Oasis Party.'

'Really, sir?' Mona said. *Clearly, senior officials had to operate on an entirely different level. Maybe political brown-nosing ought to have been part of her current course.*

'Anyway, leave all that. You'll think I'm nothing but a big gossipmonger. Or a medium-sized one, at least. What's your progress on the case?'

'Sir, still interviewing people. A bit confusing.'

'How so?'

'All four appear to have been murdered, but we have confirmation only for Sankatram Reddy. Sainath Rao, the HR manager, received what can be construed as death threats, but they were not specifically directed at him. There are hundreds of employees who are disgruntled over delayed salaries, a few of whom were on the premises at the time of the deaths, but I can't say if that's enough to draw a conclusion. There's a corporate takeover angle, but it seems far-fetched.'

'Anything else?'

'Well, sir, several outsiders visited the victims this very morning. Film producers, an industrialist, a realtor, a starlet, a cricketer and an astrologer. A low-level local activist was in the building, too, though he did not meet any of the victims. Also, there were some former employees. I have to talk to them all before drawing a clear picture.'

'Well, none of them are going anywhere.'

'Yes, sir,' Mona said. 'May I ask you for some advice?'

'Of course. Are you going to see any politicians after the commissioner?'

'Sir. Sharmila Ma'am, the chief minister's daughter, and then her brother. The minister.'

'Indeed. Do ask the commissioner about them. Be persistent. You might hear a thing or two.'

'Sir.' Mona saluted and departed.

She drove down to the Commissionerate in Basheerbagh. As her bike chugged along Tank Bund Road and skirted the Hussain Sagar Lake, Mona considered the DCP's advice. Perhaps she should be circumspect. After all, she did not belong to the Hyderabad City Police, nor was Telangana her home cadre.

At the Commissionerate, she was briskly escorted to the commissioner's room. She stepped in and saluted as smartly as she could.

'Jai Hind,' Commissioner Chandravardhan said. 'Please sit, ACP Ramteke. It's true then. You're not much bigger than your motorcycle and yet you beat up men twice your size.'

'Sir, I don't believe in third-degree interrogation. It's illegal.'

'Good. Neither does the Hyderabad City Police. We tried to eradicate it, but in this feudal society it's the only effective way to make some talk. A few tight slaps. Sometimes more. After Abu Ghraib happened, the Americans, who used to pretend to be human rights' votaries, unwittingly validated third-degree interrogation around the world.'

'Yes, sir.'

'Now all we hear from the public is "instant justice, instant justice". Until it happens to them. There is so much clamour for extrajudicial execution. Remember when the veterinarian was raped and killed last year? Every hour, C.N.T. Rao would call me and ask if I had bumped the suspects off yet. Imagine. As if I were the Phantom. Who cares about due process anymore?'

'Well, sir, you are obliged to obey the political leadership.'

'Yes, within the law. Things have gone out of hand though. Will India ever stop being feudal and casteist? If not, how will we ever catch up with China?'

Mona wanted to say that India would never catch up with China, but she kept silent. The commissioner seemed to be an intellectual. *Poor fellow, stuck in the Telangana police.*

'Such is destiny,' Commissioner Chandravardhan said, apparently reading her mind.

'Yes, sir.'

'Anyway, how's the investigation going? Are my people troubling you? Is the staff at *Deccan Testament* troubling you? Is the Hyderabadi cuisine troubling you?'

'No, no and no, sir,' Mona said before launching into a review of the investigation.

'Good, good. Any further news from Dr Dharma?'

At that very moment, Mona's phone buzzed. It was Dr Dharma. 'What a long life!' Mona murmured. The commissioner nodded to her to take the call.

'We have a second murder,' Dr Dharma said. 'Sainath Rao. But his heart attack was different than Sankatram's. Not by air injection, but by poison. Batrachotoxin in his paayasam. Note that it is not a common toxin.'

'How uncommon is it? And how fast-acting?' Mona burst out. 'How was it administered?'

'Good questions. It is not at all common here. In fact, I nearly mistook it for tetrodotoxin. In any case, batrachotoxin is extremely poisonous. One of the most potent alkaloids known to us. Paralyses the nervous system immediately, especially the heart muscles, causing an arrythmia, as in this case.'

'Where does one procure a poison like this?'

'From beetles and birds in Papua New Guinea,' Dr Dharma said. 'Frogs, too. Someone surely went to Southeast Asia recently to obtain this.'

'Well, nowadays everyone and their buddies visit Southeast Asia.'

'Yes, I agree, but beyond Indonesia and the Philippines? I doubt anyone has travelled there, or even to Australia, in the past seven or eight months since the pandemic,' Dr Dharma said. 'Whoever got a hold of it did so before the Covid outbreak, and they stored it in a carefully calibrated refrigeration system. It cannot be your average pharmacist for sure. It is probably why the COVID-19 vaccines won't be available in India for a while.'

'How was the HR manager given the toxin?'

'I'm not 100 per cent certain, but it might have entered his body through his penis, which was immersed in a pudding, I'm told. We're retrieving the pudding to confirm. His penis has abrasions, which make it seem like a possible entry point into the bloodstream and nervous system. Many nerves are, after all, bunched in that, uh, region. Otherwise, I found no fresh injection marks, or even dart marks, on the rest of his body.'

'But this means the killer knew about the abrasions on Sai's, er, thingy?'

'Well, perhaps the killer did not anticipate the victim to masturbate into the paayasam. Perhaps the killer assumed he would just eat it.'

'How could Sainath Rao have got the abrasions on his penis?'

'Perhaps he had a deviant sexual partner, though he appears to be a pious Brahmin.'

'So, what does that mean?'

'His wife could have stopped having marital relations with him decades ago,' Dr Dharma said. 'Or maybe he just masturbated too much, like three to four times a day. Actually, I don't know if that's too much or just enough for a pious Brahmin.'

Mona found it regrettable that death exposed a person's private life in such a humiliating manner. She thanked the medical examiner for the hard work and long hours.

'Don't be silly,' Dr Dharma said. 'This is so exciting. A murder mystery! I'm not sleeping till all the bodies are done.'

Mona put her phone away and summarized the conversation to the commissioner.

'Two confirmed homicides,' the commissioner said. 'I wonder how the killer put the poison into the paayasam. Doesn't it come in sealed tins?'

'Yes, sir.'

'And why these two people? What common motive links them, besides the non-payment of salaries?'

'Will find out, sir.'

'Sounds like a tough nut to crack, but you have my support. I do hope you can solve the case early rather than let it drag for weeks. Else we'll never figure it out.'

'I'll try not to let you down, sir.'

'I know. Your Mumbai police commissioner has great faith in you. And I have great faith in him.'

'Thank you, sir.'

'No doubt ACP Srinivas is seething over your involvement in the investigation. Don't worry about him.

I'll take care of any complaint he writes up, but just be careful of him.'

'Yes, sir.'

'He's aligned with C.N.T. Rao, so he can be a pain. And the minister knows that Sharmila got you involved with the case.'

That sounded ominous.

'You will probably meet CNT this evening, after you leave from here?'

'Yes, sir. Both him and Sharmila Ma'am.'

'If you can, do ask the lady about the chief minister's relationship with the Reddys. Ask CNT about each of the visitors to DT office this morning.'

'The siblings don't get along, is it, sir?'

'Worse,' Commissioner Chandravardhan said, standing up to signal that the meeting was over. 'They don't get along with the father either. And all three of them were not fond of Sankatram Reddy. Don't put this down in the case diary, but ...'

'Yes, sir?'

'One of them could have ordered these murders.'

7

UBIT minister C.N.T. Rao lived in an imposing white bungalow in Begumpet. At the left end of a colonnade was his waiting room. Reeking of disinfectant, an oil portrait of a foreigner dominated the room. Mona sat on a sofa opposite the painting, fighting a nagging feeling that she had seen the woman somewhere. The woman in question had a side parting and wide eyes, and she posed as if she were the Mona Lisa, except that the longer ACP Mona looked at her, the more her smile looked not enigmatic but mildly constipated.

A door opened and out came a short but glamorous young woman. She resembled a starlet, glowing in a bright lemon dress, canary yellow pumps and crimson lipstick. She tossed away her glossy hair in a way that her nose, looking slightly but not markedly large for her face, pointed in Mona's direction. She hurried out. Mona couldn't tear her eyes off the departing woman.

Minister Rao barrelled into the room along with two file-clutching lackeys. Mona stood up and saluted him.

'Yes, ACP Ma'am, good to see you here,' CNT said, taking the opposite sofa and putting on a mask. 'Tell me.'

'Sir, who's painting is that?' Mona asked.

CNT turned slightly to catch a glimpse. 'You don't know Ayn Rand?'

Oh, that's who! Mona remembered seeing a clothbound edition of one of Rand's hogwash in Sankatram Reddy's room. 'She posed for this painting?'

'No, this I had custom-made.'

'Why the Mona Lisa?' Mona asked. 'Why not portray her in a cubist painting, in pastel colours and with both eyes on one side of her face?'

CNT laughed. 'Or in a Raja Ravi Verma painting, as a chubby Travancore princess?'

'Or as Saraswati in an M.F. Hussain.'

At least, the minister had a sense of humour. At ease, Mona got down to business.

'About the case, sir, you might have already obtained the forensic details. I haven't finished the interviews, and so I don't have a convincing motive. At least not yet.'

'Why? Isn't the disgruntled staff motive enough?'

'If they were so disgruntled, sir, they would have publicly lynched the Reddys.'

'And poisoning the HR manager through his penis seems too elaborate for a poor press worker,' CNT agreed. 'So, you're waiting for the forensic evidence to throw up something.'

'That, and exploring if there's a strong enough motive to kill them.'

CNT nodded but said nothing.

'The motive would be easier to establish if it were just the Reddys,' Mona admitted. 'But the fact that Rao was also poisoned confuses matters. It's not just about a family, but a family and the HR manager.'

'On the other hand, had it been only the Reddys who died, it might have been more difficult to crack. The Reddys were not loved in Hyderabad. You would have had too many suspects and elimination would have been a massive exercise. Everyone could have been a suspect.'

'Everyone, sir?'

CNT laughed again. 'Yes, even me.'

'Why, sir?'

CNT seemed amused. 'I met each of the Reddys occasionally,' he said. 'I tried avoiding them, but they kept seeking appointments. A minister can't keep turning down appointments and one can't ignore the family that owns, or at least used to, the largest-selling English newspaper in the state. Now in two states. Outsized influence.'

'The *Deccan Testament* was broke, but the Reddys personally weren't,' the minister added. 'In fact, the newspaper was persistently trying to obtain funds from the state government.'

'You mean they wanted the government to book more ads?' Mona asked.

'That, of course. But they also kept bringing up invoices of nearly ₹40 crore that were supposedly due from our administration. They said it could help them pay the pending salaries and statutory dues to staff across the country. What nonsense!'

'Sir?'

'We, in the government, knew very well that those scoundrels said the money was intended for the staff, but that they siphoned every last paisa for their personal use. It happened just earlier this year when the treasury released a payment of ₹8 crore. It vanished, but the backlog of salaries didn't reduce. I cannot dictate to the Reddys what kind of a lifestyle to adopt, but their debauchery should not have come at the staff's expense.'

'Of course, sir.'

'Second, times are difficult. Everyone knows it. The economic slowdown, the pandemic. Did these people think that the government has surplus funds for non-priority disbursements? No, we don't. The central government is stalling payment of the state's share of GST. The Centre claims low collections. How is the state government supposed to pay its employees? And when we get the money, our priority will always be developmental spending, for welfare schemes. We have local elections coming up in the city and the ruling party at the Centre, the Bitterness and Grievance Party, the BGP, is breathing down our necks. Our electorate takes precedence over a newspaper, any newspaper, especially one owned by the dissolute. Paying newspapers is just not something the state can afford at the moment.'

'What did you tell them, sir?'

'I cautioned them against running anti-government reports. They repeatedly said they would stop, but that their editor-in-chief regularly slipped in one story or the other to embarrass me. What rubbish! They have two pages of readers' letters every Monday morning, called "Speak Loud", filled with complaints about civic problems. That too immediately after the front page. Makes me look bad. Makes the local government look incompetent. And every Monday. How is it that the editor-in-chief kept slipping it through so prominently every Monday morning?'

'Yes, sir.'

'The Reddys played a double-edged game. Their journalists would flex the paper's muscle and then their marketing executives would come and praise my father to the heaven, begging for the next round of government ads. I would fob them off with a promise and tell them to contact the chief secretary, who only gave the ads to their rival newspaper, the *News of India*. They could say nothing. I didn't like the Reddys, and they knew they didn't like them.'

'Yet they had no choice.'

'None whatsoever. They would try to compensate for a negative story by doing a puff for my father, but we were not going to be duped. They even sent their resident editor, Canning Sairam, to come over and brush his teeth with my dick.'

'Sir?'

'I meant, to come over and do a gushing interview,' CNT said and paused.

'Sankatram Reddy was also a member of the Congress party, which is your main opposition, sir,' Mona said.

'Yes, but where is the Congress party today? Just a Reddy party now. India is swayed by its Great Leader, whose bloody Gutka Gang is using the political vacuum to spread its influence wide and deep. Both Telangana and Andhra Pradesh are fertile soil for the BGP.'

'Isn't your party, which got statehood for your people, firmly rooted?'

'Yes, of course it is, but the Gutka Gang is relentless. They go all-out even for municipality elections. And people love the Great Leader, especially all those Telugus out in Chicago. They love his aggression. He channels their bitterness and fear and anger. They think his aggressive manner is what has been missing from India for the last seventy years.'

'In fact, sir, a low-level functionary of the BGP visited Mr Canning this morning.'

CNT looked at Mona for a moment, immersed in thought. 'Not the deputy minister from Delhi?'

'No, sir.'

'Who else visited DT?'

'Film producers.' Mona checked her notes. 'Rowdy Panja Naidu and Raghupathi Pullaiah.'

'Oh yes, one visiting the elder brother, the other visiting the younger.'

'Yes, sir.'

'You must question them. I hear that Raghupathi Pullaiah is making a film of which Rompy Reddy was a shadow financier, having invested his family's black money. Some absurd name, like most Telugu films. *Michael Reddy Eats Hot Chips*. Why can't they make meaningful films like Michael Bay or Christopher Nolan? Or even like the ones Tamil directors Cheran and Bala make?'

'Who would watch such classy movies, sir?'

'True, true,' CNT conceded, resignedly shaking his head. 'In any case, Raghupathi Pullaiah might know something about how the Reddys managed the black money they hid from creditors. The banks. Always follow the money.'

'Absolutely, sir,' Mona said. 'What about the other film producer?'

'Probably the same thing. You ought to use the third degree on Rowdy Panja Naidu.'

Mona was distressed. Either she was associated with third-degree interrogation, or it was par for the course in Hyderabad. 'Third degree is illegal, sir.'

'I grant you blanket immunity.'

'Other visitors, sir, included Maximillian Reddy,' Mona said, trying to change the subject.

'Haan haan, Maxi's got projects everywhere. Fingers in so many pies. Like a mini-Adani. There's a rumour that Sankatram Reddy was trying to persuade him to buy the newspaper from Shrek Fund, so that the Reddys could continue to run DT on Maxi's behalf. But I don't think the negotiation was getting anywhere. Even Maximillian knew what a reptile Sankatram was.'

'Then there was a realtor, Bharathi Rao, sir.'

'I think he and Rompy Reddy had grabbed some land in Jubilee Hills and also in Shamsabad. Perhaps Rompy was looking for some liquidity.'

'Yes, sir. Also, an astrologer came to visit Sankatram.'

'Ha ha. Hocus-pocus and mumbo-jumbo. Must have told him he would live for a 100 years.'

'Sir. Two others came to meet Babloo Jubilee Reddy.'

'The son,' CNT laughed. 'You know, he came to meet me maybe nine or ten days ago. He was looking for a payment of ₹10 crore in dues. Tried to be politically savvy. What a kid! An illiterate bumpkin with a cocaine habit. He threatened to expose the deal for the cable-stayed bridge over the Durgam Cheruvu. I told him he'd be encountered. He began crying, got down on the floor and massaged my feet. Made a spectacle of himself.'

'A starlet, Gurleen Kaur, visited him, sir. And a former IPL cricketer, Richard Lessness.'

'Dick is not a bad sort. I think he's filed a suit in London against the Reddys for non-payment of dues from when he coached their cricket team. You can see the details on his website. I wonder why he met BJ. Was it because of the court's judgment that the cricket board owed the Reddys $1 billion? Could they be negotiating a settlement?'

'Yes, sir. Money everywhere.'

'And yet, for the Reddys' staff, nowhere at all.'

'The starlet, sir?'

'Didn't you see her leaving? In the yellow dress?'

Oh, thought Mona. In the morning, Gurleen Kaur met Babloo Jubilee, and in the evening CNT. That certainly tangled this Hyderabadi web further.

'She's shooting for "Michael Reddy Eats Hot Chips". The usual song-and-dance sequences. She said they're shooting at Ikea tomorrow morning.'

'Yes, sir.'

'Anyone else?'

'A cardiologist visited Sankatram Reddy's widow.'

'Right,' CNT said and stood up, as did Mona. 'Well, let me know what they tell you.'

'Yes, sir,' Mona saluted and left.

As Mona got back on her Royal Enfield, she noted that though it was beginning to get late she could still make time for a chat with Ms Sharmila who lived in Banjara Hills, not far from Begumpet. The traffic was still crazy, but half an hour later she was at the former MP's apartment.

As she stepped into the flat, Mona was enveloped by the spicy smell of dinner. She was swiftly shown into a living room that was modestly furnished. A large garlanded painting of the chief minister was up on one of the walls. The artist had shrunk the man's famously bulbous black nose and had apparently applied a generous dose of a skin-lightening cream. He stared down crossly at Mona, making her wonder what she had done to encounter so many grim portraits in one day.

Sharmila was already waiting for her, so Mona saluted and accepted the invitation to sit down.

Mona looked at Sharmila and her first thought was that the brother and sister did not look alike; in fact, they could pass off as husband and wife. Then she noticed that both Sharmila and her brother had a tight-lipped smile and flared nostrils, much like their father. The chief difference was that CNT's left eye seemed set lower in his face than his right one. And the hair, of course. CNT's processed hair looked like that of a 1990s Tollywood film star, rising up in waves, whereas his sister tightly pulled hers back from the scalp to a point at the back of her head, from where it sprayed out across her shoulders.

Mona gave her a complete run-down of the case, along with the leads that Minister C.N.T. Rao had asked her to pursue.

'I hope I'm not a suspect?' Sharmila asked, smiling tightly.

The directness caught Mona off-guard. 'No, ma'am. Why would you be?'

Sharmila's smile became tighter and slightly lopsided. 'I would think that anybody who's anyone in Hyderabad would be a suspect, given the amount of hatred they had for the Reddys. Even my dad.'

'Chief Minister Sahib?'

'Yes,' Sharmila said. 'Don't look so surprised. Though he'd be lower down the list than Anna.'

'Why would your brother be higher up on the list?'

'He is, as you know, the most visible minister around town, the face of the administration. He shoulders most of the political work while our father spends his time at the farmhouse. Not that Anna takes any decisions himself. Ultimately, he goes to our father for advice.'

An attendant entered the living room with glasses of lime soda. Sharmila waited for him to serve them and leave before speaking again.

'My father had a particularly seething hatred for Sankatram Reddy,' she said. 'Though I wouldn't go so far as to say it was enough to have had him killed.'

'Yes, ma'am.'

Sankatram Reddy had long been a member of the Congress party she said, and had narrowly missed a nomination to the Rajya Sabha nearly a decade and a half ago; he had been thwarted by his own editor. Yet, Reddy was enough of a player that he saw himself as an important politician in the undivided state. But, by the time the state was bifurcated, his finances had already started unravelling and he was politically on the backfoot.

'As you may have noticed, Hyderabad is staunchly feudal and patriarchal,' Sharmila said. 'Just look at me. I was a computer scientist in the US and Anna was an investment banker. We both came home to help Dad out when it was clear that the Congress was pushing to bifurcate Andhra Pradesh and make a separate state of Telangana. I put in just as much work as he did. Yet, he's been made the heir apparent, while I was just a post office for party work in Delhi for five years. In a way, I'm glad I did not get re-elected to Parliament. It ensured that I would be right here in Hyderabad, by my father's side.'

As Sharmila spoke, Mona watched the spray of hair behind her head rising and ebbing.

'Anyway, it was political suicide for the Congress to divide the state. In a way, it also diminished Sankatram's political heft. The party did it to cut the then chief minister, Rajamohan Rao, to size. He was a powerful chief minister and basically funded the national party, thanks to businessmen from the state, including Sankatram. He was the top feudal in the unified state. They were terrified of him.'

'Too bad that he died in that chopper crash,' Mona said.

'Yes, a lot of mystery lingers behind who sabotaged his helicopter,' Sharmila said, looking away momentarily. 'But that's not the case we're discussing.'

'Yes, ma'am.'

'Sankatram, like the then chief minister, never gave Dad the time of day when he was agitating for a separate state. He would scoff at him. Dismissive. But then Telangana became a state. And Dad was the most powerful man. He never forgot the slights he received whenever he went to Sankatram for support, or for just a measly interview in DT. He began to avoid Sankatram like one would do with a superspreader. Whenever Anna would get a visit from Sankatram, Dad would utter all sorts of filthy abuses about the Reddys in front of my teenage boys.'

Sharmila took a pause before speaking again.

'Dad was uninterested in bailing the Reddys out of their financial problems. He was pleased that they had declared bankruptcy, though he said that it was not good that so many Telugu-speaking industrialists were failing one after the other. We discussed whether or not to take over the paper through a proxy, but Sankatram was such a slippery customer ...'

'And now that he's dead, it's convenient for your family to take over,' Mona said. 'Through a proxy.'

'If that were the case, I wouldn't be giving you all this information so readily. But the pandemic has shown that newspapers don't matter any more. Well, they do matter, but not as much as they used to. Not in a life-or-death way at least.'

'The de-newsification of society, ma'am?'

'It's more that everyone has news ka nasha, but they've got over the newspaper ka nasha. The addiction remains, alive and thriving, as long as we have a social media platform. That's all that matters.'

'Like WhatsApp?'

'The BGP unfortunately has a stranglehold on WhatsApp, so we have been trying to disseminate our own take on events and do our own explainers for voters on Telugu-language websites that we then flood social media with. We were doing a lot on TikTok, but then the government banned it after the clash with China in Ladakh. There would nothing better for us than to capture a popular social media app.'

'You could do that with the DT website.'

'Maybe, but no one at DT seems interested. Not the Reddys, though they are no more, not Shrek Fund. The only person interested was their editor-in-chief, whom they sacked because he called Sankatram's son an illiterate eunuch,' Sharmila giggled. 'After he said it, we all realized how well that description fit Babloo Jubilee Reddy. Why didn't we see it earlier?'

'So, you're not interested in DT any more?'

'No.'

Mona smiled and then looked down at her hands. 'Ma'am, I'd like to ask you a question.'

'Please, always, you are welcome to.'

'Why did you want me to head this investigation?'

'It's simple,' Sharmila said, looking straight at Mona. 'There should not be a whiff of suspicion about my family. We are not involved, and that is the truth. If someone were to as much as speculate about the possible role of a member of my family, our political opponents would make an issue of it. Particularly those ruthless ruffians at the BGP. They are itching to get a foot in the door in our state, and a controversy would give them that wedge.'

'Ma'am, how can I promise you something like that? I am nowhere near solving the case, and so I can't rule anyone out as a suspect, as improbable as it may be.'

'I don't care where your investigation leads you, and who all you question and suspect. There's only one thing that I want, and that's for my father to be politically insulated. You must ensure, at any cost, that my father is completely protected from this multiple murder investigation.'

8

Mona was back at the IPS Officers Mess Annexure. She made it in time for the last round at the dining hall, and then went straight to her room to freshen up and lie down. Her head was humming. She undressed and turned off the light.

She wondered if she should call Deepika. *But what was the point of talking on the phone when they had barely anything to say to each other face-to-face*?

It was the pandemic's fault. As a police official, Mona could at least get out of the flat on the pretext of duty, but for Deepika it was a case of coronavirus-induced claustrophobia.

The lockdown had initially caused Mona to marvel—the empty roads, the clear sky, the birdsong and Mumbai's reduced stink. It resembled a never-ending hartal, the kind that Banduk Singh spoke of during his CRP deputation to Kashmir, minus the bunkers at every street corner.

The flipside was that people didn't step out of their homes; Deepika was deprived of other human faces. It was vital sustenance they had previously taken for granted. Even Mona understood how much she needed to see faces other than the usual assortment of sub-inspectors and assistant sub-inspectors checking in and out of her division.

The feeling of isolation worsened when the lockdown began to lift in stages and people cautiously stepped out of their homes, in masks though. Wearing masks was critical, but it hindered Mona in reading faces, even those of unknown passers-by, something fundamental to her job. She had always relied on looking into a pair of eyes and was beginning to realize that the nose and mouth were equally fundamental to self-expression.

What Mona missed most of all was other women's faces. She hungered for it. She felt a physical pain in her gut when she saw an attractive youngster pass by without being able to drink in her full facial beauty. Especially if the young woman had an intriguing hairdo. No one seemed to be aware of her pain; they carried on, at shops, on the road, at a park, moving rapidly and purposefully. She felt she would go mad. The city felt like an open prison.

Also, the dawdling had ceased. People stepped out for chores but hurried from point-to-point. There was no more loitering. Once upon a time, Mona cursed men for idling as she felt it led to petty crimes ranging from verbal abuse to pick-pocketing to just littering or urinating against a wall. It used to bug her that you couldn't find even one deserted back alley without a couple of unemployed men loafing about, but those days had become a thing of the past. Maybe they would return in two years.

It was worse for Deepika, imprisoned in the flat and irritated over her salary reduction. Mona was also annoyed; the government had stopped the scheduled dearness allowance hike that did not amount to much, just around ₹5,000 every month, and it held back half of the March and April salaries. It wasn't unduly bothersome because the government, compelled by the financial hit because of the lockdown, promised to compensate the police at a future date. Probably just before the next election.

For the private sector, no such compensation was on the horizon. Companies took whatever advantage they could get and employees suffered. Worst off were daily wagers and support staff.

Deepika fell into a foul mood. And she began to drink.

Her colleagues had agreed not to start Zoom conferences till noon. She would wake up minutes before noon, wash her face, comb her hair, apply kajal and make herself a Bloody Mary to get the day off to a proper start. She would begin by sipping her drink, keeping it just out of her computer camera's range, ducking her head out of the frame for each sip. After concluding the first video conference, she would pour a second drink. Midway through the second video conference, she would step away and pour her third drink.

After the second conference, she would fry an egg and pop two toasts. She would switch over to a screwdriver—yes, still vodka—for her fourth drink to wash the breakfast down in time for the third conference call. The fifth drink would keep her courage up.

The calls would end by five in the evening, but not the drinking. Deepika would finish her emails and reports, but sharp at seven she would turn on Netflix and spend the next six to seven hours binge-watching the most nonsensical European police dramas, drinking and occasionally shouting advice to the characters on-screen, or merely observing: 'Woh dekho Sweden ka Mona Darling!'

Before she would lose consciousness, Deepika would become a late-night online shopper. She would buy whatever caught her fancy at the moment, losing interest long before its delivery a few days later. She bought a compact saw. She bought a carton of KN95 masks. She bought four multi-purpose storage boxes. She bought a sports bra. She bought two packets of Valaithandu powder, basically crushed banana leaves that were apparently a good diuretic and effective in reducing blood pressure, though neither of them suffered from that affliction. She bought a wireless mouse that Mona found still unpacked when she left for Hyderabad for the police course. She also bought an expensive exercise bike, with back support, which also remained unpacked and took up substantial floor space near the dining table.

Mona was not amused by the taunts comparing her to globally-famous fictional Scandinavian investigators, but she did despair over the fact that they no longer talked. They spoke, but they did not talk. Anyway there wasn't much of an opportunity for the two of them to chat in the mornings, which Mona thought to be the best time. According to her, the mornings were filled with possibility and positivity; the evenings were for reflection and catharsis. Mona was an early riser, but Deepika was a late sleeper.

Because they never talked, Mona wondered whether each was becoming allergic to the sound of the other's voice. The pandemic had accelerated a lot of things—like the flab around Deepika's abs and and perhaps the inevitable decline of a relationship.

'We're becoming like my parents,' Mona said one day, in frustration.

'Your parents, maybe, not mine,' Deepika said.

Perhaps the tension could have been sorted out with sex. But by the time Mona would return home Deepika would be in no state for intimacy. She would comment on irrelevancies loudly. When Mona would sit by her and try to reassure her with a pat on the arm or thigh, Deepika would swat her away. Mona would go to bed feeling alone, in desperate need for a kiss, but Deepika would seem completely disinterested. Once, Deepika perhaps had a fleeting moment of clarity; she tried to touch Mona's waist, but it was too late. By then, Mona had also lost interest.

With the lockdown also came unexpected phone calls from girlfriends, with whom Mona had lost touch. One after the other. They seemed to crave human contact, lonely and locked in their miniscule flats, needing to break the tedious routine. Mona accepted some calls, some she did not. But on one occasion her phone was on the coffee table and Deepika spotted an incoming call from actress Charuchitra Singh. She was livid.

'Why are your ex-girlfriends calling you?' she had screamed.

Mona had shrugged helplessly.

'Do she still have feelings for you? Or you for her?'

'No, no.'

Mona had got over Charuchitra quite quickly; the actor, she had found, was high-maintenance and low-IQ.

'Are you on Hinge? Let me check your phone.'

Mona had assured Deepika that she was faithful and there was a fragile truce. She did, however, wonder how many people trapped in the lockdown had to manage love affairs they may have been having on the side, outside their marriage or live-in relationship. *What if the affair was intense and you were trapped at home with your spouse*? She wondered if, during the lockdown, people were hatching crimes of passion: police records had shown that domestic violence cases had gone up a lot, but not murders. Not yet.

She once allowed herself to mull the possibility of Deepika's death, and how that would release each of them. The thought experiment, however, had revealed that there was little chance of Deepika dying in a car accident, a train mishap or an air crash because the pandemic had curtailed travel—even after the lockdown was lifted. The only way Deepika could die was murder. Or if she was poisoned.

Mona seemed to experience a moment of clarity about the Hyderabad case just then, but it instantly evaporated without leaving a trace.

'All this endless waiting and waiting,' Deepika had once said, which Mona had assumed was about the pandemic-related restrictions on personal mobility and socializing. Now she wondered if Deepika had referenced it to something more existential, or whether she was merely referring to their relationship.

Poor Deepika! Perhaps she would appreciate a call from her. Or maybe it would make things worse.

Mona tried to visualize Deepika in her darkened room but could not. Not even her still-enviable physique, despite its slightly visible paunch.

Mona reached for her phone on the side table. When it came alive, she went on to social media. She went to Deepika's page and began swiping through recent posts. A swarm of unasked-for ads kept popping up, the most stubborn of which was a thinly veiled BGP post about the rising number of Muslim journalists in the country. *Odd*, she thought, *there didn't seem to be any on her list of* DT *interviews, even though old Hyderabad was Muslim-majority.*

She stopped at a photo of Deepika at a bar in Four Bungalows. She wasn't wearing a mask and her mouth was open. *She might have temporarily taken the mask off*, Mona mused, *but in the picture Deepika looked as if her mouth was endlessly open.*

There was another photo of Deepika sitting by the window of their flat, wearing a bright yellow top that reminded Mona of the starlet at the minister's house that evening. She put her phone back on the side table, face-down, and remembered Gurleen Kaur.

Mona felt herself stir.

Gurleen's nose! What a sharp line it had, broken only by the bent bridge. It was a paradox: a masculine nose on an otherwise ultra-feminine face, framed by glossy hair.

And what a physique! Mona drew up a scenario in her mind where Gurleen and she were alone in a room for questioning. Gurleen volunteered to be interrogated, and somehow the term 'third degree' popped into Mona's head. Shaking it away, Mona mentally undressed Gurleen and they pressed against one another. She began to explore the starlet's body.

Suddenly, Ms Sharmila intruded. Mona tried to eject her from the interrogation room, but Sharmila opened her tight smile and reached behind for her own blouse. Mona could not believe it. This politician was hardly a ravishing beauty, but Mona could not stop herself from getting worked up as she thought increasingly about her. Before she knew it, she had given in to waves of joy and affirmation.

Mona fell asleep, dreaming of herself as a drone over Mumbai, in a pandemic lockdown, flying over the usually bustling Marine Drive that was eerily empty now, somewhat like a curfew after violence, but for some reason spookier. She was seized by a fear of the unknown. They were living in dystopia, not just through a violent interlude.

9

The Page 1 headlines the next morning, on the second day of the investigation, were:

- 'MURDER OF FREE SPEECH' (*DT*, banner headline)
- 'Newspaper family (not NoI), HR head, have cardiac arrests' (the *News of India*, second lead)
- 'Police report four deaths in Secunderabad office' (the *Iyengar*, single-column, below-the-fold)
- '*DT* decapitation portends new Telugu order' (the New Indian Success, anchor)
- 'CM offers condolences, holds meeting' (*Telangana Toady*, third lead)

Mona scanned the headlines at the entrance to the mess. The newspapers were getting desperate in this era of the coronavirus. Hyderabad's papers were arguably more ill-informed than other cities.

She joined the breakfast queue and scanned the offering. Idli, brown rice idli, bajra idli. Poori bhaji. A dosa station. Medhu vadas, dahi vadas and urad dal vadas. Poha. Oats. Muesli in yoghurt. A dry and crusty cereal. White bread for toast. Industrial jelly, but no jam or preserves. Guava juice, lime juice. Buttermilk, skimmed milk. Instant coffee. A teapot.

What Mona craved was an egg. A single egg, even hard-boiled, would do, though she preferred a two-egg mushroom omelette. But egg was not available here. Just another subtle reminder of who ran things around here. Or in India, as always.

'Good morning, Ramteke Ma'am.'

A swarm of probationers gathered at her table with their plates, cups and glasses. Mona smiled and nodded at each one of them.

'How's the case going?' asked Probationer Alka Mathur.

'You know I can't speak about it,' Mona said, laughing. 'As it is, the local police thinks of me as an interloper. And I'm a woman, which further annoys the brass. Maybe I can share facts with you in a couple of days?'

'But tell us, na, how does it feel to be investigating a case in a different city?' asked Probationer Shweta Nair.

'Is language a problem?' Probationer Rohini Anjlekar added.

'It's like a heritage walk through the city's psyche,' Mona said. 'Not knowing Telugu is not a big drawback, not in this case at least. Anyway, the people here speak Urdu. Or

Dakhni, I guess. Easier to sense when a witness is being economical with the truth.'

'Ma'am, I wish you were giving one of our courses,' Probationer Kavitha Vaidyanathan said.

'What details do the papers give?' asked Mona.

Mona came to know a lot. DT disclosed that there had been multiple murders, though only two were confirmed so far. It saw an insidious conspiracy against a family that had done much to uphold press independence and the freedom of expression in India, if not in the whole of Asia. The *News of India* found it suspicious that there were four cardiac arrests around the same time, and noted that though DT was the top-circulating newspaper in the city—in the old city, in Secunderabad, in high-tech city and in the outlying gated communities and slums—the *News of India* was the preferred paper of the influencers and young people in the Socio-Economic Class (SEC) category 1 that was targeted by advertisers. The *Iyengar* made a straight police press release even drier, revealing nothing of what lurked under the surface. The *New Indian Success* report was tangential, focusing on how the Reddys' death meant a loss to the Congress party, giving the BGP an opening to broaden its voter support. *Telangana Toady* reported only the chief minister's reaction to the deaths, which included a high-level meeting that unanimously supported his decision to levy a new newsprint duty.

'That summary saves me some bother,' Mona said. 'Thanks.'

The group then proceeded to chat about life on the academy campus till Mona's mobile phone buzzed. It was SI Pavani.

'Morning, ma'am.'

The film unit Mona and Pavani planned to visit had begun shooting at the Ikea in Hitec city, at the opposite end of Hyderabad. Ikea apparently wanted them to finish before the customers came in, though that was down to a trickle because of the pandemic. Pavani suggested that they leave early to avoid traffic.

'Yes, good. Will you pick me up from the academy?'

'Ma'am, I'm at the academy's entrance.'

Before long, Pavani's motorcycle was chugging towards Hitec city. Mona's tummy protested mildly at riding the motorized beast just minutes after breakfast. Soon, it settled down and she spent the next forty-five minutes peering at the roadside urban blight and at bored car passengers.

Suddenly, in the distance loomed a long, light blue building on which the word 'IKEA' announced itself in yellow, much like the Swedish flag. They had reached the Mindspace junction and taken a ramp to get into the superstore's multistorey parking. Pavani stopped her motorcycle and a masked guard, wearing a uniform in the brand's colours, approached hurriedly. He spoke excitedly in Telugu.

'What!' Pavani exclaimed. 'Ma'am, a leopard has entered the premises and is headed towards the film unit.'

Mona and Pavani rushed in with the guard trailing.

'Call the forest department and the local zoo,' Pavani said. The relieved guard made a U-turn. As Mona and Pavani ran across the ground floor, they heard several shouts and screams echoing in the distance.

Unfortunately, the Ikea layout allowed for no shortcuts for the outsider, so customers had to navigate the entire floor before reaching their destination. No staff was in sight to assist them. Mona and Pavani whizzed by the array of pastel-coloured dishes, shiny pots and pans, dizzying curtains, racks of bath towels, pyramids of cups and glasses, other assorted accessories and the vast hall that housed all this. Oddly, the leopard had not knocked over any of the precariously placed displays.

They reached a cavernous warehouse where floodlights were turned on, blinding the leopard that had climbed atop a display pile of foldable tables in red and grey. The animal was spinning round and round, while film hands shouted advice in Telugu from the safety of neighbouring aisles.

It was a pale and short-legged leopard with a large skull. Perhaps a female. It was disoriented and continued moving, while the crew and store staff who had not fled the set, and who wore masks, shouted and beat on Ikea pots and pans, like villagers cornering a tiger in a forest.

Mona spotted a masked Gurleen Kaur hiding behind a rack of shelving units. The starlet held a purse, from the grip of which a gun peered out. Mona scrambled over to her while Pavani commanded the unit people to stop banging the accessories. She then introduced herself.

'Is that something useful in your purse?' Mona asked Gurleen.

'A taser,' Gurleen said, taking off her mask. 'Imported.' And then, for no discernible reason, she shrieked at the leopard.

'Give, give.'

Mona estimated the leopard's weight to be around fifty kilograms at the most. She came as close as the taser's range would allow—*what was it, fifteen feet*—and aimed at the big cat. She fired, and at the same time, the leopard leapt towards her.

As soon as the taser's probes hit, the leopard convulsed and lost consciousness mid-air. It fell close to Mona's feet. The film unit cheered. Several of them rushed to get a selfie with the fallen leopard.

'Rajan, ma'am, from the Nehru Zoological Park,' a man in a mask said. He had just arrived with his team.

'Tell me, Mr Rajan, where in the world did this poor leopard come from?'

In all probability, he felt, the leopard had emerged from the forest reserve during the lockdown. There had been other instances of leopards roaming the city after the streets were emptied of people, all of whom were hiding in their homes to escape the coronavirus.

'But why come to Ikea?' Mona asked,

'For the Swedish meatballs?' an assistant holding a syringe of tranquilizer asked.

'Ma'am, we'll conduct a physical exam and then release it into the forest,' Rajan said.

The assistant tranquilized the sleeping leopard and, with the help of three others, loaded it on a gurney. Rajan waved goodbye as they departed, with the gathering spontaneously bursting into applause.

A burly man with sunglasses and a fine-tipped moustache that poked out of the sides of his mask walked over to the display where the leopard had been cornered. 'Well, we missed our chance to film the leopard, but that's okay,' he said. 'There will be good publicity, for sure. Although I hope the government doesn't shut us down.'

The crew murmured.

'Okay, everyone, back to work,' he said and clapped his hands like a schoolteacher.

'May I have my taser back?'

Mona whirled around, and there was Gurleen in her purple dress with a dangerously high hem. Mona introduced herself.

'Of course,' she said. 'Where did you get this, by the way? Imported?'

'A friend got it for me. He bought it in Bangkok.'

'A girl's best friend.'

'The taser or the friend who bought it?' Gurleen asked and stared intensely at Mona for a few seconds. 'Haven't we met?'

'At the minister's,' Mona said. Gurleen immediately nodded in recognition.

'I'm not here about that though,' Mona said. 'I need to ask about the deaths at the DT office yesterday. You were at its office near at the time, so we should speak.'

Gurleen's face fell. 'But I didn't see anyone die,' she said. 'BJ didn't look like he was having a heart attack.'

'I know, I know. It's just a formality. Can we talk now?'

'I guess it'll take them some time to set up again. I was halfway through my dance sequence when that leopard appeared. How scary! And the producer wanted me to keep dancing while the leopard prowled around the furniture.'

'Really?'

'Really. But who listened to him? At that moment, I was scared shitless. Anyway, I now have to have my make-up done again as the mask smudged it. Come on.'

Mona and Gurleen followed Coreena, the masked make-up artist, through a doorway marked 'Staff Only' to a room filled with plastic-wrapped pillows and plastic hangers, in the middle of which a plastic chair had been set up facing a large portable make-up mirror. Several Ikea lamps burned brightly to illuminate the chair. Gurleen sat down and her nose and cheeks were immediately attacked by two make-up brushes.

'Was the guy with the moustache the producer?' Mona asked, watching the artists at work.

'Yes. Raghu Sir.'

'I need to talk to him, too.'

'He was at DT yesterday?' Gurleen was genuinely surprised.

'I guess,' Mona said. 'Why were you there, Ms Kaur?'

'To pick up my taser. Babloo Jubilee had called the night before and asked me to come to the farmhouse to take it, but I figured it would be a lot safer at his office.'

'Smart lady.'

Gurleen looked at Mona and grinned. They were silent for a moment. At that moment, Pavani came and stood next to the ACP.

'He was probably coked-up when he phoned. Anyway, I was tired from shooting and reshooting a single dance sequence that day. Why must a dance sequence need so many takes? The director must think he's David Fincher.'

The name sounded familiar, but Mona struggled to place it.

'Did he take a lot of cocaine? How well did you know him?' she asked Gurleen.

'Babloo Jubilee was forever on coke. The thing is, girls in the Telugu film industry can't avoid bumping into rich industrialists and their bratty sons. Can't say much for them though. The fathers are rapists and the sons are spoilt by ayahs. Babloo Jubilee wasn't all that bad, but he was too soft to be a threat. He must have really liked me because he kept calling me to his uncle's farmhouse to party. He would snort lots of cocaine and lay sprawled on a velvet couch, while me and the other girls would spend the night dancing. Why not, you know?'

'Nothing more than that?'

'Maybe he wanted more. He was sweet enough to get me the taser. He went abroad before the lockdown, in January I think, and after he returned he invited me over to collect it. The fact that it took me many months, with a lockdown in between, to see him tells you how deep our relationship was. For all I know, he might have bought a carton of tasers for other friends. But, thankfully, he didn't ask me to reimburse him.'

'Sweet fellow,' Pavani agreed. 'As sweet as paayasam, perhaps?'

'Paayasam?' Gurleen blinked.

'Hold still, Gurleen Ma'am,' Coreena said as she got to work on the starlet's eyebrows.

Gurleen's eyes were soon transformed. The eye make-up was bright and shiny. The magenta melded with aquamarine, and the gradient shined bright with the mild glitter, which was also added later. It reminded Mona of the make-up trend in her late teens and early twenties.

Gurleen caught Mona staring at her, and with those freshly made-up eyes, she smiled. This brought Mona back to reality.

'Did Babloo Jubilee look ill when you met him yesterday morning?' Mona asked.

'No, not even hungover.'

'What did you two talk about?'

'BJ talked about himself, as men usually do. He said he was tired of the newspaper business and wanted to diversify. I suggested that he bankroll movies for me to star in. He said maybe next year, but first he wanted to set up a vaccination business. He said that he could import a COVID-19 vaccine and sell it in India, making enough money to finance the entirety of Tollywood.'

'And?'

'And nothing. He stopped talking abruptly. As if I were secretly recording him. As if I would steal his business idea or his plans. Silly, yaar. Here I am, worried that my tits are not big enough for the Telugu audience and he thought I wanted to get into pharma.'

'You mean not big enough for half of the Telugu audience?' Pavani asked.

'How long, in all, would you say you were in his office?' Mona questioned.

'Maybe twenty minutes. He offered me a cup of tea, but I said no. How can you trust putting anything in your mouth during this pandemic?'

'Isn't a film shoot illegal during the pandemic?' Pavani asked.

'You'll have to ask Raghu Sir about that. Everybody is wearing masks. Except me, because I don't want to mess up my make-up. The entire set has been tested, and everyone was negative. We're all reasonably safe.'

'That's what you think,' Pavani said.

'Let's go talk to the producer,' Mona said. And then hesitated. 'Miss Gurleen, may I have your number? I may need to ask about your other meetings.'

Gurleen stood up and rattled out her number. She was dressed to kill. She bid the police officials adieu as they went off in search of the producer.

'What other meetings, ma'am?' Pavani asked.

'I just said that,' Mona said. 'In case we have more questions for her'.

Raghupathi Pullaiah sat in a lawn chair, scratching his crotch absent-mindedly. He had a white tika on his forehead, running from his hairline to his where his eyebrows met each other. The continuity girl announced the police officials. He took off his sunglasses.

'Haaah?' he said loudly.

The continuity girl pulled her mask outwards, repeated herself and allowed the mask to snap back into place. The producer immediately stood up and ordered a lackey to pull two more lawn chairs for Mona and Pavani.

'Myself Raghupathi Pullaiah,' he said, sticking his hand out.

'Have you forgotten COVID-19 protocol?' Pavani barked at him in English.

There was a hush on the set. All eyes were on the sub-inspector.

'What the fuck?' Pavani said loudly. 'Get back to work before I haul all of you off to jail for having an assembly of over fifty persons.'

The crew returned to hurrying about like gas molecules inside a box. Three dark, lanky men continued to hover around the producer, no doubt at his beck and call.

'Raghu Sir, can we speak alone?' Mona asked.

The producer waved his hand in stylish dismissal and the three beck-and-call men vanished.

'I'm sorry to trouble you during this shoot, but time is of the essence,' Mona said. 'We're investigating the deaths of the DT's Reddys and their HR manager. You were in the building at around the time of the incident.'

Raghupathi giggled. 'DT's Reddys!'

'Is Raghu Sir a suspect? What a great idea for a plot.'

A chocolate brown, bulky, bearded fellow with a massive explosion of jet-black hair on his head had mysteriously appeared by their side. 'Writer-director,' he said to Mona, sticking his elbow out as a greeting.

'You're David Fincher?' Mona asked, ignoring his elbow.

'Thank you, ma'am. You are a cineaste, likening me to David Fincher.'

'Ma'am, don't compliment Kashinath,' Raghu said, shooting daggers at his writer-director. 'He's worse than the most spoilt leading lady.'

'Er, okay,' Mona said. 'Does your production have permission to shoot?'

'Yes, yes, paid the health minister off. What more do they want?'

'How did you manage to get your crew out so early? I thought people in the industry were late birds.'

'Ma'am, you think everyone in Hyderabad suffers from the Nawabi culture? Just because those DT journalists wake up at two in the afternoon doesn't mean that we in the film industry also do the same. No, ma'am, we are a disciplined lot. Time is money. And of the essence.'

'Impressive.'

'Also, morning was the only time available at Ikea.'

'Why Ikea?'

'Ask Mr Fincher over there. Hey, Kashinath, wake up. Tell Ma'am why Ikea.'

Kashinath looked down. 'How can a creative person fully articulate an ineffable aesthetic decision?' he asked.

'What he means to say is that there are less customers due to pandemic,' Raghupathi explained. 'Also, the company has provided generous discount to use its space and purchase any items for personal use.'

'What a resourceful man, Mr Raghu! Indeed. You were at the DT office yesterday to meet Mr Velveti Rompy Reddy. Tell us everything about it, without missing any detail.'

'I met Rompy Reddy Garu quite often, and yesterday was no different. Went early since I had to come here for the parking lot shoot-out. Yes, good scene. Just like that movie. Which was it, Kashinath, the English movie you showed me?'

'*Free Fire*.'

'Yes, that one. Intense shooting scenes. Plot so-so.'

'You were telling me about Rompy Reddy,' Mona said.

'Yes, of course. Well, we had to discuss a private matter. We talked. Had a heart-to-heart chat. Then I left. Later I heard Rompy Reddy Garu had died of a heart attack. Immediately, I booked an executive check-up at Apollo Hospital in Jubilee Hills for myself.'

'What was this heart-to-heart?'

'Really, ma'am, it was not a heart-to-heart attack.'

'Still.'

'I'd rather not say.'

'Well, if you tell me now, I'll keep it off the record. Or else, we'll have you interrogated in front of a magistrate. And I'll give the transcript over to *Telangana Toady*.'

'No need for threats,' Raghupathi said, wiping his brow. 'We didn't talk about anything serious. Just some gossip about his nephew, Babloo Jubilee, and my leading lady, Gurleen. Nothing for the police.'

'What gossip?'

'Arre, how can I say it in front of ladies?'

'It's either the ladies or a magistrate.'

'Just … well,' Raghu said, his fingers drifting to the front of his mask. 'That he was doing a good job with her.'

'Is that true?'

'No, no, I've heard he was actually an illiterate eunuch. No, I just made him look studly to please his uncle, Rompy Reddy Garu.'

'You didn't discuss further financing for this film?'

Raghupathi shot a sullen look at Kashinath. 'Director Sahib, can you just check with the DoP if there are any shots of the leopard?'

Kashinath, nonplussed, went off to check with the cinematographer.

'Pardon, ma'am, but I don't want to discuss money in front of Fincher,' Raghupathi said. 'Or else he'll start demanding real Swedish meatballs, not this Indianized version, for the crew's tiffin and lunch.'

'So, you were discussing money with Rompy Reddy?'

'Ma'am, unlike Michael Reddy, Rompy Reddy Garu has no interest in hot chips,' he said. 'No, no, ma'am, his whole family is bankrupt, how can he give funds? We needed only ₹50 crore. Low-budget, thanks to the pandemic. Got it from an off-shore company registered in the Maldives. VRR Infra Pvt. Ltd.'

Mona looked long and hard at him. 'Pavani,' she said and stood up. 'Let's take him to your police station for a cup of tea. Ginger tea.'

'Aiyyo, Amma, why are you getting angry?' Raghupathi said, joining his palms in supplication. 'I've already told you everything you wanted to hear.'

Mona sat back down, mulling his words. 'VRR Infra, I take it, was a shell company belonging to Rompy Reddy?'

Raghupathi nodded.

'That, and probably other accounts belonging to other shell companies, have undeclared money which escaped the banks' notice when the Reddys declared bankruptcy?'

Again, Raghupathi nodded.

'And if Rompy Reddy had no interest in films, then this was just a way of laundering money, isn't it?'

Raghupathi beamed. 'I win, you win, we all win. Except that bastard Rowdy Panja Naidu who is not fit to even make Doordarshan documentaries about Harappan pottery.'

'I would hold off on the gloating,' Mona said. 'If it is a money-laundering operation, and your budget is ₹50 crore, how much did you tell him and how much is the film actually costing?'

'Ma'am, just what I said.'

'I know that's not true,' Mona said. 'But I am not doing an income tax inquiry, GST audit or an enforcement directorate investigation, so I won't bother about the funds. I'm just looking into a bunch of deaths. If I feel you are being less than honest, I'll go straight to the chairman of the Central Board of Direct Taxes.'

'Aiyyo, Amma. I'm being 100 per cent, no, 200 per cent honest. What you say is true; we are cost-cutting and hoping to wrap-up in under ₹30 crore. I told Rompy Reddy Garu it would be a ₹100-crore extravaganza. Yesterday, he got angry with me and asked who is this Gurleen, and that his nephew had told him that Gurleen couldn't bring a return on that much money. So, I said that we could set him up as a distributor and let him keep ₹50 crore as profits. Money laundered. He said that was okay. Trouble is that he had only given ₹35 crore till now. Now I have no choice but to keep costs down, come what may.'

'Maybe Shrek Fund will find all this information useful,' Pavani said.

Raghupathi looked from Mona to Pavani and back at Mona again. 'Ma'am, please don't do that. They'll go to court and get a stay on my film and say that this money should be given to creditors. They will demand all of the ₹50 crore to be handed over to the banks, which I don't have, which means I'll have to give ₹15 crore from my own pocket. Om Balaji, save me.'

'Again, I might keep this off the record,' Mona said. 'Do you have any idea how much money they had stashed away?'

'Rompy Reddy Garu never spoke about their money. Sankatram Anna was more loose-lipped. I heard him mention something like ₹3,000 crore, but I can't say for sure. I have no proof. Word of mouth only.'

The mention of such a big amount jolted both Mona and Pavani. They took a long pause.

'Sounds like a motive,' Mona said. 'Who else had this information?'

'Everybody,' Raghupathi said. 'Except the banks and the central government. Those monkeys! Perhaps Shrek Fund, but I wouldn't know for sure what they know or don't know. All our local industrialists likely knew. Certainly the chief minister's son. But no one can access this money unless they have a list of the Reddys' shell companies.'

Mona looked hard at Raghupathi. 'What time did you leave Rompy Reddy's office?'

'Ma'am, in roughly twenty minutes, around 11.30 a.m. He looked fine. No sign of a heart attack. What a tragedy.'

'Was there anything else he mentioned? Try to remember. It won't look good if we find out later that you held something back.'

Kashinath returned. 'Sub-Inspector Pavani,' he said. 'You have quite an impressive personality. Why don't you make an appearance in our movie, in uniform, as an angel of vengeance?'

'Good idea,' Raghupathi said. 'She will be a stunning scene-stealer. Just a figure of speech, ma'am.'

'I have a better idea,' Pavani said. 'Why don't you have your background dancers wear masks while dancing? It will give a social message, too.'

'Fantastic idea,' Kashinath said. 'We can have masks with tiny leopards.'

'Or each mask with a sponsor's logo,' Raghupathi said.

Mona's phone buzzed then. It was the medical examiner.

'Well, it's confirmed,' Dr Dharma said. 'Mr Velveti Rompy Reddy also died because of batrachotoxin … injected into his armpit. We almost missed the puncture mark; it was in an acrochordon. It is a harmless skin flap, or tag, that comes with age, amidst the hair. He had more than one acrochordon, and the toxin was injected into the largest flap.'

Just the thought of a skin flap hanging in the armpit made Mona queasy. 'Do these flaps happen to women also?' she asked.

'Yes, but it's harmless. Just collagen.'

Mona shivered.

'By the way,' Dr Dharma continued. 'I conclude that at least three different syringes were used. I would say four, but there's a possibility that a dropper was used for the paayasam. Or it could have been added straight from the vial or a tube.'

'No traces of any of the victims in the others?'

'Absolutely. Also the entry of each syringe was shaky, so epidermal tissue was disturbed. An identical entry mark would have shown up on another body had the same needle been used.'

'Three, maybe four, injections?'

'Either one killer carried several syringes, or his accomplice, or accomplices, carried one or more of the syringes. You may ask your subordinates to hunt for them.'

Mona mulled the necessity yet inevitable futility of searching for syringes. 'The other death?' she asked.

'Yes, the youngster. He died of a cocaine overdose. Massive. Instant cardiac arrest.'

'How is that a murder? And I thought there was no residue in his nostrils.'

'We collected fluid residue from the lungs and subjected it to Raman spectroscopy,' Dr Dharma said. 'We found nanometres of benzoylecgonine. Cocaine in high concentration, of high purity. Low in sodium bicarbonate. Not the kind that is peddled on the streets. Someone took a high concentrate and injected the victim with a fatal dose. Immediate cardiac arrest, instant death. Whoever gave it was confident that his victim would die. Ergo, murder.'

10

SI Pavani received a call from lead forensics expert SI Padmaja Rao. After a few words in Telugu, she handed the phone to Mona.

'Ma'am, we will immediately search the premises for used syringes,' SI Rao said. 'Additionally, we found four sets of fingerprints on the tin of paayasam. One is likely to be Sainath Rao's.'

'No doubt. SI Pavani will give you the list of visitors to the DT office yesterday. Take all their fingerprints for matches.'

Mona handed the phone back to Pavani and they stepped out of Ikea, towards Pavani's motorcycle. 'Let's formally inform the families that murder is confirmed,' she said.

Pavani checked her notes. 'Ma'am, the Reddys lived in Jubilee Hills, not far from one another. Sainath Rao was in Tarnaka, in Secunderabad. We can go there afterwards. Unless you want to depute somebody to tell his family?'

'No, better we go ourselves. You never know what fragment of a clue might emerge.'

A quarter of an hour later, they were navigating the leafy lanes of Jubilee Hills, where lush mansions made no pretence of camouflaging their vulgar immodesty. They turned a corner and came upon Sankatram Reddy's modest bungalow, modelled on Al Pacino's lavish residence in *Scarface*.

As they dismounted from the motorcycle, a well-groomed man with a salt-and-pepper ponytail passed by, walking a large pure-bred dog. Trailing them was a black-skinned servant carrying a poop scooper for the dog.

'These savarnas can't scoop up their own pet's poop?' Mona asked.

'The servant doesn't seem overly bothered,' Pavani noted. 'The Reddys used to have two or three dozen Bentleys. I wonder where they parked them. Not at the residence, obviously.'

'I've never seen a Bentley,' Mona said. 'What happened to all of them?'

'The banks seized them after the Reddys declared bankruptcy.'

'I wonder what the banks do with all the Bentleys. Who would they auction them to?'

Mona and Pavani were escorted upstairs to a velvet-immersed bedroom with a stale smell. A slight woman in a beige kaftan sat on the bed, sobbing softly. She was unremarkable with her thinning hair, disappearing lips and a pair of beady eyes. Another woman, muscular and determined, sat at the edge of the bed and held the sobbing woman's hand. She wore a mauve salwar-kameez; her pinched face contained two bulging eyes and was framed by a bob cut whose lower half had been dyed platinum.

'Mrs Magnolia Reddy?' Pavani asked the grieving woman. Bearing no resemblance to a magnolia, she nodded through her sobs.

The half-platinum haired woman stood up and greeted them. 'Sukhi Puri,' she introduced herself, refraining from sticking either her hand or elbow out. 'Former editor of the *Deccan Testament*.'

Mona politely nodded at her and then addressed Magnolia.

'Mrs Reddy, I come with bad news,' she said and paused. This part of the job never got easy. 'Your husband, Mr Sankatram Reddy, died of a heart attack. It's been determined that it did not happen naturally, so to speak. It was induced by a person, or persons, still unknown.'

Magnolia stared at her. 'What are you saying?'

'Mrs Reddy, your husband, your brother-in-law and your son were murdered. As was Mr Sainath Rao.'

Magnolia clutched at her hair with both hands and began shrieking. A middle-aged maid and two elderly servants rushed into the bedroom. 'Babloo!' she wailed. 'Babloo!'

Sukhi and the maid tried to pry Magnolia's fingers out of her hair. They succeeded, in that she let go of her hair and began swatting their hands and faces. The servants mutely looked on.

'Maggi, Maggi, dear,' Sukhi said, soothingly.

'Didi, Didi,' the maid said.

'Give her a pill the doctor prescribed.'

The maid got the pill and a steel tumbler of water from the side table. Magnolia swatted both from the maid's hands, the water spilling on her bed. The maid searched the blanket and retrieved the tablet, which she offered to Magnolia's wailing mouth.

'Don't medicate her yet,' Pavani said. 'We need to ask a few questions. We can't afford to wait for her to wake up.'

'What kind of police officials are you?' Sukhi Puri said. 'Can't you see she's in no state to talk?'

'Whatever her state, we need to move fast if we're to nab any suspects. No luxury of time.'

'You need not worry. I don't think another pill will put her to sleep. Or make her any more incoherent than she already is.'

Magnolia swatted the pill out of the maid's hand again. 'I've wet myself,' she said.

'No, you haven't. That's spilled water.'

'Water?'

'Mrs Reddy?' Mona said, her voice firm. 'Take the pill. I have some questions for you. Do you understand?'

Magnolia looked at Mona. Their eyes met, and Mona saw a glimmer of a person shrouded by grief. Magnolia nodded her and took the pill.

'Also, later we'll have a brief word with the servants about Sankatram Reddy. For now, please send them downstairs.'

'But these aren't Ram's servants; they're Maggi's,' Sukhi said.

'Mrs Reddy, was your husband's behaviour unusual in the days leading up to his death? Was there anything out of the ordinary, be it in his conversation or his behaviour, yesterday?'

'How should I know?'

Mona and Pavani exchanged puzzled glances.

'Maggi and Ram hardly interacted,' Sukhi explained. 'They spent their evenings separately. Ate their meals separately. Never saw each other. Sankatram slept in a separate room. They woke up at different times. Dressed separately. Her mornings were spent in the prayer room, his were in the living room with the newspapers and the phone. Breakfast at different times. Went to office at different times, in separate cars. Never spoke.'

'How do you know so much about their personal life?' Pavani asked.

'Sukhi is my friend,' Magnolia said suddenly. 'We used to lunch together and exchange gossip. Until she left DT. Traitor.'

'Come on, Maggi, you know I had to leave.'

'Why did you leave DT?' Pavani asked Sukhi Puri.

'I left last year. I was sixty-four and bone-tired. I couldn't be "Big Sister" any more.'

'Big Sister?'

'She was the best akka we ever had,' Magnolia said and began wailing again.

'I was the only akka that she and Ram ever had.'

'If you left DT a year back,' Pavani said, 'what were you doing at the office yesterday morning?'

'Akka can come to the office anytime she likes,' Magnolia said.

'Did Akka come to the office to murder anyone?' Mona asked.

'No, she didn't.'

'I went to meet Maggi. We were going to have lunch.'

'Akka, we missed lunch.'

'Did Akka eat any paayasam?' Pavani asked.

'Yuck, no,' Sukhi said. 'I heard about Sai, that degenerate.'

'What did he do?' Magnolia asked.

'Forget about Sai for the moment, Mrs Reddy,' Mona said. 'Can we focus on who might have reason to kill your husband, brother-in-law or son?'

'My poor son! My poor darling priceless golden fragment of the moon,' Magnolia wailed. 'Nay, of the supermoon.'

'What about who murdered your husband?' Pavani asked.

'If she doesn't know who killed her son, how will she know who killed Ram?' Sukhi Puri asked.

'Do you mean to say that you think it was the same person who killed them?' Mona asked.

'Why would anyone want to kill my sweet Babloo?' Magnolia wailed. 'He had no enemies. None. Unlike his father, who had endless enemies.'

'I thought the father and son were alike,' Pavani said. 'How is that one had no enemies, but the other did?'

'They belonged to different generations,' Sukhi said. 'And they did different things at DT. Journalism and politics were in Ram's blood. Not in BJ's. Like Rompy, he preferred sales and marketing.'

'They didn't even look alike,' Magnolia hissed. 'My son was so handsome, so good-looking, so fit, like Bal Krishna. His father? Hmph. Resembled Yamraj himself.'

'Your baby may have died of a cocaine overdose,' Pavani said.

Magnolia stared with her mouth agape in horror. Sukhi merely shook her head in dismay.

'Pavani,' Mona said, annoyed.

'What about Ram?' Sukhi asked.

'An air bubble in his heart killed him,' Pavani said.

'Really? He died of nothing in his heart? Surprising.'

'My condolences.'

'It's Rompy's fault for getting him hooked to drugs,' Magnolia wailed again. 'Drugs, drugs, drugs. Why did they need drugs? Why didn't the police stop cocaine from coming to Jubilee Hills? That damn Rompy and his damn farmhouse. He is a rapist. Drug pusher.'

'Rapist?' Mona was curious.

'He looked like a rapist, like the ones who killed the lady veterinarian last year.'

'Not like a suave and affluent member of Hyderabad's elite?'

Magnolia simply wailed in response. 'My heart was not empty. It was full of my sweet Babloo, sweeter than paayasam. And he died of drugs!'

'True. Someone injected him with a deadly dose. Might you have any idea who?'

Magnolia stared back at Mona vacantly.

Sukhi shook her head.

'Makes no sense,' she said.

'What about his father?' Pavani asked.

'Sorry to say this, but Ram had too many enemies.'

'Maybe one of his whores,' Magnolia said.

'Maggi!'

'How many did he have?' Mona asked.

'How would she know?' Sukhi answered on Magnolia's behalf.

'All of his sluts are in the tabloid,' Magnolia said.

'Especially in DT's lifestyle supplement that Maggi edited,' Sukhi explained. 'Daily. The supplement is for its popular party page. Filled with photos of well-dressed, high-society ladies. And girls. One reason the *News of India* has never been able to catch up with DT. Every high-society party or event was covered, thanks to Maggi's contacts.'

'And yours, Akka. Some would say DT sold only because of the tabloid.'

'That's a bit of an exaggeration,' Sukhi said, amused. 'Maggi would somehow hear about Ram's latest conquest. She would then locate the most unflattering photo of that woman and splash it in on the tabloid's pages. If she captioned it with "wearing the same dress as last week", I knew it was someone Ram had recently slept with.'

'He spent too much money on his whores.'

'Ram was warm-hearted when he wanted to be.'

'I didn't see the name of any "whores" on our list of visitors to the office yesterday morning,' Pavani said.

'Perhaps you ladies can check if anyone on our visitors' list was connected to any of Sankatram Reddy's women friends?' Mona suggested.

'How would we know who else the whores were with?' Sukhi said.

'Who visited yesterday?' Magnolia asked.

Pavani read out the list.

'Didn't he sleep with Rowdy Panja Naidu's wife?' Magnolia asked. 'What was her name? Nimmi? Panja Rowdy and he shared a couple of yesteryear actresses. Also, Maximillian. He and Max had a regular whoring session once a month or so. I think Max brought them in from Bengaluru. Maybe you can talk to these men about the whores and the whoring, and who killed my son.'

'How was Sankatram Reddy with his Akka?' Pavani asked.

'You mean, did he ever try to sleep with me? Never. He was respectful.'

'Maybe you weren't his type?'

'You mean I am not a North Indian bimbo or a five-star whore? You know, I've noticed that the men who get any women they want, want the very women that they can't get.'

'There are those men who are attracted to the intensity in a woman,' Mona said.

'Ha!' Magnolia snorted. 'BJ's father wasn't deep enough for that. He was like one of Duryodhana's anonymous brothers.'

'Be that as it may, I want each of you to describe your exact movements and timings in the DT building yesterday.'

Magnolia glanced at Sukhi, who began: 'I came to the office around noon. Maggi hadn't arrived yet, so I thought I would go say hello to Ram—'

'You didn't tell me this,' Magnolia interrupted. 'I came in just after noon and went to my cabin, where I set down the tins of paayasam on my table and asked the peon, Ravi, for a glass of purified and filtered warm water.'

'You brought the paayasam to office?' Pavani asked.

'Yes. So? I recently went on a temple tour in Kerala. I picked up the paayasam there.'

'Was it one of those tins that Mr Sai was found, er, dead with?'

'Yes. I meant to give him one. Unopened. He was always bringing paayasam for me whenever he took leave and visited a temple. It was only proper that I, in return, also give him prasad.'

'But you didn't hand it to him?'

'No.'

Magnolia claimed that she had gone upstairs with the peon and given one tin to Rompy Reddy.

'My husband happened to be with Rompy at that moment, talking to Maximillian Reddy. He demanded that I give Max the tin that I had intended to give Sai. I did. I never got to hand over a tin to Sai.'

Pavani called up the lead forensics expert. 'Padmaja, did you find any other tins of paayasam?'

She listened and then spoke. 'Why didn't you say so earlier? So what? WhatsApp me a complete inventory of items from all dustbins in the building.'

'Should I be worried?' Mona asked.

'No, ma'am. Forensics found three other tins besides the one they found with Sai. All of them are from same batch and had the same date. But the others had no trace of poison in them. So they simply inventoried and packed them.'

'Whose dustbins?'

'Rompy Reddy's, Canning Sairam's and Magnolia Reddy's.'

'The last one Maggi and I shared,' Sukhi added.

Mona was lost in thought as she digested a possibly important piece of the puzzle. She shook her head in dismay. Her colleagues seemed to go about their business in a most mechanical manner. 'Let's go back to the beginning,' she said.

'I waited for Ravi to give me my glass of water—' Magnolia began.

'This must be the same Ravi we spoke to yesterday, ma'am,' Pavani noted.

Mona nodded. They would have to speak to him again. She encouraged Magnolia to continue.

'I checked my email. The government had taken my hard drive recently and erased some of my emails to the team about story ideas.'

'The government took away your hard drive?'

'Yes, some department, ED or something. They do this every few months.'

'Why?'

Magnolia paused. She needed water. The maid gave her a refilled steel tumbler.

'My husband and Rompy had cases against them and had been raided more than once,' she said. 'My husband even went to jail for a month.'

'Awful,' Sukhi said.

'Not at all. He had his own cell. Lived like the VIP that he was. Demanded home-cooked food and so it went, three times a day. I believe ...'

'Yes?'

'At least one of his whores visited him regularly.'

'What was the case, or cases, against him?' Mona asked.

'Money laundering,' Sukhi replied. 'The ED alleged that he ran a benami company. Just a few weeks ago they had attached property belonging to Ram and Rompy in Hyderabad, Delhi, Chennai, Bengaluru, etc. I think there were fourteen properties in all. They said none of these were declared during the bankruptcy, which meant the banks were cheated out of ₹800 crore, approximately.'

'Is it only an ED case?'

'No, I think there is a police case, too, and also one with SEBI. It all boils down to the Reddys not showing all their assets, of manipulating the balance sheets of their various companies, hiding loans of one bank from another bank that they had borrowed from. They said the Reddys had accessed up to ₹15,000 crore from the banks through this sort of illegal jugglery.'

'What more did they want from us? Do you know they took away my mother-in-law's house? She died six months after that,' Magnolia said.

'Tragic.'

'Yes. Even the union went and sat on a dharna outside her gate to prevent the ED vehicles from going in. They built a small makeshift temple. But did the ED care? No. It just wanted to harass wealth creators of the nation. And did the government care? No, it just wanted more and more money to fight elections.'

'Is it?' Mona asked.

'Yes. The chief minister, that black-nosed bumpkin, kept demanding money from us. I knew he would never be satisfied, that he just hated our family from the bottom of his black heart.'

They were all momentarily silent.

'You were perusing your email?' Mona prompted Magnolia.

'Yes, the resident editor had requested coverage of a school event. The usual nonsense from his son's school. I discourage these things. Also, Sairam was always pushing his own things into the tabloid. All the time pushing his agenda, as if it were his personal paper. And you brought this slime into DT,' Magnolia said, pointing a finger at Sukhi.

'Yes. I thought he'd be different.'

'At least the editor-in-chief wasn't such a relentless self-promoter, though he too had his faults. Do you know he complimented me on my hair? I had come to office with it open. I was shocked. No one ever had the gumption to comment on my hair.'

'Maybe he fancied you?' Pavani ventured.

'No, no. He liked the girls in the tabloid and would get irritated if I shouted at them or abused them. Once I sacked this chubby Bengali girl he and Sairam had hired. He told Sai that, given a chance, he would sack me. Can you imagine! He wanted to sack me. It is my family's paper, and he wanted to sack me.'

'How impertinent!' Sukhi commented.

'What do you mean?' Magnolia said to Sukhi. 'You're the one who suggested we hire him.'

'To get back to the email ...' Mona said.

'Yes, yes. I was irritated by the resident editor's email, so I went to complain to my son. I climbed the stairs to his floor, but a starlet was in his office.'

'Isn't he a married man?'

'So what? He was no less than Lord Krishna.'

'You mean Bal Krishna,' Pavani said, rolling her eyes.

Magnolia ignored her. 'I went upstairs to his father's room, but he was not in. Ravi said he was in Rompy's room. I went there, carrying the paayasam tins, and gave one to Rompy. My husband demanded one. So, I gave him the one meant for Sai. I complained about the resident editor and then came back downstairs. By coincidence, Sai landed up in office just then.'

'Oh, he wasn't usually there in the mornings?'

'No. The lazy fellow hardly showed up most days. Since the pandemic began, he came to the office maybe once a week, that too around 4 or 5 p.m. Anyway, there was a visitor in his cabin, so I told Ravi to hand him his tin.'

'Yes, this much I saw. I was waiting in her cabin when she returned,' Sukhi said.

'Then Dr Kiran Mulukutla arrived, seeking a favour. Something about a hospital opening. Sukhi went downstairs, and Kiran and I chatted a while. Then she left. Sukhi returned, and while we were trying to figure out where to have lunch, the news of my husband's death came.'

They all fell silent again.

'We ran up the stairs to see him,' Sukhi said. 'Ram was still. Nothing seemed to revive him. I told Ravi to give him mouth-to-mouth resuscitation, but he was reluctant. I had no choice but to try; his mouth stank of a recent cigar. Then Gopalaiah came in, took a look and said it was of no use.'

Magnolia began sniffling.

'Then we were told that Rompy, too, was not all right. He was also still, in his chair, and that's when I felt terrified,' Sukhi said. 'And then Maggi's motherly intuition must have kicked in because she screamed even before they gave her the news.'

Magnolia sobbed. 'Suddenly, I saw in my mind Babloo sitting in his chair, also still like his father and uncle.'

'We ran downstairs. Maggi collapsed as soon as she saw Babloo. We carried her to a sofa in the outer corridor and brought her water. When she regained consciousness, she began slapping me.'

What Sukhi probably didn't notice was that two caretakers had tried to calm Magnolia down, but she began to slap their chests. That was when Gopalaiah came in and asked the women to go home.

'So we left,' Sukhi said.

Mona looked at Sukhi. 'You had started to tell us your account,' she said.

'Yes, I came in around noon. Maggi hadn't arrived, so I went to meet Ram, but he was busy with a swami and Rowdy Panja Naidu. I went downstairs to meet Sainath Rao to ask about my gratuity. I wanted to take it out, it came to around ten lakh.'

'For what?' Pavani asked.

'None of your business,' Sukhi snapped.

'Then?' Mona said.

'Then I came back up to Ram's room, but he wasn't there. He was in Rompy's room, but I did not want to go in there, so I came back to Maggi's cabin and waited for her. I saw Sairam enter his cabin. He saw me and waved, and then he came over and started talking about how grateful he was to me for the job, how much it had enriched his life, and that even his wife told him he seemed happy. Then he saw one of his visitors approach, so he went back to his cabin. Moments later, Maggi returned and then it was as she said.'

'Do you know who this visitor was?'

'He looked like one of those Hindi pracharaks.'

'Sanskriti Suraksha Samiti?' Pavani asked.

'Probably,' Sukhi said. 'I don't mix with that lot.'

Mona stood up. 'I'm just going to have a look at the house, if you don't mind. Pavani, meanwhile, will go over the details with you before we leave.'

She walked down the corridor, towards the sweeping spiral stairway that was built around a staircase chandelier whose raindrop lights almost touched the railing. She passed by the other bedrooms and stopped at a room that was obviously the library. It was stacked with ceiling-to-floor shelves of books on each of the three walls, the smell of their leather bindings hanging in the air. The fourth wall had two narrow windows, with a large portait of Ayn Rand hanging in the middle. It was another oil painting in which Rand and Reddy held hands, looking towards the rising sun on the horizon.

A servant was in this room, wiping the books with a dustcloth. 'Who are you?' Mona asked in Hindi.

'Apparao, ma'am,' he replied in English. 'Anna's librarian.'

Mona smiled. Perhaps Reddy wasn't as loathsome as people were making him out to be.

'Here, would you like to read this?' Apparao reached over and pulled out a volume. She read the title off the spine. *Ayn Rand's Relevance in the Ramayana* by Anjyanelu Naidu.

'Are you joking?' Mona asked.

'Ma'am, there's a room with Anna's cameras. Would you like to see?'

Apparao led her to an anteroom that had no windows but several glass cabinets that displayed only cameras and lenses. Though she had never had a proper camera—her father had a very old second-hand camera from the 1980s with which he took photos of her sisters and her—and used her mobile phone for taking photos, Mona was fascinated by the variety laid out.

'Minolta SLR. Leica, very antique. Hasselblad 1600F, nice square viewfinder from above. Kodak, also a classic. Rolleiflex, with the parallax lens. Canon AE-1. Nikon F, an old SLR reliable,' Apparao listed them out while pointing to them. 'This is a Carl Zeiss lens. The best.'

'Oh, I know this one,' Mona said, pointing to a camera.

'Yes, Polaroid. Making a comeback. Fuji also has an instamatic, over here.'

'What a museum!'

'Anna had hobbies. Horses, cigars, Bentleys, brandies ...'

'And ladies?' Mona asked.

Apparao said nothing and silently followed her down the stairs. Mona stared at the sparkling chandelier. Despite Sankatram's hobbies, his large house and its ostentatious decor were the true evidence of what he and his family were. Like plastic surgery, class and sophistication had been grafted on to their essential barbarism.

In the family room, Mona found many big photo frames of the family—Sankatram Reddy; his wife; BJ Reddy and his wife; and the daughter, Deepthi, with her baby and husband. They all wore silks and jewellery. Only the two Reddy men did not smile. Sankatram looked off-camera, perhaps at the Ayn Rand portrait upstairs, while BJ Reddy looked askance, as if wondering whether it was necessary for him to be there at all.

Mona passed by the dining room and stepped into the kitchen, where a team of cooks was chopping onions and whispering quietly. They went quiet when they saw a police official. Mona quietly withdrew.

There was a guest bedroom that was empty but smelled of fresh linen. Mona peeked into the attached bathroom. It had a large mirror above the basin, and to the side was a shelf with porcelain dispensers of liquid soap and shampoo. There was also a vial.

Mona picked up the vial and examined its label. The writing on it was presumably Chinese, except for a single English word: Sinopharm.

The vial's cap was sealed shut; below it was presumably a rubber top, through which the needle of an injection could be inserted. A clear liquid sat inside the vial.

Maybe there was a syringe with this vial. But Mona noticed that there was none. It seemed odd.

11

Mona phoned Dr Dharma. 'If someone associated with this case is missing a syringe, should they be a suspect?'

'Why not? It's odd, however. Who keeps a syringe at home besides diabetics? And keep in mind that there are a variety of syringe barrels. Some are 10 ml, some are 5 ml and others are as much as 20 ml or as little as 2.5 ml. I think the air injection probably used a larger barrel than the toxin,' Dr Dharma said.

'Is that a problem?'

'If you used a small syringe, you would have to pump it several times to inject a fatal amount of air into the artery. During an attempted murder, it would not be easy. To first inject, then pull out the syringe, pull up the plunger and then re-inject? No. Moreover, the victim would struggle for his life. He was big, not easy to overpower. I think a specific syringe was used for him.'

'What kind of syringes would be needed for the toxin and the cocaine?'

'Given the amount traced in the bloodstream, the 2.5 ml syringe would have been more than enough for the batrachotoxin. A 5 ml syringe would have been sufficient for the cocaine.'

Mona told the medical examiner about the vial with the Chinese label that she found in Sankatram's guest bathroom.

'Curious,' Dr Dharma said. 'If I were to guess without seeing the vial, or without knowing Putonghua, I would say it is a sample vaccination against SARS-CoV-2 developed by the Chinese.'

'Oh,' Mona said, crestfallen. 'I thought it might be the toxin.'

'That would not be in a labelled pharmacological vial. Still, why don't you send it across for analysis?'

'Immediately,' Mona said and ended the call.

She summoned everyone present in the mansion to the guestroom. About seven maids and servants followed Magnolia, Sukhi Puri and SI Pavani.

'Pavani, have this sent over to the medical examiner asap,' she said. 'I want to know from anybody here where the syringe that possibly accompanied this might be.'

The domestic staff shrugged in unison. Both Magnolia and Sukhi stared cluelessly.

'Have either of you been to Bangkok recently?'

'What? In the lockdown?' Sukhi asked. 'I haven't been abroad in ages.'

'I was in Dubai last winter, in January,' Magnolia said. 'Does that count?'

Mona said nothing. Pavani returned after dispatching the vial to the medical examiner. 'Ma'am, there may have been no syringe,' she murmured to the ACP.

'True,' Mona said. 'But something here doesn't seem right.'

'Should we stay or move on?'

'I suspect we'll be back here at some point. Who's next on our list?'

'Ma'am, Rompy Reddy's wife.'

'Oh yes, Sulochana,' Sukhi said. 'What a classical beauty she is. Was. The kind that men would travel from all corners of Andhra Pradesh to catch a glimpse of. She has a daughter, Sanjana. Quite a handful. Very much her father's daughter.'

Soon, Mona and Pavani arrived at a modern-looking mansion with glass terraces and balconies. Inside, they were led to a bedroom that smelled like a perfume factory. Sulochana Reddy was sprawled on her bed in a silk salwar-kameez, weeping tragically, her hair open and spread out. Two masked middle-aged maids waited on her.

'You've arrived,' Sulochana wailed. Then she paused. 'Who are you?'

The police officials introduced themselves and delivered the grim news about her husband being murdered. They offered their condolences.

Sulochana's tears inevitably dried. 'He was killed?' she sniffed.

'Yes,' Mona said. 'And we need to ask questions.'

'Why?' Sulochana asked. 'I didn't kill him.'

'Mrs Reddy, you're not a suspect at the moment. But we are determining who his killer was. You can help. Tell us about any changes in his behaviour lately, any known enemies, any recent developments in his life, anything at the DT office. Anything will help us.'

'I don't know anything about his businesses. You will have to ask Sanjana, our daughter, about that. She was involved in some business activity. The only thing I know is that he was, once upon a time, desperate to marry me. Kept telling me I was the most beautiful girl in undivided Andhra Pradesh. In the last few years, however, when the money gushed in, he neglected me.'

'How so?'

'He was never home. Always at his farmhouse, always throwing parties awash with alcohol and drugs and cheap whores. When the money ran out, the whores got cheaper. The worst was when we had a cricket team. Then he was always with one of the Eastern European cheerleaders. I told him not to come near me; I didn't want any Western venereal disease.'

Sulochana noisily burst into a fresh round of tears. Mona and Pavani stood and looked at the maids, who remained stoic, looking towards Sulochana.

'The worst was when he was seduced by Magnolia,' Sulochana exploded. 'That whore!'

Mona and Pavani exchanged surprised glances. Mona found it odd that this beautiful, glamorous, sexy, well-turned-out woman should call her plain Jane sister-in-law a whore. Magnolia, compared to her, seemed wilting, or at best, a wallflower.

'Beg your pardon?' Pavani said.

'When we were married, she was the senior daughter-in-law. Still, Rompy would say to me, "She may be Magnolia, but you are magnificent." And then, at the height of all the money and debauchery and cheerleaders, she seduced him. I confronted her, you know. She claimed that she had been raped by my husband.'

Mona and Pavani exchanged another glance.

'But I knew that my Rompy wouldn't want to rape such a sack of emaciated potatoes. I knew that she had done some black magic on him. Even her own husband did not believe her.'

Again, Sulochana burst into a tears.

It gave Mona a moment to reflect. There was motive for Magnolia to kill Rompy. But why kill the others? It was too neat, yet at the same time incomplete. As a piece of the puzzle, it was more misleading than missing.

Without warning, the weeping woman shouted, 'Sanjana!'

Her daughter, with open hair, mascara-streaked face, wearing stylish slacks, chiffon top, and high heels, came running into the room. She collapsed on top of her mother. 'Daddy!' she bawled. 'Daddy!'

Mona and Pavani stood silently while the two women hugged and wept, neither of them wearing masks.

Finally, Mona said, 'Ladies, we need to ask more questions.'

'I told you, we didn't kill the bastard,' Sulochana said.

'Amma,' Sanjana cried in protest.

Sulochana stopped sniffling. 'Rompy was a terrible businessman,' she said. 'Ask Sanjana.'

'True. Daddy tried his hand at many businesses for a long time, since I was a baby,' she said. 'Poultry breeding, a hotel, sports equipment, aluminium foil manufacturing, pharmaceutical trading, bookshops ... he even tried a business of mail-order sex toys.'

'He failed at mail-order sex toys?' Pavani was astounded.

'Yes. Each customer apparently had a busybody at home who opened their courier packages, discouraging them and others from ordering. My pedananna, SRR, was indulgent since Daddy was his younger brother, and anyway he looked after the newspaper. He seeded each of Daddy's ventures.'

'But none of the businesses took off?'

'None.'

'Then?'

'Then Pedananna brought him into DT.'

'How come?'

'The paper was flourishing; it was the time when cash was flowing freely. You know, in the early 2000s. Businessmen took bank loans and built mega businesses. Pedananna wanted to diversify and roped Daddy in to do so. They started a cricket team, a chain of bookshops, an infra company, and they were going to start an airline.

That's when the promised licence vanished, the money dried up and the good times ended.'

'So he killed this business as well?' Mona asked.

'Nobody in our social circle seemed worried,' Sulochana said.

'Yes, everyone we knew simply stopped repaying the banks. Like that MP who took ₹8,000 crore. I heard Daddy say so many times that the banks would never get their hands on the family's money. Trouble is, now that he's dead, neither will we,' Sanjana noted.

Sulochana bawled again on hearing her daughter's words.

'After the success of the cricket team, Daddy wanted to hold a Formula 1 race in Hyderabad. I was in the business with him. But we had to fold up because the airline deal did not come through.'

'You're in the business as well?' Pavani asked.

'I was, but now I'm on my own,' Sanjana said. 'I have my own fashion label and boutique. But yes, this vindictive government of lowlifes has registered a fraud case against me. In the Formula 1 project, some investors claimed they never got their money back. Can you imagine the nerve to file such a case against me?'

'Who was this?'

Sanjana, who was on a roll, ignored Pavani. 'Then there were the land deals. Daddy was accused of selling property he did not own to a third party. All he did was invest the bank money into properties around the country. I don't know why they went after Daddy when Pedananna was the real land-grabber.'

'He was?'

'You know my cousin Deepthi? Maggi Aunty's daughter? She was to be married long back. To the son of industrialist K.K.K. Reddy, who owns a big power group called Powerful Reddy. About two weeks before the wedding, she broke it off. Told us that KKK's son was gay. So, Pedananna sold a plot of land that he had bought from the software guy, the one that went to jail, and then put out a story in DT that KKK had bought the land from the scamster software fellow. KKK was publicly humiliated. He had to surrender the land to the government, which seized the software guy's assets to compensate the banks for their losses.'

'This is just one land deal you're talking about,' Mona said.

'Hello! This is what they did all the time,' Sanjana said. 'I wonder where they got time to run their newspaper.'

'That's what that dry cow Sukhi was for,' Sulochana said.

'Deepthi got married, isn't it?' Pavani asked.

'Yes, but not to that fellow,' Sanjana said. 'She was involved with the cricket team for some years. You might have seen her during the matches, cheering the team on. She looks like her mother. Some rich guy in Delhi, a divorcee, saw her on TV and courted and married her. The son of another businessman. Guess it worked out okay for her.'

'One of the last people to see your father was a realtor. Bharathi Rao,' Pavani asked.

'Yes, yes, Bhobho Uncle. He was one of the main fronts for the property business. Always trying to pump Daddy for political gossip. Always trying to get him to buy land on the outskirts, saying that the CNT was going to start a health-city like Hitech city. No wonder Daddy and Pedananna took loans from the banks to buy the land. Appreciation. Values will shoot sky-high. Demonetization, though, froze that process for a few years.'

'Rompy Reddy and Bharathi Rao were great pals?'

'I don't know if "pals" is the right word, but they got along and were always trying to get some scheme going. Lately, I heard they were talking about importing coronavirus vaccines from Russia or China. Or both.'

'We've been hearing that,' Mona said. 'Isn't there a ban on importing things from China?'

Sanjana laughed so loudly that Mona, Pavani and the two maids stepped back, lest she spray an unknown virus on them.

'Bans don't apply in Andhra Pradesh or Telangana.'

'Is it?' Mona thought for a moment before asking the next question. 'If you were to suspect someone for your father, uncle, cousin and Sainath Rao's murders, who would it be?'

'Shrek Fund,' Sanjana said promptly. 'They were going to take everything from us, but Daddy and Pedananna put up a good fight. Of course, there was the bankruptcy process and the NCLT order, but Pedananna was fond of saying he knew how to juggle these things.'

'How did he plan on doing that?'

'Maybe find a new shadow financier to pay off Shrek Fund and allow us to run the paper. Or keep up one legal challenge or another, so that Shrek Fund could never take possession of the paper.'

'But what if Shrek Fund did take over finally?'

'Daddy would have paralysed the paper, even had the union stop publication. That would leave Shrek Fund in a mess; they would have to run away, go back to Kolkata. Pedananna had also planned to take all the assets, the printing press and the staff, and simply start a new newspaper called *Daily Testament*. They weren't going to give up the family heirloom so easily. It is a cash cow.'

Mona scrutinized the two women. 'Did either of you go out of the country in the months before the lockdown?'

'Rompy kept promising he would take me to Sri Lanka for a holiday,' Sulochana said. 'But he never did, that cheapskate.'

'Amma.'

'What? Can't I say anything?'

'I went to Singapore for a shopping weekend in January,' Sanjana said.

Mona and Pavani stared at her.

'What did you buy?' Pavani asked.

'I beg your pardon. What does that have to do with my Appa's death?'

'Just answer the question, please,' Mona said.

Sanjana pouted. 'I bought some tops and dresses. No slacks. All the women there are stick-thin.'

'What else?'

'Well, some underwear. Silky ones, from some Hong Kong designer.'

'You mean to say that those fit you?' Pavani asked.

'Go look at your own dickey,' Sanjana retorted, glancing at Pavani's backside.

'What else?'

'What else, what else ... oh yes, a dildo.'

'You can get those in Madhapur,' Pavani said.

'Really? That East European crap? I prefer the Made-in-Philippines kind.'

'What else?' Mona persisted.

Sanjana looked dazed. 'Maybe a charger for my phone. I don't know.'

'Nothing from Papua New Guinea?'

'Uff, that's not even a country.'

'You didn't bring back any toxins?'

Sanjana did not take long to figure out what the police were after. 'You mean the poison used to kill Appa? Are you insane? Why I would kill Appa?'

'So, that's a no,' Pavani said.

'I wouldn't even know how to go about getting a poison if I managed to reach New Papua one day.'

'Papua New Guinea.'

'Yes, yes. But no. And how dare you! I'm going to complain to the police chief.'

Mona sensed that they had reached a dead end here. She took leave of the two ladies who again burst into tears.

'Poor Rompy Reddy,' Mona said after Pavani and she had stepped outside.

'Babloo Jubilee Reddy's widow?' Pavani asked.

Mona nodded.

They arrived at the gate of a modern one-storeyed bungalow. A long-haired young woman, attired in a peach chiffon sari, stood in the garden examining the pink and off-white hibiscus, oleanders, peach crossandra and yellow roses. Up close, she had eyebrows that lingered dangerously close to one another, a flat nose and a double chin. She did not look as if she had been crying. She immediately put on a mask when the police officials walked up to her.

'Indira,' she introduced herself. She pointed to an older couple standing on the verandah. 'Those are my parents.'

She waved them indoors. Then she and the two police officers sat on chairs laid out on the verandah, still in range of the flowers' ambrosia.

Mona gave her the grim news. 'Your husband died of a heart attack that may have been induced.'

'How? A cocaine overdose?' Indira asked matter-of-factly.

'As a matter of fact, yes.'

'It was bound to happen. Thank God. Now I'm free. I'm still young enough to remarry.'

'Shouldn't you at least pretend to be a grieving and shattered young widow?'

'Why? It wasn't as if our life together was filled with warmth and liveliness.'

'I wish you all the best,' Mona said. 'My priority, however, is to solve the case of four dead people in the DT building asap. I couldn't care less about anything else.'

'I didn't kill them. Neither did my parents.'

'None of you are suspects, but we thought you might shed some light on who could have been the murderer, or who could have been behind it.'

'Wouldn't that be one and the same?'

'Not necessarily,' Mona said. 'Indira Gandhi was assassinated by her bodyguards, but no one believes they were behind the plot to kill her.'

'My husband and his family were not the prime minister.'

'Yes, indeed. But we do need your help.'

Indira shrugged.

'Did your husband behave differently in the past few days? Did he meet anyone out of his usual circle?' Pavani asked.

'No.'

Mona and Pavani were brought to an impasse by the young widow. They were silent for a few moments.

'Well, your husband's cousin—' Mona began but was interrupted by Indira.

'You mean Sanjana, that slut?' Indira said. 'Fancied herself a businesswoman. My appa is a better businessman than her, and I could have been a better businesswoman if the family had allowed me. Whore. Do you know how long her marriage lasted? A fortnight. They spread the word that the husband was gay, but he wasn't. Do you know how I know? Because a good friend of mine slept with him. Before I got married. Nothing was wrong with him.'

Mona seemed to recall that Sukhi had referred to Sanjana as 'quite a handful'.

'Every week she's with a new guy at a five-star coffee shop, thrusting her boobs at him, practically begging him to climb into her bed. Spends each weekend with a different guy. An insatiable libido. Just like her dad.'

'Miss Sanjana referred to a business deal that might have led to this series of murders.'

'You mean Creamy Stock Broking killed my lifeless husband? Because of the Chinese vaccine?'

'Creamy Stock Broking?'

'Yes, it accused Babloo Jubilee of pledging non-existent shares of DT for some ₹200 crore. They were pissed as hell. They were buddies with some film producer. I don't know which one though.'

'Raghupathi Pullaiah? Or Rowdy Panja Naidu?'

'Yes, that's it, the second one.'

'That's a good tip. Thank you, ma'am,' Pavani said.

'You said something about a Chinese vaccine?' Mona asked.

'I heard something in passing. They were going to import the vaccine and sell it across the country. Cheaper than the Western vaccines. Babloo Jubilee said it would be the biggest windfall in decades. We were supposed to make lakhs of crores of rupees.'

'I see.'

'I don't know though,' Indira said, 'Babloo Jubilee was all talk and no action. We had been married for years, but look, no baby. Or babies. But I won't accuse him of being gay. I know he was too fond of cocaine and the whores.

That was his preference, not some demure wife or even a feisty one.'

'I'm sorry to hear that.'

'It isn't your fault. Or mine for that matter. These were habits he picked up when they had a cricket team … partying with rich businessmen and the film stars. Do you know, Babloo once saw a cricket match on the TV, because his tummy was upset, and he saw this Australian player, Richard Lessness, and said that his hair looked too long for TV. So, the next day they took the family airplane—'

'The family had an airplane?' Mona asked.

'Used to. A Jetstream that has now been seized by the banks. Anyway, the next morning Babloo and Dick went by air to Mumbai to get a haircut. Dick protested saying that he had a match to play that evening, but Babloo assured him that they would be back in time. And they were, but the match went badly for Dick. It was as if his vital energy had been sucked out of him. By a whore. On the airplane.'

'Dick Lessness met your husband yesterday morning.'

'Yes, but he was harmless,' Indira said and then paused. 'Or maybe it was favourable court judgment on behalf of the cricket team. Maybe Dick had dues pending.'

'Your husband went to Bangkok in January. Did you accompany him?'

Indira laughed. 'Are you joking? Of course I didn't. He did not want me with him while he did his ... well, whatever it is that men go to Bangkok for.'

'He didn't bring you back anything?'

'You mean like a taser? That was for his starlet, his "slutlet", so that the producer wouldn't try to rape her.'

'He told you that?' Pavani asked.

'No, don't be silly.'

'Anyway. You think your husband would not have gone through with the Chinese vaccine?' Mona asked.

'That's my opinion. But what do I know? His father would definitely have.'

'Why do you say that?'

Indira paused. 'Do you know what my last dinner at my in-laws' place was like? Well, let me tell you.'

❧

It was a Thursday evening when Indira arrived with Babloo Jubilee at her in-laws' house.

'Hi, Amma,' Indira said, stepping into the sprawling living room where Magnolia and Sankatram sat with Rompy, Sulochana and Sanjana. There were two sofa sets, one in each half of the room—the men were on one set, the women were on the other. Husbands and wives sat with their backs to each other.

An attendant appeared and asked the new arrivals in Telugu: 'Sir, ma'am, the usual?'

Babloo Jubilee sat in a single-seater adjacent to his uncle. Indira sat in a single-seater adjacent to her mother-in-law, across from Sanjana. The couple were not in each other's line of sight.

'I told Agarwal that he should just take over his father's jewellery showroom this instant, corona or no corona,'

Sankatram was telling Rompy. 'The fellow says he's in mourning. I went like hello! There's no time for mourning.'

'Why doesn't Agarwal Uncle give us more ads?' Babloo Jubilee asked.

'Bobo, let's stick to the big players for the big ads,' Sankatram said. 'Anyway, I thought you'd be at office this morning.'

'Anna, I heard that the union is demanding we pay any corona-related hospital bills,' Rompy butted in.

On the other sofa, meanwhile, Magnolia said,

'I always buy so much from Agarwal, but his people don't how to make the traditional gold sets.'

'Like bridal designs?' Sulochana asked. 'For whom?'

'Like kasulaperu,' Magnolia said. 'It might be a bride's gift, but in the tabloid we've carried photos of even actresses wearing them.'

'The one with the row of hanging Lakshmis?' Sanjana asked.

'Hanging Lakshmi coins,' Indira said.

'I personally prefer the designer kasulapera,' Magnolia said.

'I like the ones with stones,' Sulochana said. 'Especially precious stones.'

'Why not a triple-layer kasulapera?' Indira asked.

Back on the men's sofa, Sankatram said, 'I was telling your uncle about the Chinese vaccine proposal, Bobo.'

'This is a once-in-a-lifetime opportunity to make some serious money,' Rompy said. 'This is the chance we've been waiting for. We'll be the wealthiest Reddys on either side of the Godavari.'

'I was wondering, we need not price it under Moderna or Pfizer, or even that Pune lab. We could just scale up while the government is still importing. It will take them a while; the Western countries are buying billions of doses. That leaves us with the Chinese vaccine that we can sell on a mass scale, earning crores,' Sankatram said.

'How will we purchase it?' Babloo Jubilee asked.

'That's where our partner comes in,' Sankatram said. 'We'll use the Mauritius funds to get letters of credit at the Export-Import Bank (EXIM) of China. Our partner will be the front. Then we use Waiting for Godown as the chief distributing agency.'

'Fantastic solution for washing our money and bringing it in,' Rompy said. 'That way, we can also keep DT by buying off Shrek Fund and clearing the paper of liabilities.'

Babloo Jubilee looked doubtful. 'I don't know. You have to be clearer about how you intend to move the money from Mauritius to EXIM.'

'Bobo dear, you worry too much,' Sankatram said. He stood up and clapped his hands twice, announcing: 'Time for dinner.'

Everyone stood up, all of them leaving their glasses behind except Rompy, and staggered to the dining room where, under a tiered crystal chandelier, an eight-chair dining table had been set. At each place was a Chinese porcelain plate whose edge was gilded with gold. The fork, knife and spoons were all golden. A crystal glass and tumbler sat guarding each person's cutlery from the other diners.

Sankatram took the head of the table, Rompy sat on his right and Babloo Jubilee sat on his father's left. Magnolia took the other end with Indira on her right and Sulochana on her left. Sanjana sat between her parents.

The attendants served them an appetizer: crispy caviar pakoda with mint chutney. 'My favourite,' Sankatram announced as he rubbed his palms in anticipation.

'No corona pakoda from the kitchen?' Sanjana asked.

'Calm down, Sanju,' Magnolia said.

'But your head chef did come down with Covid, isn't it?' Sulochana asked.

'Why don't we try the Chinese vaccine on him?' Babloo Jubilee said.

'Good idea, Bobo,' Sankatram said. 'I'll get a vial and syringe, and we'll inject him with it ourselves.'

'Maybe we'll get a professional,' Babloo Jubilee said.

'You want to call someone from China?' Rompy asked. 'From Wuhan?'

The attendants came in just then with raw tamarind soup.

'You can go to Wuhan and fetch him,' Sulochana said to her husband.

'I would never go to Wuhan,' Magnolia said. 'Don't they eat dogs there? How did Covid start? Came from a bat, right?'

'You're thinking of that film, *Contagion*, Amma,' Indira said. 'This started from a pangolin.'

'What's a pangolin?'

'A scaly anteater, I think.'

'Thank God it didn't start from monkeys,' Rompy said. 'Or else it would have spread from the DT newsdesk first.'

Everyone laughed. 'Don't remind me of those morons,' Sankatram said.

'Those monkeys are under your charge, no one else's.'

'What do I do?' Sankatram was slipping into a foul mood.

'They make our lives impossible,' Babloo Jubilee said. 'I met CNT and he went on and on about this story and that story. How do I explain that we're not responsible for these out-of-control journalists?'

The attendants came in again and served jackfruit curry, crispy bhindi, tamarind rice, a Pulasa fish curry and a sorrel leaves chutney.

'It's that damn editor-in-chief,' Sankatram said. 'He keeps misleading me with the story list. Each story says one thing, but then it turns out to be another anti-government hitjob.'

'No wonder the chief minister and his family are always pissed at us,' Babloo Jubilee said.

'No, that's because Pedananna was never nice to them,' Sanjana said.

'What? You want Appa to be as friendly with the politicians as you are?'

'Bobo, stop it at once!' Magnolia said.

'What do you mean by that, Babloo Jubilee?' Sulochana demanded.

'I mean, why can't you ladies just go get some more Botox done and leave me in peace.'

'Please, Bobo, can't we just eat in peace?' Indira pleaded.

'At least we don't look as dry as your whores,' Sanjana retorted. 'Your herd of dry cows, Baby Krishna.'

Indira's chin dropped down to her mangalsutra.

'Your faces look like they will crack if you smile,' Babloo Jubilee said.

'Is this why you came here?' Magnolia asked. 'To fight?'

'Who started the nasty remarks?' Sulochana said.

'Let's just agree that the journalists are the clowns who keep landing us in a mess,' Sankatram said.

'You hired the editor-in-chief,' Magnolia said.

'He looked like an intellectual, so I thought he would stay away from anything controversial and just stick to writing his editorials. I didn't know he was such an idealist.'

'What do you mean?'

'I don't know. He has this fucking fixation with Kashmir.'

'Language,' Magnolia cautioned her husband.

'The fellow got his father to Hyderabad for a month and started bringing him to office, taking him for lunch and all. Apparently has Alzheimer's, like Amma.'

'I know. How sweet.'

'I told him, why don't you leave your father with your wife. He started to laugh.'

'He's a sly one,' Rompy agreed.

'What kind of Reddys can't deal with a sly intellectual?' Sulochana said.

'You mean, I should get tough with him?' Sankatram asked. 'I did, and he went to pieces. Any tougher and I don't know what will happen.'

'Besides, we're not gangsters,' Babloo Jubilee added.

'What a shame!' Sanjana said. 'Perhaps that's what's missing from the Reddys. A bit of rough stuff.'

'Is that what you like from your men? The rough stuff?' Babloo Jubilee said.

'You should try it with your next cow,' Sanjana shot back.

'Only after your Dad is done with her.'

Indira could not take it any more. She got up without finishing her food and went back to the living room.

'What about your sweet dish, dear?' Sulochana called after her. 'Pineapple halwa.'

Babloo Jubilee did not come after her; he continued eating as if nothing had happened. His father began talking about the Chinese vaccine again.

'That was what life was like with this family,' Indira told Mona and Pavani. 'And now the men are gone. Good riddance.'

'Ma'am,' Pavani said. 'Are you expecting?'

Indira paused and nodded reluctantly. Mona was taken aback. *How did Pavani guess*, she wondered.

'I can tell from your colour of your skin,' Pavani said. 'How many months?'

'Nearly five.'

'That means you got pregnant after the lockdown began,' Pavani said. 'At least your mother-in-law will be happy.'

Indira looked at the two police officers. She smiled wryly.

'My father-in-law would have been happier,' she said.

'No,' Mona said.

'Yes.'

'Did you ever tell your husband?'

'I did. He laughed and said, "Now you'll have your baby."'

Everyone fell silent. Mona was getting sick of this mess.

'Before we go,' she said, 'you know, your husband's cousin is certain that Shrek Fund was behind the murder.'

'What? Why?'

'She said that they can now take control of the cash cow, DT.'

'Sounds good in theory, but she neglected to tell you an important fact.'

'What's that?'

'That with the passing of the brothers and my husband, the person who has inherited control of DT is my mother-in-law. Mrs Magnolia Reddy will now run the show.'

12

By lunchtime, Mona and Pavani were famished. They decided to stop for a bite on the way to Tarnaka, to talk to the late Sainath Rao's widow.

'Ma'am, vegetarian or non-vegetarian?'

'I would prefer non-vegetarian,' Mona said. 'Some Hyderabadi biryani?'

Pavani took a detour to Basheerbagh, past the Commissionerate, and on to Hyderguda road. They got down from the bike near a nursery and walked down a nondescript lane until they were enveloped by an invisible cloud of cinnamon. Lovely. Several cars in front of the cafe appeared to be trapped in the same cloud.

'They have an open area on the ground floor and an AC dining room on the first floor,' Pavani said. 'It's usually very crowded in the open restaurant. You have to wait to share a table. Brutally efficient; people don't linger. They eat, wash at the communal sinks and leave.'

That day, however, the cafe had more than a few empty tables. Men milled around the takeaway counter. Despite the social distancing, the people sat at the very edge of the benches, as if the virus might enter their bodies through their pants. Seeing Pavani's uniform, a waiter led them to a table away from the others. They ordered two mutton biryanis and a bottle of mineral water.

'What does it look like to you?' Mona asked.

'Ma'am? The case? It's pointing to Magnolia Reddy. Hard to believe that such a small-built and frail-looking woman could pull off such a thing, but we've seen stranger things on *CID*.'

'True, but there are many inconsistencies. First of all, there's the poison. How did she get it? Even if her son obtained it in Bangkok, which isn't exactly next door to Indonesia, and brought it back before the pandemic and kept it refrigerated, why would he hand it to her so that she could kill his father or uncle?'

'Yes, ma'am.'

'Then, let's assume she wanted to bump off her husband and her brother-in-law, not just as a crime of passion but also to take over the family business. Why would she kill her son? She looked deeply distraught over his death.'

'Maybe she didn't kill him. Maybe it was an accidental death that coincided with the other induced heart attacks.'

'There are no coincidences in life. And why would Magnolia kill Sai? No motive as far as I can tell.'

Pavani was quiet. On cue, their biryanis arrived.

'This is so much,' Mona said. She took a bite without either the raita or the mirchi salan. She was in heaven. 'Saffron,' she said.

'Kewda too,' Pavani said.

They ate in silence for a few moments.

'Ma'am, most police officers would start wrapping up the case on the basis of just this.'

'I know. They would no doubt leak stories to the press about her guilt, arrest her, go to court for police custody so that they could interrogate her, give her a few slaps and make her confess. Case closed.'

'Yes, ma'am.'

'But that would be a travesty of justice in this case. Though I don't mind handing out a few slaps to those who've got wealthy by stealing from banks.'

'When do we arrest her?'

'We won't until we crack the case. Too many messy loose ends. For instance, this Chinese vaccination thing that keeps popping up. Is it linked to the poison from Southeast Asia? And then there's Shrek Fund. There's also the messy fact that the Reddys, despite being bankrupt, owed money to different people. Also, what happens to their black money, wherever it may be stashed?'

'We'll need help from the Economic Offences Wing.'

'Let's see,' Mona said, tossing another piece of mutton into her mouth. 'You know, I often think another course should be added to police training, especially for investigation.'

'Like what, ma'am?'

'One way would be to make them read crime fiction from around the world,' Mona said. 'I know, it sounds frivolous. But the fact is that most crime novels, in an attempt to be clever and tease their readers, throw red herrings. All plausible. In any given murder mystery, readers keep changing their minds about who might be the murderer.'

Mona chewed another mouthful and then said, 'At the very least, it will ingrain some scepticism in investigators about their first suspicions and help them avoid wrapping up a case as soon as they have the first suspect.'

'But, ma'am, hunches, especially those of seasoned investigators, are often correct.'

'I agree, but that should not become a cause for laziness in following through with the investigation. It should not mean that you stop searching for suspects. What if you get a fresh hunch after interrogating a different person connected to the crime?'

'What books would you recommend, ma'am?'

Mona sighed. 'I'm not an expert,' she said. 'There are so many books. We are hardly in the age of Aristotle, who had read all the books published in his time. Even as we speak, so many murder mysteries are being written or published or being rolled out for sale. It is hard to keep track of all that is available, and even harder to find out what suits one's tastes.'

'Still.'

'I think there is some good Scandinavian crime fiction despite the hype over one particular Swedish writer. I like French crime fiction, always some convoluted crime of passion. American crime fiction, I don't know, always about murdered children nowadays. I like crime writing by a couple of Scots, like Ian Rankin and Val McDermid. Oh yes, there's also a lot of Japanese detective novels, but I don't know, they're all such intricate puzzle boxes. Good for the brain, I guess, but a bit impractical.'

'Like Sudoku puzzles?'

'I don't mind Sudoku. One of my sisters has been trying to get my father to do Sudoku daily, to keep his brain active and ward off senility. I guess you have to like puzzles. Most cops don't, I suspect.'

'What about local-language crime? In Indian languages? We have some in Telugu.'

'Yes, there is Marathi and Bengali, too, but Hindi relies more on magazines and serialization. The real "serial" killers, ha ha. Somehow the thrust is not so much on the twists and turns as it is on the lurid aspects, or in aping a Western writer like James Hadley Chase.'

They finished, cleaned up, paid and got the leftovers packed, which they handed to a homeless woman and her children on the roadside. They were then off to Sainath Rao's house.

Sainath's family lived on the ground floor of a modest house in a treeless lane, hidden away deep inside a concrete neighbourhood. On the verandah stood a unique young man. As soon as he saw the two police officials, he panicked. He tore off his mask and ran inside. Out came his mother, a woman with more than a few silver strands in her oiled and tightly tied hair, a white blouse and sari and a white mask that could not hide her despair.

'Namaste,' she said, her palms joined. 'I'm Rajyalakshmi.'

Mona and Pavani introduced themselves and sat down on cane chairs. A strong smell of sambar wafted out from the house. The young man peered from behind a curtain on the main doorway.

'That's Vijay,' Rajyalakshmi said. The boy giggled. 'He's a special child,' she added.

Mona winked at the boy, making him run inside. Then she steeled herself and gave the widow the news that Sai had been poisoned. She did not mention the condition in which Sai's body was discovered.

'Why Sai?' Rajyalakshmi asked, crying softly. 'What am I to do now? How will I look after Vijay on my own? He was so close to his father. They were like best friends.'

Vijay peeped from behind the curtain. His smile had vanished; he had sensed things were not right. His mother reached out, took his hand and wept.

'He's twenty years old, but his mind is like that of an impatient child,' she said. 'I'm not getting younger. Once his sister is married off, it'll be just the two of us.'

Mona was at a loss for words. Rajyalakshmi asked her son to stay inside.

'Is there anything that you can tell us, which will help us catch the culprit who did this to your family?' Pavani asked.

'What can I tell you? We are simple, God-fearing Brahmins. We don't fight with anyone, not even with neighbours. We were planning a trip to Tirupathi next month.'

'Yes, ma'am.'

There was silence for a few moments.

'Sai must have felt angry over the delayed salaries?' Pavani asked.

'He wasn't as angry as I was. I stopped asking him about his salary, you know. What was the point? Those Reddys, God will punish them for sure! Sometimes I would get so angry that I would pray the chief minister would pour molten wax into their ears.'

'What about the threats from other staffers? Did he ever speak of that?'

'Yes, once in a while. He wasn't scared; he was just frustrated that he was being blamed for matters not in his control. What to do, I told him. This comes with the position. An important executive gets blamed for such things. No one dares to abuse the owners, except the former editor-in-chief, Sai would say. Sai disapproved but said that he was an educated yet uncouth north Indian.'

'Yes, but the former editor-in-chief didn't kill anyone,' Pavani pointed out.

'Your husband was unconcerned about the hostile email from disgruntled staffers?' Mona asked.

'Totally. He would come home, sit with Vijay and play carrom with him like there wasn't a worry in his world at that moment.'

They again fell silent.

Finally, Mona spoke in a whisper. 'What about your marital life?'

Rajyalakshmi looked puzzled. 'What about my marital life? Normal, like everyone else's.'

'No, I mean, your ... marital life.'

The widow didn't seem to be catching on.

'At night?' Pavani asked.

'What nonsense!' Rajyalakshmi roared. 'What does that have to do with anything? What business is it of yours? Is nothing sacred any more? How dare you come to my house and speak such filth? You're like a shameless TV news channel.'

'Calm down, ma'am' Mona said sternly. The widow began sobbing into the hem of her sari. 'There's a reason I ask,' Mona added and then revealed how Sai's body had been found in his cabin.

'What are you saying?'

'The poison was in the paayasam,' Pavani said. 'And that's how it got into his bloodstream.'

Rajyalakshmi took a while to compose herself. Vijay peeped out, saw his mother in distress and ran back inside again, shouting anxiously for his grandmother. His mother followed him inside and the police officials heard her try to calm him down. It took a while, but finally they heard him whimpering, somewhere indoors, unseen.

'We were like any couple in their fifties,' Rajyalakshmi said after she returned and sat down. 'More like roommates. Comfortable, quiet. At night we shared a bed, though lately

I was thinking of sleeping in a separate room. I know a man has needs, but I don't have them any more. I don't know anyone my age who does. Our bodies have changed and we just want to be left alone. Thankfully, my husband was not a forceful fellow. And yes ...'

'Yes?'

'He liked to relieve himself in bed. You understand, right? Yes, that. At night, before going to sleep. In the morning, before getting out of bed. I got used to it because he stayed on his side of the bed and did not trouble me. I never imagined he did it in office. I did wonder though how many times a day he did that. Maybe it was because of Magnolia Madam.'

Both Mona and Pavani sat up.

'Yes. Sai began working at DT seventeen years ago. At that time, Magnolia had silky hair and was pretty, in a delicate way. I always suspected that he lusted after her. I suspected that for so many years she had been in our bed, in a manner of speaking, while he, you know, relieved himself at night and in the morning.'

Everyone fell silent.

'Did anyone know about this, um, passion he had for Magnolia Reddy?' Mona asked.

'Well, I never told anybody, and I doubt he told anyone. Being such a polite man, I doubt he would ever have told her,' Rajyalakshmi said and burst into tears. 'Are they going to publish this in the newspaper? How he was found? Will they show it on TV? I hate those TV re-enactments. They're so scary. We will be ruined. How will I ever show my face to the world? Everyone in his family will blame me. They will say I should have gone to him at night.'

'Madam, do not worry,' Mona said. 'We will not tell the media or the general public. I can't control his colleagues, but I'm sure they will be discreet.'

'How can you be sure? Didn't they blame him for the delayed salaries even though it wasn't his fault? He was just a convenient target for everyone.'

She had a point. It depressed Mona, especially when she saw Vijay look out from behind the curtain, his wide eyes big with fear and his cheeks streaked by tears.

Mona had one last question. 'Did your husband ever talk about Shrek Fund?'

'Oh yes, all the time.'

'Really?'

'Yes, he was often angry with the people there. He said they just wanted to come in and sack all the staff. That they would come and strip down the assets of the newspapers group that the Reddys had built over the decades.'

'Sai was loyal to the Reddys, is it?'

'Very much. He always reported to them anything that he suspected Shrek Fund was up to. He told me that if Shrek Fund took over, it would sack him and he would have to find a new job. But who would give a fifty-three-year-old a job at this time, especially with the economy so down?'

'Was he planning anything specific?'

'I don't know,' Rajyalakshmi said. 'But I do know that he talked to me, and that he also talked to some people in the office about Shrek Fund.'

'Who?'

'I think Gopalaiah. Maybe Canning Sairam, the resident editor.'

'Saying what?'

'Saying that Shrek Fund had to be stopped under any circumstance,' Rajyalakshmi said. 'At any cost.'

13

As they got back on to the Inner Ring Road and left Tarnaka behind, Mona marvelled at some of the greenery they came across. Government land, naturally. Wherever people settled, they made the trees vanish and poured cement even into drains that were centuries old. Hadn't she read somewhere that even the chief minister wanted to take over the cantonment, with its lovely green cover and quiet walkways, and subject it to more urban blight? Well, everyone deserved a place to live. That's how she had made it into the police, wasn't it, instead of staying in a village and being subject to the whims and fancies of the upper-caste landlords.

They followed the road till it reached the DT office. Inside the gate, a constable stood up and saluted. Mona and Pavani dismounted from the motorcycle.

'Ma'am, should we see Lord Canning?' Pavani asked Mona.

Mona considered this. 'Let him stew a while. Why don't we set up, as yesterday, on the fourth floor and meet the representative from Shrek Fund?'

'Yes, ma'am. I'll get Mrs Srilatha.'

Srilatha entered the late Sankatram Reddy's room with trepidation. She was a stumpy woman, wearing functional metallic frames. Her hair, with a functional middle parting, was drawn into an oily plait. She wore a KN95 mask and a pale brown salwar-kameez that appeared to squash her bosom. She carried a soft briefcase made of a waterproof fabric, which likely contained a laptop.

'You met all four of the dead yesterday morning,' Mona said even before Srilatha sat on the chair brought out for her.

'What a coincidence!' Pavani remarked.

Srilatha looked from one to the other. 'Yes, ma'ams, that's my job,' she said.

When asked about Sainath Rao, whom she had met first, she said,

'Looked normal to me, though I later found out he was not so normal.'

'What did you talk about?'

'Nothing important. The usual. Yesterday we were talking about the Bengaluru office. The paper has been shut down there, but the staff is yet to be reduced to a minimum. Also, we pay rent for the current office, which is too much space. The local manager has identified a new site at a fraction of the rent, but he says we need ₹20 lakh to renovate it.'

'He didn't seem distracted or unhappy?'

'No, not at all. He had received an email from a Mumbai staffer, demanding backpay of seven months. He shook his head and laughed. "What can I do?" he said. I knew that he told me about the email only to keep putting pressure on Shrek Fund to give more money for the pending salaries.'

'Why didn't you?'

Srilatha gave a wry smile. 'Not so simple, ma'am. We are waiting to take control. Then we will pump money into the company and pay the genuine liabilities.'

'Genuine liabilities? Are there liabilities that are fake?'

'Yes, ma'am. For instance, there a huge bills pending from a newsprint trading company. Now that he is dead, I can tell you that we know the trading company was a front for Rompy Reddy to siphon off DT money by producing fake invoices. The newsprint would come directly from the producer or importer, but this trading company showed that it was storing the newsprint in its godown before unloading it at the printing press as per requirement.'

'What was the name of the company? How do you know it was fake?'

'The trading company is called Waiting for Godown Pvt. Ltd.'

Mona rolled her eyes.

'We always suspected it was fake because Rompy Reddy would insist that payments of Waiting for Godown be made a priority, more than paying the newsprint manufacturers. It was confirmed when I was sitting in the former editor-in-chief's cabin one day. He got a call from Gopalaiah that a truck of their newsprint had been stopped at the city border due to the coronavirus lockdown. Gopalaiah wanted the editor's help in releasing the truck from police custody. It was headed straight here, not to this so-called godown.'

'Perhaps it was a one-time matter?' Pavani asked.

'I asked the former editor-in-chief about it. He casually said it was a regular matter. The trucks would arrive during the day, violating entry rules for heavy vehicles. This confirmed that there was no trading company, no Waiting for Godown. I looked up its registered office, and it is in a building in Balanagar that belongs to Rompy Reddy.'

Mona and Pavani were momentarily quiet. 'This is why you didn't give them money for the pending salaries?' Mona asked.

'Yes. Also, a huge part of the money we would have given would have gone to the Reddys and their family members as salaries.'

'What?'

'Yes, ma'am. Each of them held multiple titles and was paid separate salaries for each designation. For instance, Rompy Reddy was also the editor of the Telugu monthly magazine that closed down this year. Separate salary for that. Sankatram Reddy was also the editor-in-chief for the Telugu newspaper *Telugu Prabha*, which now only appears as an e-paper. It misses a few days here and there, but no one seems to complain, so low is its readership. Separate salary for that. Rompy's wife and daughter are employed as consultants drawing exorbitant salaries, as are Magnolia's daughter and Babloo Jubilee's wife. Quite a drain on the salary account.'

'Okay,' Mona said. 'You had a daily ritual where the executives put on a show of how desperate they were for an infusion of funds, and you went through with the ritual though you were not convinced?'

'Exactly right, ma'am.'

'Was it the same when you met the three Reddys?'

'More or less,' Srilatha said. 'I met Babloo Jubilee first. He was quite excited about having met CNT, the minister, and said the paper would finally get its much-needed dues.'

'That must have been a relief.'

'Quite the contrary, ma'am. He wanted to impress on me that I should convince my higher-ups at Shrek Fund that since the Reddys had managed to get this money, some ₹8–10 crore, they should be allowed to direct the spending according to their priorities.'

'I see,' Mona said. 'Did his behaviour seem unusual?'

Srilatha thought for a second. 'Maybe he was a bit excited that early in the day,' she said. 'I thought it was because of the starlet who had visited him first thing in the morning.'

Mona and Pavani exchanged a glance.

'In fact, he looked so happy with life that I was keen to get out of his room. Is that how he got the heart attack?'

'Which Reddy did you meet next?' Mona asked, ignoring Srilatha's question.

'I went to Rompy's room. Both the brothers were there. Rompy must have heard that we suspected Waiting for Godown, so he tried to browbeat me as to how I had the gall to suspect Waiting for Godown, that it was a company that paid its GST on time. I asked him how payment of GST was relevant, since it is anyway computerized so you have to pay it on time in order to get the releases. Then he tried to be velvet-voiced and said how it was necessary to pay the dues to loyal companies like Waiting for Godown.'

'He was Velveti Rompy, after all. And Sankatram?'

'He was quiet, smoking his cigar, creating a lot of smoke that somehow wafted towards me.'

'Any difference in their behaviour?'

'None. I also didn't say anything to Sankatram. I just sat there, looking out of the window. Then Sankatram finally addressed me, explaining why part of the next infusion of funds had to go to the Delhi edition of the newspaper. It was an old complaint, so I just listened and then left.'

'And both men were still alive?'

'At that moment, yes. It is amazing how God works. No prior warning.'

'You don't seem too put out,' Pavani said.

'I'm not, but that's nothing. I had a Zoom call this morning with the Shrek Fund headquarters and it was like Diwali, Christmas and Eid all rolled into one.'

Mona yawned. 'Even I need to speak to Shrek Fund at some point.'

'You can speak now,' Srilatha said, opening her briefcase and pulling out her laptop. 'Shrek Fund is on a conference call at this moment. Manish Manaktala and the others are there. We can join in.'

'My first Zoom interrogation,' Pavani said.

'This is an interrogation?' Srilatha was alarmed.

'No, of course not,' Mona said, shooting an angry glance at Pavani. 'Get us Mr Manaktala.'

Srilatha opened the Zoom application and clicked on the invite to an ongoing call. Immediately, she was one of over a dozen faces in as many boxes on the screen.

It appeared that a raucous online party was in progress. In each box, people wore party hats and were sipping from martini glasses. Some of the revellers noisily used their festive blowouts. Virtual balloons flew up across the screen and paper streamers ran across.

'You can do that?' Pavani wondered aloud.

Mona leaned into the laptop to search for Manish Manaktala. There he was, third row, last column.

Manaktala had a broad forehead and wide-set eyes that hid behind rimless rectangular eyeglasses. He wore a party hat, under which was trapped bushy but steel grey hair. A magenta paper streamer lay across his shoulder. He raised a glass of orange juice.

'Cheers, Srilatha!' he shouted and recklessly downed the juice in a single gulp.

'Cheers, Mr Manaktala,' Mona said. 'If you don't mind, what exactly are you celebrating?'

'Dr Bina Rehman can answer your question. She's the resolution professional who is managing the DT bankruptcy till Shrek Fund moves in. We invited her to the party.'

A stringy-haired woman, with crow's feet around brown eyes that trained a canny look towards the camera, waved from the second column, first row. 'Hi-i-i-i-i!' she called out. She then lifted a cowbell into the frame and rang it, its loud clang amplified by the computer.

'Ma'am, what's the celebration about?' Mona asked.

'It seems that DT will soon be handed over to Shrek Fund,' she said. 'Hence the celebrations. Here, talk to Mr Manaktala.'

With that, her box disappeared. She had left the call.

'She's a bit unhappy because she will no longer hold meetings of the Supervisory Committee,' Manaktala said. 'She gets a tidy little sum for each meeting.'

'So, she's not a suspect,' Pavani murmured under her breath.

'What was that?' Manaktala asked cheerfully.

'Was it such a big deal for Shrek Fund to get rid of the Reddys that it is celebrating their deaths?' Mona asked.

'Let's do this on a private call,' Manaktala said. His box disappeared.

Srilatha also left the Zoom party and received an invite for another call from Manish Manaktala. She accepted it. This time, there were only two boxes on the screen: Srilatha and Manaktala.

'Oh, you don't know. You don't know,' Manaktala said, 'what a terrible time it has been! Besides the fact that the Reddys absolutely refused to yield the managing of the newspaper to us, in contravention of the statutory order of the constitutionally mandated National Company Law Tribunal under the Insolvency and Bankruptcy Code, and besides the fact that they continually siphoned off money for personal use, they were also quite nasty to us. The effing family is, or should I say was, far from noble in its intent or conduct.'

'Makes me think that you would have wanted them bumped off,' Mona said.

'We are an investment fund, not a mafia family,' Manaktaka said. 'I mean, let me put it this way. If I wanted to kill them, how would I do it sitting here in Kolkata?'

'No assassination is the brainchild of the person pulling the trigger. There are always larger forces in the shadows who usually get away with it.'

'You're giving us too much credit, ma'am. Also, you're giving the Reddys too much credit. Perhaps it was not an assassination but simply an act of revenge? Locally? Granted, we are thrilled to bits, but I don't think you can accuse us of masterminding the deaths. Or the killings, whatever be the case.'

Mona paused. She decided to change tack.

'Mr Manaktala, what do you intend to do with the newspaper once you get a hold of it?'

'Good question, ma'am. We intend to make some money.'

'But don't you have to put in money first?'

'Yes, once that is done, we put into effect our plans. We stop the losses. That means cutting staff, closing the Delhi edition ...'

'Why are you after the Delhi edition? Don't you need that for national advertising, or at least national-level influence?'

'That is a fallacy. The Delhi edition was strong when it started twenty-five years ago, a must-read, but that was another era and a different ownership. Now it is just Sankatram's vanity edition.'

'Vanity edition?'

'Yes, the paper was a way to get to attend high-level get-togethers and meetings and say that he was the owner of a national newspaper. He just wanted meetings with ministers, income tax commissioners and top businessmen. The brand has a name that still lingers in people's minds, even if they haven't seen the paper in more than a decade. The paper itself serves no purpose.'

'How so?'

'It has no readership. Maybe an oddball here or there. It used to be read by the diplomatic crowd, but even they've stopped nowadays, except for the Caribbean missions. We're not even printing a thousand copies these days. The pandemic was the last nail in the coffin for the Delhi edition.'

'What about national advertising?'

'Come on, even the advertisers aren't that stupid. Do you think the *News of India* gets advertising for all its editions? The companies look at their best markets and sell ads according to those. We might have offered the metros and the entire south, but they sold DT the ads only because of the Hyderabad edition. There are no add-ons for having a Delhi edition. In fact, we will still get national ads even after closing the Delhi edition because we're number one in Hyderabad.'

'And influence with the political class?'

'Do you think the home minister will ever talk to us because of just the Delhi edition? Hell no. The party wants to muscle in on Telangana and Andhra Pradesh and grab power in these states. So, if Big Boss ever gives an interview, it will be because through DT he can address the voters in these states. Not because of a silly, unread paper in Delhi.'

'You're really against having a paper in the national capital,' Mona observed.

'Do you how many lakhs per month, how many crores per year we're burning just so Sankatram Reddy could tell Lutyens' Delhi that he has an edition there? I need to bring the bottom line up before I can focus on raising the top line, so to say. Losses have to be cut. Only then can we climb out of the hole that the Reddys have put us in.'

'But they disagreed?'

'DT has a glorious legacy,' Manaktala said, 'but the Reddys didn't act like they cared about it. Forget about the past, they were not even interested in building the future, which is the online brand. Everybody in the media business has used the pandemic to leap forward with their online bouquet and strategies of retaining and grabbing more eyeballs. The Reddys? They were only interested in taking a used lemon and squeezing whatever was left in them.'

'With the Reddys out of the way,' Mona said, 'you can now take over and begin running the paper the way you want? Closing the Delhi edition, upgrading the online presence, cutting staff, etc.'

'Absolutely. I can't tell you how much I'm looking forward to tackling this challenge head-on.'

'The Reddys no longer stand in your way. What a happy coincidence.'

'Well, I don't know if it is tactful to use the word "happy". But certainly, I am optimistic that the Reddys will do better in death for the newspaper they once upon a time built and owned than they could have done in life.'

'You are the man with the motive,' Mona said.

'But not the culprit the Reddys deserved.'

'I think,' Mona said, 'I think it would be best if you came down here for an in-person interview. Can you do so tomorrow morning?'

Manaktala frowned. 'It's difficult for me.'

'We need you. This is a murder investigation.'

'I understand, I understand. But it's not like you're asking me to fly to Bali for the weekend. And I just came back from Hyderabad.'

Mona and Pavani exchanged an alarmed glance. 'What?' Mona asked. 'When? And why Bali?'

'I was en route to Lombok, to Gili Islands, for a destination wedding. This was in January, for a friend's daughter's wedding. I love Indonesia.'

Mona was quiet. 'And Hyderabad?'

'Yes, I was there the day before,' Manaktala said. 'I flew back to Kolkata yesterday afternoon.'

'You were in the office?'

'Indeed. I left for the airport just as the three Reddys arrived at the DT building.'

14

Manish Manaktala agreed to reach the next day. Srilatha ended the Zoom call and was excused.

'Should I get Lord Canning?' Pavani asked.

'Let's go to his cabin. See him in his full form.'

They went down to the second floor of the DT office. The worn-out red industrial carpeting was freshly vacuumed. Two caretakers sprayed the vast newsroom with a disinfectant, as a measure against the coronavirus. Less than a handful of journalists sat in each of the newsroom's far corners. The middle of three glass cabins standing side-by-side at one end was Canning's.

A midget Bakasura-like man stood up and smiled. Under a Chinese bowl haircut, his square horn-rimmed glasses hid two leery and beady eyes. His misaligned teeth jutted out and his flat nostrils flared. His tongue shot out, lizard-like, licking his lips and vanishing again. His portly torso wobbled as he stumbled forward to shake their hands.

'Mask on, please,' Pavani said.

They sat without shaking hands and Sairam ordered adrak chai.

'Your name is Canning,' Mona said. 'Unusual.'

'My father was a great admirer of Charles John Canning, the governor-general of the East India Company who put down the 1857 mutiny and became the first viceroy when Queen Victoria took over,' Canning said. 'A strong figure. The man who subdued India. My father wanted me to be as strong as Earl Canning, so he named me after him.'

'Some people in the office refer to you as Cunning Sairam.'

'I know, thanks to Rocky. He was popular around here. Taught all the peons to call me Lord Cunning. I hope you won't be so rude.'

'You're a Brahmin from coastal Andhra, is it?' Pavani asked. 'Where? Vizag?'

'How does that matter in this crazy year? COVID-19 knows no caste. It's now a level playing field.'

'Crises make the field more uneven,' Pavani said.

'We have a big story today,' Canning said. 'I mean, beside your investigation.'

'Oh?'

'Yes, I don't know if you heard, but a leopard strayed into Ikea this morning. Apparently a film shoot was going on.'

'It was a film about wildlife?'

'I don't know.' Canning rubbed his fleshy chin. 'I was under the impression that film shoots were prohibited during the lockdown. Or Unlock 4.0. Or is it Unlock 5.0?'

'Unlock 6.0.'

'Anyway, the police apparently tased the leopard. A taser, can you believe it? The Hyderabad City Police is equipping its force well. I do hope our crime reporter gets an interview with the officials involved. What a dope! These reporters are so lazy. Always relying on press releases on social media. They couldn't get a story even if it was delivered to their desks.'

'True. Someone has to be incompetent to have a story come to their desk and they not recognize it.'

'That's the level of mediocrity and incompetence a leader such as myself finds himself bogged down with. It is tough running the newspaper. It's during times like these that I wish the former editor-in-chief, Rocky Borkataki, was here to kick some inept ass.'

'He'd probably start with yours, no doubt.'

Canning shot Pavani a dirty look. 'I know the police commissioner,' he said.

'Tell us your exact movements from yesterday morning,' Mona said.

'You mean I'm a suspect? How can I be a suspect? I never did anything.'

'Standard procedure. Answer in as much detail as possible.'

'I came in a bit early, around noon. I had called a friend over for tea, and I wanted to catch the chairman before he left for lunch.'

'Chairman?'

'Mr S.R. Reddy. Or former chairman, I guess. I caught a glimpse of Rocky and former editor Sukhi Puri. She was in the next cabin with Mrs Magnolia Reddy. I was about to head across the street for lunch when I heard about the deaths. Then the police came. That would have been you and your team. I waited to talk to you, but my turn didn't come. Then I got busy with bringing out the newspaper.'

'Did you get to meet Mr Sankatram?'

'The chairman? Yes, briefly. He offered me a tin of paayasam, but I declined. Thank God.'

'Why "Thank God"?'

'I heard that Sai Garu was, er, caught in it.'

'Sainath Rao was masturbating into the pudding.'

'What he was imagining it to be is beyond my imagination,' Canning said. 'Some people will surprise you.'

'Did you know him well?'

'I had never even seen him till a few weeks ago. Only spoken to him on the phone for work. I emailed him when people demanded their salaries. I sent him a few applications for recruitment, but all were stalled by the Shrek Fund people. Nothing beyond that.'

'A purely professional relationship?'

'I knew I had to stay clear of him. He was Janus-faced, pretending to be polite and God-fearing and pious but ready to stick the knife in your back. I know that he reported whatever the editor-in-chief said, word-for-word, to the Reddys. Especially to Babloo Jubilee Reddy.'

'You kept your distance from him?'

'Yes, and what a wise decision in retrospect. Considering his fetish for paayasam.'

'Speaking of the editor-in-chief, how was your relationship with Mr Borkataki?'

Canning squirmed. 'Well, he was my boss. Brilliant fellow, but very strict. Focused on work and the paper. An intellectual. Every day, I learned something new and profound from him. A bit foul-mouthed at times. Do you know what he said about the vice president's girlfriend?'

'We're not interested in gossip,' Mona said.

Pavani looked disappointed.

'Well, he was friendly and caring,' Canning continued. 'Once, when I was feeling low, he took me across the street for a beer. Just imagine, there was a time when we could go out and have a beer at the drop of a hat. Now, with the COVID-19, my wife won't even let me come to the office. Thankfully, Rocky allowed me to work from home all these months. Till he was terminated.'

'I hear you had a hand in that.'

'No, no, not at all. Never.'

'Didn't you forward a private message from him, in which he called Babloo Jubilee Reddy an "illiterate eunuch", to him directly? Isn't that what got him terminated?'

'No, no, never. I swear on my son. I don't know how the management got a hold of our messages, but I never sent it. Maybe someone hacked it. I have sworn to Rocky that one day I will get to the bottom of it.'

'How can someone hack a sixty-four-bit encrypted messaging app and forward only one message that got the editor-in-chief fired?'

'I don't know.'

'Should we get the cyber cell to investigate this so-called hack? Now that we have Babloo Jubilee's phone as part of evidence?'

Canning's forehead was suddenly streaked with perspiration. 'Are you threatening me?'

'Yes,' Mona said.

'You have to understand my position,' Canning said, looking down at his desk. 'Babloo Jubilee called me in one morning. The editor-in-chief had gone to the hospital for an MRI of his head. He had suddenly developed high blood pressure. I felt really bad for him.'

'Is it?'

'But Babloo Jubilee put me in a tough position. Prisoner's dilemma, you must have heard of it?'

'Of course. It was either your neck, or you betray him.'

'Babloo Jubilee said one of us was to be sacked. Either it was me, or I had to give the management incriminating evidence against the editor-in-chief.'

'So you threw your boss under the bus. You could have resigned. That way, he wouldn't have been humiliated.'

'I mentioned prisoner's dilemma to him in our last conversation, but I don't think he understood.'

'What does it say about your character?'

'Ma'am, it's part of the nawab–nizam culture,' Pavani said. 'Being a chamcha is the default mode of Hyderabadi men.'

'Oh, come on,' Sairam said in a phoney American accent. 'How did it matter to him? He was from the north. He could return and carry on with his life. Me? Hyderabad is my turf. I can't afford to fail here. And where will I get a job again? He's so accomplished, I'm sure he can fend for himself. He often said over the summer that he felt like quitting and going to Mumbai to write scripts for web series.'

'You liked the job that much?'

'In the first few months, I was very stressed by the work and the commute. I live in Madhapur; my wife, Leena, is with a software company. The chairman was quite rude, always calling me a monkey or an idiot or a fucking this-and-that. Salaries weren't being paid on time.'

'So, you hated the Reddys?'

'Not really,' Sairam said, drawing out his words. 'They were thugs, and the chairman was abusive, but he could also be warm-hearted. Or so I'm told. The only person I didn't like was Mrs Reddy. Who, by the way, is still alive.'

'Why didn't you get along with her?'

'I didn't like the way she ran the tabloid. Feudal. Territorial. Never published articles I requested. Always obliged her circle of friends and acquaintances. The tabloid matters the most in the city because it is purely focused on the people and well-known personalities. I'm a resident editor, which is why many people, not just friends of mine, come to me to be featured in the tabloid. Except Mrs Reddy does not allow even a line.'

'Is it?'

'Once, Leena went to a bakery in Jubilee Hills and the staff refused to serve her. They said that they only served genuine customers and that domestic help should wait outside. I posted about it on Facebook and many people responded. It's quite common among Hyderabad's A-listers. I wanted to carry an article about the classist behaviour of this bakery, but Mrs Reddy refused. The bakery owner must be in cohorts with her.'

'This is ironic. A turf war among forward castes.'

'She is also unsympathetic to staff,' Canning continued. 'Rocky used to tell me of emails, that he was cc-ed on, in which staff would beg for their salaries, which were unpaid for five to six months. She would accuse them of playing victims, of whining endlessly or playing the complaining game. She told them to find other jobs if they were unhappy.'

'Nasty.'

'She wears different hats as per convenience. If she has to throw her weight around, she is the proprietor's wife, but if someone begs her for salary, she becomes features editor and says she will forward their request to the accounts department. She is a wicked, ruthless woman.'

'Wicked and ruthless?' Mona sounded surprised.

'I do feel sorry for her though. I can't imagine what it's like for the women married to the Reddys. Listening to their bloviating, know-it-all, dime store intellectualism day after day after day.'

'Probably the same as it is for your wife,' Pavani said.

Canning glared at her. 'I feel sorry for women whose husbands don't come home for nights on end.'

'You know this for a fact?' Mona asked.

'Obviously. Their domestic staff would tell the union leaders so many things.' Then he leaned forward and whispered. 'Like about when Rompy Reddy raped Magnolia Reddy.'

'That's enough.'

'If you were unhappy, why didn't you quit?' Pavani asked.

'Oh I thought about it many times, believe me. Yet, one day, right at the beginning of my time, I complained to Leena. She laughed and said she'd never seen me happier in my life, that my face shone every day. She knew I liked being the resident editor, that I enjoyed featuring on local news channels to give expert comments.'

'You'd better not blab about this case on TV.'

'What's with the constable? Why are her knickers in a twist?'

Pavani stood up and loomed over Canning, ready to slap him across his oily forehead. The resident editor looked up in terror. Pavani stood, coiled and ready to strike, for what seemed like an endless moment. Then she sat back down.

'Anyway, Rocky wasn't flawless,' Canning said. 'He once loomed over me in the same way as this lady constable.'

'Why?' Mona said.

'I was making fun of a sub-editor. He never allowed me to sack anyone, always said that we had to work with everyone, with all types. I did manage to throw a couple of people out of the paper though. One was Syed Masroor

Ali, a hothead who disobeyed my orders. Thought he knew better English than me. Though I am a bestselling author.'

'You are?'

'Here, take this.' Canning reached behind to a row of books and pulled out a paperback. Mona had never heard of it. It was dedicated to the memory of Ayn Rand. Mona looked up and saw the rest of the books that comprised the libertarian's entire oeuvre.

'What is it with Telugus and Ayn Rand?'

'Why? Ayn Rand is the most sensible twentieth-century philosopher.'

'Oh yes. She helps Telugu men harness their inner John Galt,' Mona said. 'But didn't she loathe US President Ronald Reagan, the most successful champion of reducing government?'

Canning rubbed his doughy chin for a few moments before snatching back his book.

'Anyway,' he continued, 'I brought Leena and our son to office one Sunday and introduced them to Rocky. I suggested that we get a photo for Facebook. While they posed, he cupped Leena's right buttock. Just imagine!'

'Did your wife protest?'

Canning stared at Pavani. 'In any case, after he left, he's been avoiding me and yesterday was no different. Thank God, even though I'm an atheist. I actually do feel bad that he was unceremoniously let go.'

'Not that bad, I guess.'

'Well, he was unreasonable about certain things. Like Kashmir. The government basically ended the special treatment of that state on the day I joined DT. Rocky joined four days later. I suggested that we support the government in this important decision, as a trade-off for opposing them on other issues. He wouldn't hear of it.'

'His prerogative, no?'

'We journalists are a more democratic lot than the cops. Flatter culture, not as hierarchical. We get less things wrong.'

'That's not true,' Pavani said. 'I saw your front-page story on the Dubakka bypoll. You got it wrong.'

'I was made to do that story by the Reddys. They wanted to make CNT happy.'

'Why put *your* name to such a story?' Mona asked.

'He wanted his name there so that the minister would be happy,' Pavani said.

'And was he happy?' Mona asked Canning. 'Or did he continue to hold you in contempt?'

'Did it make your SSS friend happy?' Pavani asked. 'The one who visited yesterday?'

Canning smiled as unctuous a smile as Mona had ever seen.

'You mean Nageshwar Rao? Why not? If the BGP is trying to take power in Telangana and in Andhra Pradesh, believe me it will eventually. It's a determined, unstoppable party, something like the "Terminator".

'Does the BGP also read Ayn Rand as if it were ancient scripture?'

Canning sighed. 'Who makes more sense than Ayn Rand? Amartya Sen? Communist! Campus Naxal! Looting the public for false temples of bureaucracy.'

'Who you politically support is none of my business,' Mona said. 'I'm here for these four deaths.'

'Even if you don't support our regional party,' Pavani said.

'Isn't it time India moved into higher gear?' Canning said. 'We've been muddling along, and finally we've got a tough leader to take tough decisions without succumbing to popular opinion. To put the nation on the path of fast growth.'

'Indeed,' Mona said. 'So that we can catch up with China?'

'Yes,' Canning said. His enthusiasm waned. 'Are you making fun of me?'

'No, no. We're all angry that China came into Ladakh and grabbed our land,' Pavani said.

'Yes, that Xitler,' Canning spat out, as if he had choked on Sainath's paayasam. 'Duplicitous chinkies! Giving us the virus, grabbing our land.'

'What did you and Nageshwar Rao discuss?' Mona asked.

'This only. China. Perfidy. Maoists.'

'Muslims?'

Canning looked away. 'Eh,' he said. 'They make too much noise. Kashmir. JNU. CAA. Why can't they sit quietly and let us run the country? They'll end up making good money as well.'

'Indeed. Is that why the *Deccan Testament*, the number one paper read by many of the city's Muslims, has almost no Muslim employees?'

'We have two,' Canning said.

'You just said you got rid of a desk hand, Syed Masroor Ali.'

'He gave anti-BGP headlines all the time. Always trying to sneak in articles that spoke of the oppression against his community. Unprofessional. He should have stuck to the work he was given, under editorial guidelines, following the editorial line.'

'Is that the kind of thing that Nageshwar Rao asks you to do?'

'He doesn't interfere with how I run the newspaper. He only occasionally suggests story ideas.'

'He suggests ideas, or he tells you how to portray reality?' Pavani asked. 'Like if the Muslims rally against the Citizenship Act then it is menacing, it is anti-national, it disrupts traffic. But if the SSS parades through L.B. Nagar with twenty thousand men, then it is stirring, it is a show of patriotism, it is done in an orderly manner with no traffic disruption.'

'Facts are facts. I can't help it if, in an anti-government protest, buses are torched and shops are set on fire, while the pro-government demonstrations show miscreants the errors of their ways.'

'Sounds like you're trying to turn the city's number one English-language newspaper into a vernacular newspaper,' Mona said.

'What do you think news is about nowadays?' Canning asked. 'It's an instrument of competitive politics created to feed an audience. We are quite clear that we want the kind of audience our advertisers want, the kind of audience the BGP wants. Gone are the days that news was an instrument of investigation into what's wrong with society. No one cares. At least no one looking at an ad for jewellery or white consumer goods.'

'Basically you gave Nageshwar Rao a lecture in contemporary journalism, politics and society?'

'No, no. He's an old friend. Once upon a time, twenty years ago, we worked together. Putting together an encyclopaedia of Hinduism.'

'You mean, you made this encyclopaedia in question?'

'No, the man in charge threw me out. Someone had sent me an email containing a worm that spread to all my contacts. Without me doing anything. Our in-charge was furious. So, I left.'

'Fine, but what about yesterday morning?' Mona asked.

'Nothing. Some function tomorrow morning at Mahboob College nearby. A meeting of BGP leaders with Muslim women. He was inviting me.'

'That's it?'

'Nageshwar Garu was slightly annoyed,' Canning said. 'He said that even with the editor-in-chief gone why was the newspaper still publishing anti-BGP pieces, why weren't there more positive pieces about the party and its government's policies.'

'And what did you say?'

'That I don't control editorials, that they're done by the new editor in Delhi. He is the Reddys' man. The Reddys are still, at heart, a Congress family, though they are sucking up to the current state government. Until the BGP poses a direct threat, the Reddys won't bother about them.'

'How did he respond?'

'Nageshwar Garu said it would be better if Shrek Fund took over as soon as possible, before the GHMC elections even.'

Mona raised her eyebrows. 'So the SSS or the BGP wanted the Reddys removed from the scene, is it?'

'They wanted them out of the scene, sure. They wanted a more pliable or sympathetic newspaper management. But I don't know if they wanted the Reddys removed with heart attacks.'

'What exactly did he say?'

'Just what I said. I told him of my meeting with the chairman, who berated me for carrying a BGP story about how it was preparing well for the municipal elections and the kind of middle-class candidates it was fielding.'

'That's all you talked to Sankatram Reddy about?'

'I tried to convince him to strengthen our bridges with the SSS and the BGP, but he was not interested. He told me not to get too smart and to keep to the brief, or I would end up like the former editor-in-chief and have my ass kicked out on to the road.'

'What a sweet man. Did you say anything in response?'

'Are you joking?'

'What else did he say?'

'He also said that his wife had complained that I was trying to bully her into carrying an article and photo about my son's school. He got angry and told me to stay the fuck away from his wife and the tabloid.'

'Then?'

'Then I got the hell out of there as fast as I could.'

Mona nodded for a few seconds. 'What about Rao? He didn't drop in to see any of the Reddys, did he?'

'He didn't,' Canning said, 'but his guru ji did. His comrade-in-arms, so to speak.'

'His guru ji-in-arms?'

'Swami Bonanand.'

15

It was late by the time the police officers agreed to call it a day. Pavani returned to her office to type up the summary of the day's interviews and email them to ACP Mona, who proceeded to give her briefings to the senior officers. They planned to catch up in the morning.

Mona did not have a vehicle. It was dusk and pedestrians were thinning so she decided to walk to the Commissionerate, despite Hyderabad's drivers apparent and wrongful presumption that they had the right of way over pedestrians.

ACP Chittla Srinivas Kumar grunted without looking up from the file on his desk as Mona walked in and saluted. She remained standing, so he looked up. 'Any progress?' he asked.

She summarized the day's interviews. 'At the moment, the only certainty is that Sainath Rao was an accidental victim,' Mona said. 'I believe the poisoned paayasam was for Sankatram Reddy, but it went to Rao by mistake.'

'It's the timeline that is problematic.'

'Yes, whoever wanted to poison Sankatram later found out that it did not happen, and the suspect then injected air into Reddy to induce a heart attack.'

'The killer went to his room twice?'

'Or stayed long enough to see the tin of paayasam leave the room.'

'And Rompy Reddy?'

'The murderer visited Rompy Reddy's room and administered the same poison either immediately before or immediately after seeing Sankatram.'

'Prime suspect?'

'Right now it's Magnolia Reddy, though others have motive as well. Shrek Fund wanted control of *Deccan Testament*. There's a political angle, too, as the Reddys were pro-Congress and the Bitterness and Grievance Party was keen on controlling DT to effect an electoral breakthrough in the state.'

'Magnolia wouldn't kill her son.'

'I agree. Also, he didn't die of a heart attack; he overdosed on narcotics. Perhaps she did not murder them, and whoever did had a separate MO for Babloo Jubilee to throw us off-track.'

'In which case, who would you suspect?'

'The former editor-in-chief was terminated during the pandemic and had reason to kill all four. Shrek Fund's representative, Mrs Srilatha, had the opportunity. Perhaps

Swami Bonanand could be responsible, though I will only see him tomorrow morning.'

'What about the film people?'

'They provided important clues, but they don't strike me as the type to to murder anyone, much less four people. Also, they don't have the courage or the strength for it.'

'They had the balls to shoot a film while pandemic restrictions are still in place.'

'Sir, they said they had permission.'

'I checked with the licensing department. No permission.'

'Sir, they said they had political permission. They appeared to keep the unit limited to fifty people.'

'I can't believe that's possible, not with the Tollywood unions.'

'Sir, I was more concerned with interviewing those who met the victims than with checking permits.'

'I hear you tasered a cheetah.'

'Yes, sir, a leopard.'

ACP Kumar scrutinized her. 'Whoever you meet after me, and you will no doubt meet some very important people, do yourself a favour,' he said. 'Don't play up the political angle. In fact, be dismissive about it. Trivialize it.'

This made little sense to Mona. The politicians she would meet would be far from irritated, or interfering, if the biggest political threat in the state, the BGP, was a suspect. They might even leak it to the media—which was their business, not hers. She was merely interested in solving the case.

She looked at ACP Kumar who had gone back to his file. Perhaps he had an interest in keeping the BGP out of controversy. She should have not told him.

Mona saluted. He grunted. She turned around and left.

The next stop was DCP Chittla Suresh Kumar. She entered his room and found him laughing at the TV screen.

'Sir.'

'ACP Ramteke, come in, come in. Sit down, sit down. What's this, you again look a bit shaken. Are you going to fight with my twin every time you come and see me?'

Mona was puzzled. She was not the least bit shaken, merely cautious. 'I'll try not to, sir.'

She told him what had transpired that day.

'No worries, no worries,' he said, cheerfully. 'They all hated the Reddys, so they all seem to have motive. You must pin down the timeline. You said Magnolia was the prime suspect?'

'Sir, I'm not a 100 per cent certain, but at the moment she seems the likeliest.'

'Bring her in and slap her around,' he said enthusiastically.

'Sir, I'd like to complete my interviews. She isn't a flight risk, what with the pandemic and airline restrictions.'

'True. What about that resident editor, Canning? You don't suspect him?'

'His motive is weak. Also, he has even less courage than the Tollywood people. Though he did threaten to go to the commissioner during the questioning.'

DCP Kumar laughed. 'Don't worry. Canning only stabs in the back; he doesn't attack from the front.'

'Yes, sir.'

'Do you think there might be a political motive?'

Mona paused. The DCP's eyes turned serious. 'It seems a bit far-fetched, but I won't eliminate it as yet,' she said.

'If you do feel that such a line of inquiry needs to be looked into, please let me know first,' he said. 'Before anyone else. Okay?'

Mona nodded.

'In the meantime, would you like to join me for a drink this evening?' he asked, without guile. 'I have a non-police friend joining me. He sings harmoniously. A male nightingale. Ha, that rhymes.'

'I'd love to, sir, but I'm exhausted. Plus, I still have a couple of visits to make.'

'Of course, of course. Well, all the best. Keep me posted.'

Mona left his office, walked to the main road and caught an autorickshaw to the commissioner's office. Half an hour later, she was shown into Commissioner Chandravardhan's room.

The police commissioner sat on a three-seater sofa with a bearded man who wore a dark pinstripe suit and shining leather shoes. This man's receding hair, straggly beard and pointed eyebrows appeared to be dyed. He did not wear a mask. His face was dominated by a shrewd gaze and a hawk-like nose.

'Come, Ramteke, come,' Commissioner Chandravardhan said. 'At the right moment, I might add. Do you know this gentleman? An MLA from the Oasis Party, the Honourable Syed Imtiaz Akbaruddin. Powerful man. Janab, this is a visiting ACP who is working on the DT case. Mona Ramteke.'

The man threw a sharp look in her direction. 'Is Mona your given name?' he asked.

'No,' she said.

The two men waited for an elaboration.

'Should I brief you on the case, sir?' she asked.

'The DCP gave me a summary while you were on your way here,' the commissioner said. 'I just have a couple of questions.'

'Yes, sir.'

'First. What does your gut say?'

'Sir, my gut says that it's too early to ask it to say something.'

Chandravardhan laughed.

'Is there a political angle?' Akbaruddin asked.

Mona looked at the commissioner, who gestured for her to go ahead. 'It's low on my list of possible motives,' she said.

'It's well known in all circles that the BGP and the SSS, with their majoritarian agenda, were not too keen on the Reddys, a family that still believed in legal niceties and constitutional proprieties,' Akbaruddin said.

'Is it?'

'Look at the whole Tablighi Jamaat controversy. The way they banged their drums about this group, you would have thought that the members of the Tablighi Jamaat brought the coronavirus to India, when actually the first documented case was in Kerala, of a medical student from Wuhan University.'

'Yes, I remember.'

'Do you remember the way the members of the Tablighi Jamaat were vilified? They were hunted down in districts and small towns. Fake videos were spread of men spitting, saying it was infected Tablighi Jamaat members who were deliberately spreading the coronavirus. It was turned into a Muslim disease. The only true disease in India right now is majoritarianism.'

'One could assume, then, that the BGP and SSS would want the number one paper in the city, *Deccan Testament*, under their control?' Commissioner Chandravardhan said.

'Yes, the Urdu press will never side with them. Not even *Inquilaab* or *Siyasat*,' Akbaruddin said. 'The Telugu-language papers are fortunately so craven to the state party that they ignore the right-wingers. Though that may change if the BGP ever comes to power.'

'MLA Sahib, I wonder if the BGP's political fortunes and yours align?' Mona asked.

'An old conspiracy theory,' the MLA said. 'But it is untrue. My party cannot help it if others in north India call us a puppet of the BGP. We are no one's puppet. We merely articulate the demands of Muslims. For too long, we have been taken for granted by parties that scare our millat, our community, by raising the majoritarian bogey. Well, the bogey is here. And still the prejudice against us remains. Call us vote-katuas.'

'But quite a coincidence that it helps polarize the voters and drives them into the BGP's arms?'

'So what? You mean to say that we should remain mute? Allow the others to keep treating us like a captive vote bank and do nothing for us? The Sachar Committee report's recommendations on ameliorating the low social and educational indices that bedevil Indian Muslims came out during the so-called decade of secular rule. But was any of it, even one comma, implemented?'

'MLA Sahib, some are saying that you are a second Jinnah.'

'Yes, yes. They say I spread coronavirus, I am anti-national, I am a jihadi, I am Junior Jinnah,' Akbaruddin spat. 'But I always swore on the Constitution of India whenever I took my place in the assembly, while these Hindu saviours talk about doing away with the Constitution.'

Both Mona and Commissioner Chandravardhan were silent for a moment.

'I hardly think the BGP would kill a newspaper family in order to have a more sympathetic management in place to promote its political agenda,' Mona said finally.

'True, it only kills judges, state ministers, leftist journalists, Dalit labourers and Muslims.'

'You have a point, MLA Sahib, but I will let the investigation proceed and see where the evidence leads us.'

'Do what you must, but the damage has already been done.'

'Don't be pessimistic,' Commissioner Chandravardhan said to his friend.

'With the editor-in-chief gone and that "cunning" resident editor in place, the newspaper will drift towards the BGP's agenda slowly,' Akbaruddin said. 'When Shrek Fund comes in, it will drift faster. After all, what is Shrek Fund? Another member of the Hindu mercantile class that already dominates publishing and mass media in India. The Banias and Marwaris have always been the most steadfast supporters of Hindutva. Their agenda is more hardline than the government's. And now DT, once a fair and balanced newspaper, will merge into that herd.'

Again, everyone was at a loss for words.

'Speaking of Canning, sir, he threatened to complain to you about his interview today,' Mona said. 'He felt we were aggressive. I'm not scared of him, but I wanted to inform you.'

'Don't worry, Ramteke,' the commissioner said. 'Work freely and fearlessly.'

'Now that you mention this, I have a way of keeping Cunning busy for the next few days,' Akbaruddin said.

'How will you do that?' Commissioner Chandravardhan asked.

'He's easily distracted by local issues, especially those featuring on Facebook. We'll play to his weakness.'

'Well, I don't want to know anything about it,' the commissioner said with a grin.

'Sir, I'll take your leave,' Mona stood up and saluted.

'ACP Ma'am, it was an honour and privilege to meet you,' Akbaruddin said, also standing up. 'I do hope that I get another chance to chat with you. If not, then khuda hafiz.'

As Mona departed, she mulled over what the MLA had said. No doubt he had been authentic and sincere, but at the moment the political angle seemed to be an unnecessary distraction. She had to stay focussed on the main line of inquiry. She wished the politics of the situation had never come up, that it wasn't involved. Whenever a political angle surfaced, a case became infinitely impossible to bring to a close. She hoped it would stay low-key.

She flagged down an autorickshaw. 'Hindi?' she asked.

'Haan haan. Hindi, Urdu, Telugu, English, Tamil, Odiya,' the driver said.

'Begumpet.'

CNT was not home, but he was expected to arrive any minute. Mona stood in the waiting room, looking at Ayn Rand's painting. *How crazy*, she mused. Suddenly, Rand winked at her.

Impossible! Mona sat down and asked for a glass of water. She leaned her head back and closed her eyes. She was exhausted.

She was a drone again, over Mumbai. This time, she was somewhere in Dadar, perhaps over Dadar TT Circle. It was deserted. Not a soul was in sight, not even the cops. It was a sight unimaginable before the pandemic. She was gripped by uncertainty.

There was the sound of tyres screeching to a halt on the asphalt. Mona opened her eyes. CNT strode in. Ushered into his office, she saluted the minister.

'Had a busy day?' CNT said to Mona. 'Heard you were battling leopards in Hitech city.'

'Sir, I was all over the city throughout the day for interviews.'

'Any closer to nailing the culprit?'

'Getting there, sir,' Mona said and then briefed him on what she had learned so far. 'There is apparently more than one person with motive to kill the Reddys.'

'That's true of most big businessmen in the Telugu-speaking states,' he said. 'A completely cynical bunch. Cheating and thieving is their default mode. Instead of comparing who has the most Bentleys, they compare who has siphoned off the most from banks and who is responsible for the most non-performing assets, or NPAs.'

'Only businessmen?'

CNT laughed. 'Point taken. There are politicians who have also turned illegal loans into NPAs. And if there's a family that many would like to bump off, more than any industrialist's, it's probably mine, or rather, my father's.'

'Sir, today I spent most of the time talking to the Reddy family. Even within the family, there was no love lost.'

'The big, fat, happy, traditional Indian family?'

'Yes, sir. Tomorrow, Shrek Fund's head honcho is arriving. He should help clarify some points. I'll also be talking to other businessmen who were at the DT office yesterday morning,' Mona said and then paused. 'Also, I'll talk to two figures from the Sanskriti Suraksha Sangh. Well, one actually. The other's a godman who was one of the last people to meet Sankatram Reddy.'

'The SSS? Is the BGP also under suspicion?'

Mona hesitated. 'No, sir.'

'You hesitated. If there's a political angle, I want to know.'

Mona felt like kicking herself. 'Sir, it's nothing more than an opposition party wanting more favourable press coverage. Apparently, the Reddys were not cooperative, being an old Congress family.'

'I know,' the minister said. He then burst into laughter. 'Sankatram fancied himself as a Rajya Sabha member once upon a time.'

'It would seem that the BGP, too, did not offer him a parliamentary seat,' Mona said. 'Despite the BGP juggernaut sweeping the country, the Reddys remained Congress supporters.'

'Yet they recruited a BGP mole into their editorial leadership. Who? Come on, you can guess. "Cunning", of course. He might constantly call my office to offer a blow job, but we are aware who's agenda he's pushing. That's why he stabbed the editor-in-chief in the back and had him fired.'

'But Canning is not at the top of our list of suspects.'

'Still, the BGP is getting more aggressive.' The minister became pensive. 'And until he died, even Babloo Jubilee was not enamoured by his family's traditional political leaning. He was, like many brats nowadays, an admirer of the BGP for its alleged toughness. Probably wasn't allowed to discuss it at his parents' house.'

'If that's the case, the BGP wouldn't have wanted him out of the way.'

'True. They would have wanted him to take over.'

Both CNT and Mona were silent for a moment. Then the minister dismissed her.

Mona had just stepped off the verandah when a scarlet Skoda sedan pulled up and Gurleen stepped out. She had changed out of her dance costume and was wearing a shimmery red party dress, covered with sequins. Her pumps and lipstick were crimson.

'Your shoot is over?' Mona asked.

'Yeah, I was on my way to a party but had to drop in here.'

'Oh.'

'It's not what you think,' Gurleen said. 'If it were, I'd not be coming to the residence.'

True, Mona thought. Any lurid rendezvous between a film personality and a politician would have to be discreet. At a guest house, or a five-star hotel.

'Come to the party,' Gurleen smiled and WhatsApped the party's location to Mona. 'As my guest.'

Mona checked the location: Film Nagar. She could go. She hopped into the waiting autorickshaw and left for Jubilee Hills.

Inside the apartment complex, Sharmila was taking a walk in the lawns. Mona joined her.

'How's it going, ma'am?' the legislator asked, breathing in a lungful of the evening air that was saturated with the smell of recently cut grass and awakening jasmine.

'Ma'am, please don't call me "ma'am",' Mona replied. 'As I was telling the minister, your brother, there seem to be several potential motives.'

'Several?'

'Starting with a crime of passion. If that is the case, then Magnolia Reddy is our prime suspect.'

'If so, she'd be the rare Hyderabadi socialite who acted on her violent desires. Most others would simply get even.'

'It could also be a killing because of corporate rivalry, with Shrek Fund as the main conspirator.'

'But Shrek Fund wouldn't have an employee commit the crime, would it? It would outsource the assassination to a professional. Take out a supari as they say in your hometown?'

'Yes, ma'am,' Mona said. 'In which case, Sainath Rao, who appears to be collateral damage, wouldn't have died. A professional would have made a clean hit. A supari killing is usually more dramatic, something like a drive-by, contracted out to street-level thugs.'

'Whereas these killings seem to be in-house.'

'Yes, ma'am. The next potential motive has to do with a business dealing. It seems that within the family there was a difference of opinion over a possible collaboration to smuggle in Chinese vaccines against the coronavirus.'

'That would have been lucrative if they beat the Oxford vaccine or Pfizer's vaccine,' Sharmila said. 'Or even the Russian vaccine. They could clean up in the countryside, making hundreds, even thousands, of crores.'

'Yes, ma'am, big money. Enough for a motive. I still have to dig in on that front though. I may get something tomorrow.'

'That's it with the motives?'

'No, ma'am. There's one that got the minister excited.'

'Is it?'

'There could have been a political angle.'

Sharmila froze and stared coldly at Mona. 'Go on,' she said.

'The BGP had an interest in removing the Reddys from the number one paper in Telangana and Andhra Pradesh.'

Sharmila relaxed. 'Both are states where the BGP hopes to capture power in the coming years, as the next step in its southern strategy,' she said. 'But the Reddys are, I mean were, a Congress family.'

'Yes, ma'am. The minister said Canning was a BGP mole, and that he conspired to have the editor-in-chief removed because the latter was anti-BGP.'

'Yet the paper played up the state government, of course, in its greed for state advertising and exchequer funds, all the while also playing up the state Congress party chief, another Reddy.'

'Yes, ma'am. Even if Shrek Fund takes over the running of the newspaper and turns it into a pro-BGP mouthpiece, I'm doubtful that a national political party would go so far as to murder a family. They're just not that important in the larger scheme of things. They weren't posing an immediate threat to a top BGP functionary, unlike a certain judge back home.'

'And yet my brother was excited over the prospect of the BGP as a suspect?'

'Yes, ma'am. I'm to interview two people connected with the party's mothership, the SSS, tomorrow morning.'

'Indeed,' Sharmila said. 'And that's not all.'

'No?'

'I'm sure that when you look into the Reddys' cricket interests, you'll find yet another angle.'

'Is it, ma'am? I will be talking to Richard Lessness, hopefully tomorrow. Before he returns to Australia.'

'It's interesting that given so many varying possible motives, there is only one thread that could tie them together.'

'Ma'am?'

'Who would find it easy to be at the centre of all these different strands of activity involving the Reddys? Cricket, corporate, commercial? Even Magnolia Reddy, despite the wallflower that she is.'

'Who, ma'am?'

'As much as you might not like to hear this, the common thread might be politics. I am saying to you that for all these diverse strands, it might be a politician or a political party that is the common thread.'

Sharmila is right, Mona mused.

'However, I want that whatever lead you pursue, do not go off-track. I've already given you my brief, the reason I asked the police academy to depute you to the Hyderabad City Police for this investigation.'

'Yes, ma'am.'

'It was to, at any cost, keep my father walled off from your investigation. Everyone else, me included, is fair game. But this inquiry must not touch my father, come what may.'

'Right, ma'am. Understood.'

16

To Mona's surprise, her autorickshaw stopped before a house, guarded by a massive wrought-iron gate, that belonged to Rowdy Panja Naidu. It was his party. The guards scoffed at Mona as she climbed out of the autorickshaw for she was not dressed for a party, much less one for the vulgarly affluent. She produced her identification card, sending them into a panic until she said she was a guest of a guest.

Pavani ought to have been here, Mona mused as she walked towards the house, a gleaming stack of giant white cubes bathed in outdoor landscape lights, security flood lights and motion-sensor lights. Each cube was dominated by a floor-to-ceiling plate-glass window. A string of LED lights led her not to the front verandah but down a path abutting the house to the back, a pool party was in progress smothered by a thick and sweet smell of cannabis.

Surrounded by silks and jewels, Mona felt naked in her off-white shirt and black trousers. The men resembled walruses pretending to be peacocks while the women were like Barbie dolls, or rather, Telugu-speaking Barbie dolls. There was a single aunty-type. She was probably the hostess.

Mona spotted Gurleen near the bar. They clasped hands in greeting. 'So glad you could make it,' Gurleen said.

'Actually, I lucked out,' Mona responded, looking around. 'Rowdy Panja Naidu is on the list of people to be interviewed.'

'He is?'

Mona looked into Gurleen's large eyes to see whether the starlet was pretending to be naïve. Maybe not. Tollywood actors were not much of thespians. 'Which one is he?' Mona asked.

Gurleen pointed to the largest walrus. He had a jet-black hairdo that towered over his guests. His moustache daunted the party, putting even the young men's bushy beards to shame. He wore a powder blue suit, under which was a lemon-yellow shirt and a dark blue bow-tie. Mona realized that she did not know how to tie a bow-tie. Perhaps the walrus did not either and had clipped it on.

Suddenly, the background music changed, making everyone conscious that music was playing in the background. The volume was high enough, as if the music was trying to assert itself over the guests and even the host. A Telugu disco number began playing. Several women began carelessly gyrating to the music, joined by some walruses who rocked their elbows from side to side while keeping their upper bodies stiff. A youngster who looked like a character actor pulled the main aunty's hand and overcame her faux-reluctance to shimmy at a clearing near the swimming pool steps.

Mona ignored everything and everyone and approached Rowdy Panja. He said to her: 'Hey, you! Go get some more of the non-veg snacks. Hurry.'

She grabbed his right wrist and twisted it ever so slightly. The other walrus whom he was lecturing immediately vanished. 'Would you like to be waterboarded in your own swimming pool?' she whispered, twisting Rowdy Panja's hand further, triggering a spasm in his arm.

Finally, she let go and he straightened up, rubbing his wrist. She whipped out her ID card.

'Who invited you?' he asked.

'I invited myself,' Mona said. 'I'm looking into the murders at the DT office.'

Rowdy Panja was still sullen but said, 'Let's go inside and talk.'

He led her to a brightly lit living room loaded with life-size sandalwood baby elephants and giant statues of the dancing Lord Shiva. Framed film posters lay stacked in a corner. They sat down, Mona choosing to sink into a plush beige sofa. A tumbler of whiskey and a plate of fried brinjal appeared on the crystal-cut coffee table in front of them. The coffee table was supported by an animal's bulky feet. Mona stared at it.

'Rhinoceros feet,' Rowdy Panja said. He gestured to the whiskey and snack. 'Please.'

'I prefer sherbet,' Mona said. Magically, the whiskey was replaced by a tall glass of rose sherbet.

'Yes, I was with Sankatram yesterday,' Rowdy Panja said, still rubbing his right wrist. 'Poor bugger. Didn't believe in exercise.'

'He was murdered.'

'By his heart?'

'Tell me about your visit.'

'Nothing. I went early. Maybe a quarter to noon. We chatted for about ten minutes. Nothing much. No tea even. Something must have been on his mind.'

'What did you discuss?'

'Same old. He wanted to finance films. He wanted me to be the producer; and he would fund a film or two. Or more.'

'He was a film buff?'

Rowdy Panja looked stumped. 'You know, I don't know if he was a film buff or not. He was a whiskey buff for sure. He was a cheerleader buff, too. Actually, a cheerleader-in-the-buff buff. But films? I don't think he had the patience to sit through a film, even till the interval. Not even if you strapped him to a chair and hooked him to an intravenous bag filled with single malt.'

'Strapped him, like in *A Clockwork Orange*?'

'Who?'

'Look, I'm not from the enforcement directorate or income tax office,' Mona said. 'Or anything remotely connected to the finance ministry or the economic offenses wing of the Hyderabad City Police. In fact, I'm not even part of the Telangana Police.'

'You're not?'

'I'm on deputation to investigate a possible multiple murder. If something was going on between the two of you, which had a commercial aspect, then I need to know about it and understand it. Not to incriminate you. I will not use it against you. Unless you killed Sankatram Reddy and the others.'

'How can I give someone a heart attack? I'm not an up-and-coming actress,' Rowdy Panja said. 'But this coincidence of four simultaneous heart attacks sounds like divine intervention. Like a modern mythological movie. And there's police investigation also. No doubt a potential superhit of superhits.'

Mona was momentarily distracted by the disco songs playing outside. *A dance scene for this superhit film, perhaps.*

'You producers are all alike,' she said. 'Even Raghupathi Pullaiah said the same thing.'

Rowdy Panja's jaw dropped. 'You were at Ikea today? Are you the one who took down the leopard?'

'Can we stick to the business on hand?'

'Now I definitely want to make a film with a character based on you. Have you already signed with Raghu?'

'Can we focus here?'

'Yes, on the condition that you do not sign with Raghu.'

'Did Sankatram launder money through your film productions?' Mona asked.

'I don't know what you're talking about.'

'If you don't know what I'm talking about, I shall leave. But you can be sure that I'll get the central agencies to do a forensic analysis of the financing for each of your films. Something is bound to turn up that will have you paying GST, plus tax, plus interest, plus penalty for the next decade.'

'Ma'am, ma'am, ma'am,' Rowdy Panja roared, as if Mona was his long-lost BFF. 'No need for such a dire scenario. I am not a villain. I will tell you everything.'

'Go on.'

Soon, Mona learnt that Rowdy Panja and Sankatram had been pals for over two decades. Rowdy Panja gave Magnolia Reddy unfettered access to his sets and parties, photos of which helped make the DT tabloid the institution that it was in Hyderabad, nay, in all of Telangana and Andhra Pradesh.

The two of them dined at each other's houses, slept with the same starlets, slept with each other's girlfriends and occasionally went on the same vacations. When the roll-out of easy money happened in 2009, the two began to think big. For Rowdy Panja, that meant bigger films and multi-starrer blockbusters until Sankatram came up with the idea for a TV channel.

'Bigger than Eenadu or Sakshi,' Rowdy Panja said. 'With movies from select catalogues and libraries. I wanted to call it "TV is Maya" channel.'

But Sankatram had overextended himself with his cricket team, his racing horses, his private jet, his planned airline, his bookshops. He wanted to launch a business in every sector and be like the Tata group.

'The ministry did not allow his aircraft purchase, his team was banned by the cricket board and the debts began to pile up. He and Rompy took out new loans to pay previous loans, but the breakthrough never happened. They went into bankruptcy. The TV channel plan was dumped.'

'Tough luck.'

'No, good in a way,' Rowdy Panja said. 'Too much capital investment is required in TV. Too much uplinking charges. And no one watches. TRPs are manipulated. And now, in the time of corona, everyone wants to watch web series. Everyone wants to watch Netflix. So, Sankatram one day said that we start Telugu OTT platform—Teluflix—to stream the news channel .'

'I wonder where he got that idea.'

'His former editor-in-chief suggested it. I said great idea, let's do it.'

'Is that what you were talking about?'

'Not at all. To go ahead with the streaming app, Sankatram first needed to sort out the DT bankruptcy issue and get it back from Shrek Fund, in the legal sense that is, raise capital for the infrastructure and develop the software required to stream. Sankatram had an idea, and that's what we were discussing yesterday.'

'Another idea from his former editor-in-chief?'

'What? No, no. This was from another friend. About importing Chinese vaccines against the coronavirus and mass inoculation in the countryside. Before the Western vaccines came or even before the Pune lab started production.'

Mona shook her head. 'You are a vaccine expert as well?'

'Not at all,' Rowdy Panja said. 'But I know a good business opportunity when I hear one.'

'What exactly did you discuss?'

'Recently, we went on a foreign trip—'

'I thought flights were not operating.'

'There are ways around it,' Rowdy Panja said with a wave of his hand and without elaborating.

'Where did you gentlemen go?'

Rowdy Panja looked at her strangely. Something was odd, but Mona couldn't put her finger on it. He stared for a few moments. 'We went to Tianjin. North China. Near the Bohai Sea. Long flight,' he said. 'We had a discussion with executives at CanSino Biologics. Then we returned, after stopping in Brunei on the way back.'

'What? Sankatram Reddy was in Southeast Asia? Near Papua New Guinea?'

'Yes, so? It was his idea. He wanted to see the Sultan of Brunei's car collection. Do you know the sultan has close to 2,500 cars, or thereabouts? Sankatram only had fifty-six Bentleys at the height of his glory.'

'Was he happy to see the cars?'

'No, the sultan told us to get the fuck out of his country. No cars. Some shopping and we came home.'

'What was it about this trip that you discussed with Sankatram Reddy?'

'We agreed that the Chinese were playing hard to get, and also it was a bit dicey given the recent clash in Ladakh. The Bihar Regiment commander who died was from Suryapet, not far from here. It would be bad publicity. But Sankatram told me not to worry. He planned to plaster the newspaper with positive news about the Chinese vaccine and downplay the colonel's death.'

'Really?'

'Also, he suggested we meet other Chinese vaccine manufacturers. Sinovac Biotech, Sinopharm, etc. I was afraid of so many trips to China. The government could ban us, you know.'

'You didn't pick up anything else? In China, or in Brunei?'

'No, nothing. What if we caught the virus from it?'

'What about Sankatram?'

'Can't say. Maybe he bought something. A scent, or some ittar, or something else.'

'In a small vial?'

'Yes, I think. I am not sure though.'

'Anything suspicious in Sankatram's manner when you came back?'

Rowdy thought about it. 'He did seem a bit preoccupied lately,' he said. 'As I told you, he forgot to offer me a cup of tea at his office. Most unlike him. Poor fellow.'

'How will you carry on with this illegal import of Chinese vaccines without your buddy?'

Rowdy Panja shifted uncomfortably in his sofa. 'I'll find a way, I guess.'

'Was there anything else that the two of you discussed that day?'

'Nothing much. Just that he was wondering how to get rid of Shrek Fund as soon as possible without handing the newspaper over.' Rowdy Panja smiled. 'He even mentioned killing the promoters. What an irony.'

Mona paused. 'Did you kill Sankatram Reddy, Rompy Reddy, Babloo Jubilee Reddy or Sainath Rao?'

'What? No.' Rowdy Panja was genuinely shocked.

'Do you know who did?'

'How can I know? I am not Lord Brahma.'

'Just answer the question.'

'No,' Rowdy Panja said, looking outside at the party that was in full swing.

'Okay,' Mona said, pushing herself up from the sofa only to have her hand sink in. 'Hang around till the case is over. Don't fly off to Brunei or anything. And don't mention our conversation to anyone.'

'What about your film contract?' Rowdy Panja called after her.

Mona thought of calling Pavani, but then she decided that it could wait till morning. She went outside and saw Gurleen dancing. Perhaps it was time to slip away quietly.

But Gurleen had spotted her and danced over. 'Come, join me,' she said.

'I'm tired.'

'No, come on.'

Mona stood rooted on the spot while Gurleen danced around her, snaking her arms towards her and twirling so that Mona got a 360-degree view. Mona felt clumsy even while standing still. She looked around to see if anyone was watching, but no one was.

'I can't,' Mona said. 'Not here. Not now.'

'We can go somewhere else,' Gurleen said. She continued to move her arms as if she were trying to hypnotize the police officer, her feet keeping time. 'We can go have tea somewhere. Or something else.'

She was pretty. *No wonder she was in films*, Mona thought. *Otherwise, she'd be in the police.*

'Something else sounds good,' Mona said. 'Do you live close by?'

'Why yes, I do. Right here in Film Nagar. Not far at all.'

'Let's go, then.'

17

It was almost midnight. The two women were trying to catch their breath. Mona looked at the ceiling fan. Ordinary and functional. Like the two-bedroom apartment Gurleen lived in. Neat and clean, a large photo of herself, no books, framed posters of films she had appeared in, pink sofas and a French press on the kitchen counter.

Deepika briefly intruded Mona's thoughts, so she shifted her focus on the case.

'You're not thinking of that stupid case, are you?' Gurleen asked.

Mona turned towards Gurleen, put a hand on her waist and then traced a line upwards to the hollow under her arm. Mona never shaved her underarms; Gurleen's were smooth and clean.

'You shave every day?' Mona asked.

'It's my job, remember?'

Mona was suddenly seized by hunger and she attacked the hollow of Gurleen's arm. 'Midnight snack,' she said, her words muffled. Her lips travelled upwards, to Gurleen's neck. And then she raised her head and looked at Gurleen's smile and closed eyelids.

'How old are you?' Mona asked.

'Twenty.'

'No, you're not.'

Both of them giggled. 'You're at least a decade younger than I am. I'd say you're around twenty-three.'

'Don't do this guessing in public,' Gurleen said. 'If anyone hears, it'll stick. It'll come out in the DT tabloid and shorten my career. The industry is unforgiving.'

'Don't you ever consider going to Mumbai?'

'All the time. Even if I do, I'll have to "struggle" again.'

'You don't have to "struggle" if you're friends with the minister.'

'Or a supercop.'

'Is that why you lured me back to your place? To get a toe into Bollywood?'

'It's not a woman's toe that gets her into the film industry,' Gurleen said.

'You've got a gorgeous toe,' Mona said. Both of them laughed.

'Just a couple of goddesses in bed.'

Mona turned over and marvelled at Gurleen's glossy hair.

'Queen Gurleen,' she said. 'You're not the only Hyderabadi actor I've lusted after.'

'I knew it. Who?'

'Tabu. She's the goddess.'

'She is amazing, I agree. From the old city, I think. Visits occasionally.'

A few silent, satisfied moments passed by and then Mona tensed up ever so slightly.

'The first night that I saw you, when you came out of the minister's residence,' she said, 'what were you doing there?'

'Can't we leave that aside for the moment? Like JLo and George Clooney in that film? A time-out?'

'I don't know what movie you're talking about.'

'You don't like movies?'

'Who has the time? I prefer books. More intimate.'

'I wish I was as smart as you.'

Mona laughed. 'If I were smart, I wouldn't be a cop. I'd be Kalpana Chawla.'

'How come male astronauts are bald or have buzz cuts, but women astronauts keep long hair?' Gurleen asked. 'On Instagram, I've seen several with their hair down. It never seems to fly up in zero gravity.'

'You follow women astronauts on social media?'

'Why? Should I only follow actors from all of India's film industries?'

'Is your minister on social media?'

'Of course. All the time inaugurating something, or meeting with party workers, or with his dad. The chief minister.'

Mona reached over Gurleen's bosom, to the side table, and grabbed her phone. She opened the app and searched for CNT. *There he was*!

'What boring photos, na?' Gurleen said, examining the back of her hands.

'I might fall asleep looking at them,' Mona said, scrolling down.

Then she stopped. A photo intrigued her. She took a screenshot, lest it was deleted in the near future.

Mona scrolled some more and then went to Gurleen's account. She had no photos with the minister. Mona sighed, put the phone down and turned so that she and Gurleen were face to face.

'What were you doing there yesterday? And this evening?'

Gurleen told Mona her story. The minister had helped her get a break in Tollywood. They had been good friends for a while and then he, unsurprisingly, had moved on. But not until she had a solid foot in the industry with several signings under her belt and a superhit. He moved on not for her sake, but for his own. He did not want to be embroiled in a film industry scandal, especially considering how the BGP was going after actors all over the country.

'How did you bear all this?' Mona asked.

'I meditate.'

'Do you meditate while doing yoga?'

'That of course, but I meant during ...'

Mona felt a little uncomfortable. Interrogation was her forte, but not in intimate quarters. 'How many surya namaskars do you do?'

'What? Why do you ask?'

'I read that back when she was size zero, Kareena did 100 surya namaskars a day.'

'Maybe I should, too.'

'If it's over, why do you keep meeting him?' Mona asked. 'Not for meditation, obviously.'

'He phoned me some months back, just before the coronavirus hit India. He'd heard I was close to Babloo Jubilee Reddy.'

'How did he hear that?'

'Not that BJ and I were close in any way though. It was after BJ bought me a taser and called me to pick it up. I don't know how, but CNT knew. He never told me. Neither did BJ. Maybe it was through someone at the airport. Maybe it was BJ himself, but I doubt it.'

'Why is that?'

Gurleen said nothing and looked away.

'Are you scared of the minister?' Mona asked.

Gurleen nodded.

'Don't worry, I'm here to protect you,' Mona said. 'He can't touch or harm you. Trust me.'

'He can end my film career.'

'In which case, it will be time for you to move to Mumbai. You stay with me. I'll look after you while you're "struggling". I'll introduce you to a couple of my contacts. Nothing big.'

Gurleen looked back at her, a little apprehensive.

'The minister asked me to spy on BJ,' she said finally.

Mona was taken aback.

'What? Spy? How?'

'Nothing like Carrie Mathison.'

'Who?'

Gurleen's expression relaxed. 'When this case is over, you have to spend time watching stuff with me.'

'Okay.' Mona smiled as her mind raced to process the information and its implications.

'Just to keep him informed on who BJ met at his farmhouse. What he spoke about. His plans.'

'I thought you didn't meet BJ much, especially during the pandemic.'

Gurleen bit her lower lip. 'He sent a car with the DT sticker on it,' she said. 'The cops never stopped us.'

'So, you lied to me?'

'What else could I do when it concerns a minister?'

This was true. Mona backed off.

'What meetings did he take interest in?'

'The ones he was most interested in were about this cricketer who flew in from Australia as soon as the lockdown lifted.'

'Richard Lessness?'

'Yes. He and BJ really liked each other's company. They talked about online gambling. The minister was keen to hear about that. And about some court judgment. DT had sued the cricket board for suspending its one-day team. Both Richard and BJ talked about the big pay-off that would surely come.'

'How much?'

'I don't remember. Then there was Maximillian Reddy, who came to the farmhouse to meet Rompy Reddy, not BJ.

I never heard what they spoke about. They were suspicious of everyone. The minister was quite keen to know whenever they met.'

'What else?'

'The minister was keen to hear about the internal struggle at DT, any conversation about support for the BGP. He laughed and said the BGP would get nowhere in the state. Still, he wanted to know what BJ thought about the newspaper's traditional political stand.'

Mona looked at Gurleen.

'I would meet the minister for a few minutes every day and brief him about the latest information. Yesterday I told him about my meeting with BJ. This evening, I told him about you.'

'Me?'

'Yes, he wanted to know what kind of questions you asked me. He was amazed that you tasered a leopard.'

'Why, in fact, did you go to BJ's office yesterday?' Mona asked.

Gurleen looked embarrassed. 'To get a vial of cocaine from him.'

'What?' Mona said, alarmed. 'You didn't use it, I hope?'

'We did. At the party.'

'Who all did it?'

'Many people. I took it. My pal Samantha took it. Even Rowdy Panja Sir took it.'

'You took it?' Mona looked at her, furious. 'Is that what this thing here, tonight, is all about?'

'No. Tonight is good, it's awesome. You're awesome. The only thing that's not awesome is that I'm now coming down with something. Feeling a terrible headache coming on.'

Gurleen got out of bed and headed to the bathroom. Mona did not want to know whether she was looking for Calpol or for an opioid. She mulled over what Gurleen had said.

If the cocaine was not fatal, then it did not kill BJ. But he had high levels in his blood. Plus, his body had the sign of intravenous entry. Was it something else? It could not have been the toxin ... that would have shown up. Was there something else?

She would have to wake up early and ask Dr Dharma. She would have to call Pavani as well about checking up on a couple of things.

'Are you going to arrest me?' Gurleen said, peeking out of the bathroom.

'What good will that do?'

'I don't know. When I told the minister, he said he would tell Sub-Inspector Pavani to arrest me.'

'Pavani?' Mona said. 'He probably meant he would tell me.'

'No, Pavani,' Gurleen said, emerging from the bathroom and getting back into bed. 'He speaks to her every evening. You came much later. Didn't you know that?'

18

The third day of the investigation dawned.

The shock took time to wear off. Gurleen had tried to help, but Mona could not relax. It had been of no use. Gurleen had turned off the lamp and turned over and begun snoring lightly within minutes. Mona had listened to the periodic rasp and gradually fallen off the precipice into sleep.

She woke up with a jerk. She had been a drone again, flying over Mumbai, feeling utter panic. She couldn't seem to remember where she had been. Near a deserted Worli Naka, perhaps? The emptiness of the roads had deepened her panic.

Then there was a ping. She looked at her phone and saw a message notification. Pavani had fixed a morning meeting with Richard Lessness at Uppal.

'Uppal?' Mona messaged back.

'Rajiv Gandhi International Stadium. Where the cricket team, Deccan Terminators, used to play. Home of the Hyderabad Cricket Association.'

'When?'

'Nine. Plenty of time to finish and head over to Mahboob College for a BGP Mahila Manch meeting that Bonanand and Rao will attend.'

Mona felt sleep-deprived looking at Gurleen, who was still snoring in the exact manner and position as a few hours ago.

Mona pulled the blanket down slowly and lightly pressed her face against Gurleen's smooth, wondrous back. She did not want to go see an Australian cricket player. She only wished to return to sleep. Or spend all morning in bed.

Gurleen woke up with a jolt. 'Fuck,' she wailed. 'Six a.m.'

'It's still early.'

'Are you kidding? I have to drink an entire copper jug of water. Then yoga. Then the treadmill and the weights. Then shower and at least two hours with my make-up. Coffee. Maybe I'll put make-up on at the location. Still, I have to do the foundation. Might as well do the whole thing here. Second coffee. And what do I wear? Fuck! Fuck! Fuck!'

'Oh well!' Mona groaned. There was no evading the day ahead. First thing she would do is call ACP Sandesh Solvekar to help clarify a few things. He could make a few phone calls. Solvekar Sir was trustworthy; also, he was not from Hyderabad.

Mona showered and ate some papaya, toast and fried egg, while Gurleen did her surya namaskars. 'I never imagined that a cop would spy on another cop,' Mona said.

'In India? Are you kidding? Who says "no" to a minister?'

'Still.'

'I wouldn't see it as something personal against you,' Gurleen said, halting her stretch. 'She's a local.'

'You're not a local.'

'Yeah, but she has to continue her career here. You just air-dropped in. You will leave once this is over; you will go back home. For her, this is home. So, if the minister, or her commissioner, ask her to keep them informally updated, she has no choice.'

'She could have told me.'

'And what? You would have done what? Has she interfered with your investigation? Doesn't she do whatever you tell her to?'

'Okay, I'm off.' Mona kissed the top of Gurleen's head before heading out of the door.

Mona returned to her hostel to change and pick up her bike. At the entrance, she saw the morning newspapers hanging from a rack. She looked at the front pages with trepidation:

The *Deccan Testament*'s lead story had a banner headline: POLITICS KILLED REDDYS. The strap read: 'Four cremations tomorrow'.

Mona sighed. The powers that be were milking it for all the electoral advantage it was worth. Alongside the lead story was a four-column photo of a leopard being tasered by Mona, grabbed from an Ikea CCTV. Its headline read 'Curiosity Tasered the Cat'. The caption detailed the leopard's disruption of the shooting of 'Michael Reddy Eats Hot Chips'. The third lead story's headline was: 'Gops Pooh-Poohs Vax Fears'. It was essentially a Zoom press briefing by Dr Gopal Sharma of Satyam Biotech addressing doubts about the trials for his firm's COVID-19 vaccine. It had a single-column photo of his face where he looked as if he, too, had been tasered earlier that day.

The *News of India*'s lead story was 'Cheetah Tasered by Seeta at Ikea'. A photo of the film unit's hands surrounding the prostrate leopard and taking selfies from various angles accompanied the story. The second lead was: 'Gops Gabs Lab's Tabs on Covid Jabs', a headline that baffled Mona. It had the same mugshot of Dr Gopal Sharma. The third lead story was: 'Reddys' Killing Politically Motivated: Sources'.

The *Iyengar*'s lead story was: 'Biotech Head Quells Doubts Over Vaccine Trials', accompanied by the same mugshot of Gopal Sharma. The second lead was: 'Leopard Enters IKEA, No One Injured', with a photo of the unconscious leopard being carted on a gurney to the zoo's ambulance. The third lead was: 'Reddys' Final Journey Tomorrow'.

The *New Indian Success*'s lead story was: 'Wildcat Strike at Film Shoot'. The second lead had a photo of a bearded Swami Bonanand with the headline: 'Valued Vedic Vax Vaunted'. The story suggested that the swami's injectable ayurvedic potion was more effective than Gops' troubled vaccination. *Hmph*, Mona thought, *Babloo Jubilee probably injected himself with this snake oil.* She alarmedly read that it was concocted from an actual snake. Then came another story: 'Cops' Political Colour to Reddy Deaths?'

Telangana Toady's lead story said: 'CNT Inaugurates More Hospital Covid Beds' with a photo of CNT and a row of empty beds in a ward. He was not wearing a mask. The second story was: 'Gurleen Is the Girl with a Golden Gun' with a photo of Gurleen putting her taser back in her purse, while the unconscious leopard was being wheeled away in the background. She looked fabulous, Mona noted. The third story was: 'Anti-Telangana Agenda in Reddy Killings?'. It explored the Hindutva angle.

Mona shook her head in resignation.

Later, in the parking lot, Mona asked Pavani, 'Isn't the stadium closed due to the pandemic?'

'It's supposed to be, ma'am. Maybe they allow individual use. Privately. Quietly.'

When their eyes met, Pavani instantly sensed something wrong. Mona immediately picked up on it, too. *Something was off. Well, let Pavani sense it.* Mona didn't plan to get into it till the moment was right.

A steel grey Audi pulled up and a tall, bulky white man stepped out, dressed in a parrot green t-shirt and canary yellow trousers. He was bald, reminding Mona of the astronaut conversation with Gurleen. He had blonde eyebrows, an easy smile and blue eyes that fascinated Mona with their texture and colour. She stared until he caught her. He no doubt misunderstood. *Let him*, Mona thought.

'Thank you for coming, Mr Lessness,' Pavani said.

'Please, no "mister". I have a first name.'

'Okay, Richard.'

'Stop with the formality. Call me Dick. Shall we walk around the ground? It was mowed recently.'

'Let's,' Mona said. Pavani frowned.

They entered the stadium and Lessness remarked on the surrounding concrete beams, walls and ramps. 'Looks pretty ugly, if you ask me,' he said. 'Dusty, too.'

'What are stadiums like back home?' Mona asked him.

'Clean. Colourful. You see the steel facade, not the concrete superstructure.'

They came on to the empty ground and walked in a clockwise direction.

'What brings you to India in the middle of a pandemic?'

'Yeah, just the court award that we've been expecting for years. Also, DT owes me some payment.'

The newspaper and the cricket team had the same initials, Mona realized. She certainly was slow this morning. Perhaps another coffee. Soon.

Richard Lessness explained that he was owed over $5 million—US, not Australian—by the Reddys for the cricket he had played as a part of their team, first as a player and then as the batting coach. The Reddys had persistently claimed that they went bankrupt, but that did not matter to him; he merely wanted his money. So, he decided to sue them.

'Here or in Australia?'

'Neither,' he said. 'In London. Ten million pounds sounds a lot better than ₹10 million, or even $10 million. Australian not US.'

'Wow,' Pavani said.

'Then they blamed me for the sting operation,' Lessness said.

'Which sting? India is the land of the sting since time immemorial,' Mona said.

'Is it? Well, some idiotic TV station that broadcast in Indian. Or is it Hindi? They offered one of the bowlers ₹1 crore. I don't even know what that means in dollars, US not Australian, to throw a no-ball in a game towards the end of the league matches.'

'Were you involved?'

'Get the hell out of here,' Lessness said, increasing his pace. Both Mona and Pavani were breathing hard to keep up. 'I had nothing to do with that shite. No way. This racket was like small potatoes, but there was a police case. And what a coincidence, the team was suspended! The Reddys blamed me. Then they said they couldn't pay because they were bankrupt and also because the matter was sub judice. I have to say, your courts are as slow as turtles on the verge of extinction. Not an exaggeration, eh?'

'Sounds like you were not on the best of terms with the Reddys?'

'No, it wasn't bad. We kept the personal separate from business. Though you Indians keep mixing the two. Sloppy. But with the Reddys, I shared some great times. They could be a real barrel.'

'A barrel of what?'

'BJ once took me in their private jet to Mumbai for a haircut,' Lessness continued. 'Can you imagine? To

Mumbai for a haircut. And some other stuff. We got back in time, but I was in no shape to play that evening.'

'What happened?'

'The Terminators lost that game.'

'No, I mean in Mumbai.'

'You know, a bit of fun.' Lessness winked. He then closed one nostril with his right forefinger and inhaled sharply through the other.

'Cocaine is a dangerous substance, forbidden under the NDPS Act,' Pavani said. 'Possession or use is a non-bailable offense.'

'Yes, well, I never took any,' Lessness grinned. 'I just watched.'

'Did you get cocaine from Babloo Jubilee Reddy when you met him two mornings ago?' Mona asked.

Lessness faltered. 'Well, now that would be a dangerous question to answer, considering the PDS Act and all,' he said.

'It's NDPS. And don't worry, we're not going to charge you for it if it happened. We're merely interested in solving the murder case.'

'But I read the papers this morning. I got the impression that the Reddy murders were about politics, not cricket.'

'I think sport is an effeminate version of politics,' Mona said. 'Competition without the midnight knives and the blood on the steps.'

'You're being too literal,' Lessness said. 'In any case, I know nothing about your domestic politics.'

'Right. If you weren't on bad terms with the Reddys, you must be saddened by their deaths?'

'I guess. I mean, I didn't know the HR manager. Sainath, right? I dealt with the team's corporate management about my contract and cricketing matters. Can't say I'm sad about Sainath's death if I didn't know him, right? The paper's sports editor called up and told me that the Sai fella was milking his lizard when he died. Into a tin of pudding no less! What a weirdo.'

'He wasn't milking his lizard,' Pavani said. 'He was engaged in masturbation. With his own penis.'

'Right,' Lessness said, looking warily at Pavani's heaving bosom. 'Am I walking too fast?' he asked and then resumed walking at the same rapid pace.

'You weren't on the best of terms, and you weren't saddened by their deaths?' Mona asked.

'Who has time for sadness when there are business plans? I helped them set up an online gambling portal. You Indians are as big on gambling as the Chinese. You should see the Chinese, all over the casinos in Brisbane, Melbourne, Sydney, on the Gold Coast, even at the Great Barrier Reef. They're everywhere. Spending buckets of money.'

'DT's online gambling portal?'

'I told BJ when I met him that the portal's receipts didn't quite tally with the total activity. I figured there was a bit of, you know, laundry spinning around. He denied it. But, you know, I wasn't born yesterday.'

'Am I to understand that when you met Babloo Jubilee Reddy two days ago, you took cocaine and discussed gambling?'

'Sounds sinister, doesn't it? 'Lessness scratched the back of his head. 'Actually, as I said at the beginning, I had heard that the court judgment came through.'

'Which court judgment is this?'

'Bombay High Court. Or is it Mumbai now? Anyway. DT had sued the cricket board for suspending the Terminators. We hadn't played a game since 2012, and they allowed a new franchise for Secunderabad, the Secunderabad Sunspots. Yeah, silly, ain't it? Sunspots! The Reddys, quite rightly, sued the cricket board for ₹3,000 crore and won. Simply because the board had messed up procedurally. Served them right. The court also awarded interest and penalties, and it came to around ₹8,000 crore, which the sports editor said was around $1 billion. Imagine, $1 billion! US, not Australian.'

Both Mona and Pavani quietly considered the amount.

'That would solve all their problems,' Mona said.

'Well, I don't know anyone who would be willing to part with $1 billion without a fight,' Lessness said. 'The board appealed. The high court is hearing the appeal, that's what BJ told me. Now he'll never see that money.'

'A billion-dollar motive,' Pavani said.

'Wouldn't the creditors, the banks, get that money though?' Mona asked.

'That's what I asked BJ. He said the banks would only get twenty per cent of whatever the court awarded. The remaining, though, would not come to his family as things stood.'

'Who would get it then?'

'The rest of it would go to Shrek Fund. They would walk off with $800 million. US.'

'Yes, and they wouldn't even need the paper any more.'

'That's what occurred to me as well. I was thinking of talking to Shrek Fund to resurrect the Terminators. I don't know though.'

'If Shrek Fund stepped away, who would be in control of the paper?' Mona wondered out loud, though the answer was obvious.

'Magnolia Reddy,' Lessness said. 'Now there's a woman who stands to inherit a gold mine.'

19

Mona's motorcycle chugged down the road, across from the Secunderabad clock tower, from one locked gate to another until she found Mahboob College's main entrance, an arched concrete gateway covered with banners and buntings. Standing at the gateway was a hoarding featuring a woman's giant face with a pinched expression, closely set eyes, heavily oiled hair parted in the middle, a generous application of sindoor in that parting and a large crimson bindi that dominated her forehead.

She was the chief guest that day, BGP's Mahila Morcha national president Gunjan Patel. Next to her grim visage were smaller faces, including those of both Swami Bonanand and Nageshwar Rao. The programme, announced in Telugu, Urdu and English, was 'Explaining recent initiatives for Muslim women by the central government'.

Mona drove through the arch and down a lane lined with students in their finest salwar suits, holding palm-sized plastic tricolours. The lane opened to a circular path in front of an auditorium at whose entrance milled a modest crowd. Pavani was already parked and locking her helmet on to her bike's handlebars.

Mona stood in the lane, looking at a poster where Gunjan Patel appeared to be walking hand-in-hand with Swami Vivekanand and film director Shyam Benegal, when she heard rude and impatient honking behind her. She turned to see an oversized white SUV with a red siren on its roof and an angry driver gesticulating at her. She did not budge.

The bulky driver tumbled out, shrieking in Telugu. With thinning hair and a thinner moustache, his face resembled a wild animal. He wore a white safari suit. He walked menacingly towards Mona, but Pavani materialized just then and grabbed his collar. With one sweep, she threw him to the ground. His head made a thud as it hit the gravel. Pavani looked at the vehicle and the presumed VIP inside and then spat on the prostrate driver. The SUV's engine shut off.

'Pavani,' Mona said wearily. She parked her bike and dismounted.

A hush descended. The students and party workers stepped back and allowed the two police officials to enter the auditorium. They surveyed the hall. On their left was a raised stage with six chairs, none currently occupied. In the backdrop was a large version of the hoarding they had just encountered at the gateway, but it included the prime minister's and the deputy prime minister's beatific faces. At the front of the stage, behind a microphone, stood a bald, purple man with a white walrus-like moustache, dressed in a white shirt and lungi. He was flanked by two purple women wearing bright orange saris. Together, the three sang melodiously in Telugu; Mona could only periodically discern the chanting of the prime minister's name.

Facing the stage were chairs arranged in rows of twenty, with an aisle running down the middle. Half the hall was empty, yet there were easily 300 women in the audience, half of them in burqas. More women steadily streamed in and out of the auditorium, as if they were scrupulously maintaining a numerical balance.

On the right corner, sat a group of dishevelled men eating from palm-sized packets made of recycled newspapers. Out of each packet emerged a giant samosa. The men took large mouthfuls, huffing from the heat of each bite while also arguing with great passion.

'Media,' Pavani said.

Mona sat at the back of the audience, while Pavani went to see if their persons of interest had arrived. Two pre-teen girls in pink frocks, knee-high white polyester socks and greasy pigtails ran around Mona, shyly staring from eyes liberally dabbed with kohl. *Who knew what they would wear when they grew up? Burqas or saris? And how did it matter?* Mona flashed them a full smile that she reserved for very few people.

Mona phoned Dr Dharma.

'Hello,' the medical examiner sang out. 'Where are you? It's so noisy there.'

'Dr Dharma, have you prepared the bodies to be returned to the relatives? Specifically BJ's?'

'His is the last one we're working on, as we speak.'

'It may not be a cocaine overdose that killed him. Not cocaine alone at least.'

'Others took the same cocaine, is it?'

'Some film stars, and even a cricketer. It was the same in all likelihood, but I am not 100 per cent sure.'

'And they're alive and kicking?'

'Alive, yes.'

'We'll go through toxicology right away. Lucky you called. Nick of time and all that.'

Mona ended the call and went back to watching the girls.

Pavani peeped out of a door at the back of the stage and waved Mona over. She took a path behind the journalists, who were still arguing instead of watching the programme. The only word she understood in all the Telugu was 'leopard'.

In the green room sat almost a dozen gruff elderly men. A barrel of unclejis. They were the BGP's state-level office-bearers; Swami Bonanand and Nageshwar Rao sat among them, awaiting Gunjan Patel's arrival.

'May we speak in private?' Mona asked the two men.

'Yes, there is a room behind this,' Rao said. 'I just talked to Gunjan Madam's husband. They are still ten or fifteen minutes away.'

'Is he also in the party? What's his name?'

'Gunjan.'

'He's also Gunjan Patel?'

Rao shrugged. They entered a smaller room that apparently stored auditorium equipment. They sat on four plastic chairs like those arrayed out in the hall.

'We want to ask you about the four deaths at the DT office two mornings ago,' Mona said.

'Om shanti, om shanti,' Swami Bonanand said, shutting his eyes. When he opened them, he found Pavani staring at him.

'Those stupids,' Rao said. 'Putting Shyam Benegal's photo on that poster with Gunjan Patel ji and Swami Vivekanand. A film director, that too one who made a TV serial on Nehru's book. Thoo.'

'But Benegal is an illustrious product of Mahboob College,' Pavani said.

'Pah!' Rao said. 'Go on. Interrogate me.'

'Swami ji,' Mona said, turning to Swami Bonanand. 'You met Sankatram Reddy the morning he died?'

'Yes.'

Mona and Pavani waited. Swami Bonanand also waited, possibly for the next question.

'What did you discuss?'

'Reddy Garu wanted to build a temple. Wanted me to be in charge.'

'Wait,' Pavani said. 'Weren't you associated with another temple earlier?'

Swami Bonanand stopped staring at Pavani and looked at the ceiling. 'I follow the path fate has chosen,' he said.

'You were at Visa Balaji temple.'

Swami Bonanand said nothing. Instead, he put his right foot across his left knee and began to pick at the dry skin from his heel.

'What's Visa Balaji?' Mona asked.

'There's a Balaji temple about thirty-five kilometres southwest from here, in Rangareddy district,' Rao said. 'A Chilkur Balaji temple. People go there to ask Lord Vishnu for visas. To the US.'

'Lots of Telugus live in the US,' Pavani said. 'There's a neighbourhood in Chicago that is called mini-Hyderabad.'

'Swami ji is no longer stamping visas?' Mona asked.

'Swami ji was caught in a scandal.'

'Lies,' Swami Bonanand said.

'People used to put dollars in the temple hundi.'

'No hundi at Visa Balaji,' Swami Bonanand said. 'How could anyone put dollars?'

'No official hundi,' Pavani said. 'Swamiji here was caught selling the dollars received at the temple in the forex black market at a premium. He was dismissed from Visa Balaji temple.'

'Shocking,' Mona said without a trace of shock in her voice.

'What you want to ask?' Swami Bonanand said. 'Ask. Go on.'

'You mentioned a temple project.'

'Yes, yes. Reddy Garu wanted to build a temple. Not for Lord Venkateshwar though.'

'Yes, there are more gods than upper castes,' Mona said. 'For which god?'

'Reddy Garu wanted an Ayn Rand temple. And he wanted me as the temple priest.'

Mona and Pavani were left temporarily speechless.

Rao's mobile phone pinged just then. 'Gunjan Madam and Gunjan Sir have arrived.'

'You can join them in a while,' Pavani said.

'Sure, sure. Lot of songs, lot of speeches to come. We have plenty of time.'

'How big was this temple going to be? Where was Sankatram going to get the money for it?' Mona asked.

'Big temple, big temple,' Swami Bonanand said.

'In Pharma City,' Rao added.

'What Pharma City?' Mona asked.

'The state is building a Pharma City about seventy kilometres south of Hyderabad,' Pavani said. 'Filled with life sciences companies. Hyderabad is going to be the "vaccine capital of the world". Maybe it already is. CNT Sir is taking keen interest.'

'How did the Reddys get land in this proposed Pharma City?' Mona asked.

'One pious property dealer,' Swami said. 'Name, Bharathi Rao.'

'Okay. Why Ayn Rand?'

Swami Bonanand shrugged and looked at Rao.

'Maybe Reddy Garu saw a glimpse of Goddess Lakshmi in her,' Rao said. 'Many believe libertarianism supports personal wealth, as does the goddess.'

'Why do so many Telugu men think of Ayn Rand as a goddess?' Mona asked.

'The world is maya, only maya,' Swami Bonanand said. 'Reality is TV show. TV is the third eye. Window to being the ultimate Brahman.'

'Let's get back to your meeting.'

'What to say? Reddy Garu wanted a temple, said he will set up vaccine company. Made in China. I said no, Chinese have evil faces. Inscrutable. They live beyond Kailash Parvat, like Lord Shiva's lost hordes.'

'When was this temple project to launch?'

Swami Bonanand shrugged again. 'Soon,' he said. 'In Kali Yuga only. I hope his wife will continue it. She is more pious than him. Visits many temples, fasts on auspicious days.'

'What else did you talk about?'

Swami Bonanand looked at the ceiling again. 'I told him to stop supporting Congress. I told him he would get chests of money from the BGP.'

'Are you a member of the BGP?'

'No, but my fast friend Rao told me to tell him that.'

'What did he say?'

'He laughed and told me to eat paayasam. I said no, tummy already like a temple hundi.'

Mona paused. Outside the room, they heard laughter and applause.

'Did you kill Sankatram Reddy?'

'What!' Swami Bonanand shouted. 'How dare you? What nerve! How can you ask a holy man such an unholy question? Have you no shame?'

'Well?'

'No.'

'Do you know who did?'

Swami Bonanand shot a rapid glance at Rao. 'No,' he said.

'Okay,' Mona said. 'Go make your speech.'

Swami Bonanand quickly departed. Now it was just Rao.

'Tell us about your visit to the DT office,' Mona said.

Rao told Mona that he had escorted Swami Bonanand to the office for the latter's meeting. While he waited, Rao visited his friend Canning Sairam. When the swami came downstairs, they left. They did not witness any cardiac arrest.

'What interest did you have in Pharma City?' Mona asked. 'I thought you people were busy marching around in shorts. Like you did last December, through L.B. Nagar.'

'I take it you're referring to the Vijay Sankalp Sabha for the benefit of all 130 crore civilizational Hindus,' Rao said. 'We no longer wear only shorts, by the way, but also full pants.'

'I wonder if there actually was a right-wing conspiracy to kill the Reddys, as the papers claim.'

'The police must have planted that story. At the behest of the chief minister. He's so worried about the BGP snatching power. Trying to make this a Hindu–Muslim controversy. In league with Junior Jinnah.'

'You mean the Oasis party?'

'Hindus are now an unstoppable juggernaut. Our march to absolute power is almost complete. We don't need to kill anyone. We know how to control our voters and add new ones. We will bend history to our will.'

'True, giving everyone the vaccination of fear and anger and bitterness, producing the mother of all endorphin rushes, must be addictive.'

Rao shrugged. 'Sairam is sympathetic to our grievance about the meagre media coverage in the city. He said, however, that he had to play it carefully, that CNT watches him closely. Like Garuda. And the paper needed funds from the state government. I offered to have the Centre give money if he cleanly broke it off with the local administration, but he said it was not in his hands. That it was in the hands of Sankatram Reddy.'

'You and the minister are shadow boxing?'

Rao ignored the question. 'Take the temple. Once the Reddys got legal possession and documents for the land, there would be a foundation stone-laying ceremony. The prime minister wanted to do it.'

'The prime minister is a fan of Ayn Rand?'

'No, I don't think so,' Rao said uncertainly rubbing his chin. 'He worships a Kamakhya temple model in his residence. He offers it a drop of blood every morning.'

'No,' Pavani gasped.

'If the prime minister isn't a fan of Ayn Rand, then why did he want to lay the foundation stone?' Mona asked. 'It's not like there's a demolished mosque in Pharma City, is there?'

'The prime minister wants all Telugu-speaking voters to know that he is with them, always.'

'You mean Telugu-speaking savarnas.'

'Even scheduled castes. They will be allowed in the temple if they know Ayn Rand,' Rao said with a laugh. 'But why should that bother you?'

'But CNT is against the prime minister coming to Hyderabad and laying the foundation stone of a temple, is it?'

'Yes. It is a local event. He wants his father to do the honours and deny the BGP any publicity. He had been pressing Reddy. He wants it to be an event focused not just on Ayn Rand, but on the proposed Pharma City and how his father's administration is bringing Hyderabad at par with the top-tier cities of the world.'

'A political struggle over the newspaper and the temple.'

'Yes. But when Swami Bonanand went to the DT office, Reddy wouldn't budge. He said he had financial problems and needed the state government at this moment. He couldn't rely on someone sitting in Delhi. He lived here and now in Hyderabad. He could not wait for the state elections to see if circumstances changed.'

'CNT would not have been in favour of removing the Reddys in this scenario,' Mona said.

'Sounds logical,' Rao said.

'Who would have been more amenable to the newspaper changing course and allowing the prime minister to lay the temple's foundation stone? Magnolia Reddy?'

'No, not her at all. Someone else.'

'Who else? BJ Reddy?'

'The day before the deaths, a man visited me and said he would re-orient the newspaper and personally invite the prime minister to lay the foundation stone.'

'Who was this man?'

'Manish Manaktala,' Rao said. 'Of Shrek Fund.'

20

'What next, ma'am?' Pavani asked Mona.

Mona thought about what Gurleen had said that morning. Perhaps, Pavani had no choice but to quietly brief the minister every evening, keeping Mona out of the loop. It annoyed her though. *Was that because her subordinate was violating the chain of command or because she was obsessive-compulsive? Was she? After all, so many policemen around the country were lackeys to politicians, without the knowledge of their immediate superiors, or at least with the superiors' tacit acquiescence. Whatever it was, perhaps it was time for a brief break.*

'Find out where Maximillian Reddy and Bharathi Rao are. Tell them, or their staff, that we are on the way,' she said.

Pavani made the phone calls while Mona looked at the cloudless azure sky above, thinking about Gurleen.

Both men were at home in Jubilee Hills and Banjara Hills, respectively.

'Why don't we split up?' Mona asked. 'I'll go and see Maximillian Reddy and you go see Bharathi Rao.'

Pavani looked at Mona in alarm.

'We can cover more ground faster,' Mona said. 'Is there a problem?'

'No, ma'am. I just thought I should stick to you for the entire investigation.'

'You have.'

'Ma'am, I'm grateful for it. Being on this case with you, a decorated officer who rose through the ranks, not just the ranks of the police but also our society, is of advantage to me. Just being on this case helps my career.'

'Don't get too caught up in the hype.'

'It's true, ma'am. My batchmates and other colleagues are envious. Each and every one. One sub-inspector, Mukundan, even asked if I would also go to the police academy. I laughed. This case, with you, is a giant step for me.'

Mona sighed. 'Well then, earn the giant step,' she said. 'You know this case sufficiently well by now. Use that in your interview. I'll listen to your recording later.'

'Yes, ma'am.'

They mounted their motorcycles and Mona followed Pavani out of the Mahboob College campus. At the main road, she watched Pavani turn left and then waited for her motorcycle to be out of sight. Mona turned right, went around the clock tower and headed back to the DT office.

At the bottom of the building, still on her motorcycle, she summoned the receptionist. 'Please call Ravi here,' she told the receptionist.

Within moments, the peon came running down the stairs and saluted Mona.

'No need to salute,' she said. He saluted again in response. Mona gave up. 'Is there anything from the list of visitors that you omitted to tell us on the day of the deaths?' she asked both Ravi and the receptionist.

'Whatever SI Ma'am told you,' the receptionist said.

Mona scrutinized her. 'Take my number down,' she said. 'Call me if you notice or remember anything I should know.'

Ravi took out his worn ancient mobile phone and keyed in her number. Mona checked, made him call her, saved his number and then left the DT compound. With the GPS's help, she proceeded towards Jubilee Hills.

Fifty minutes later, she was parking against the outer wall of a grand stone mansion with Doric columns. She thought such columns looked comical in desi homes. *As if Homer was inside, ready to turn her interrogation into a Socratic dialogue, when in reality the house would be a warehouse for ill-gotten wealth, concealed income and tax evasion.*

A battery of private security guards stood inside the gate and outside the portico. A fleet of cars lined the gravel driveway. Mona felt that these tall and bulky men in charcoal safari suits were eying her as she walked down. She was shown inside by a neat, quiet man in a white safari suit, who showed her into the living room that smelled of leather and polish.

As she sank into the sofa, her eyes were drawn to a gigantic painting of Ayn Rand, depicted here as a goddess with a blue lotus in her right hand, her left hand held up in a mudra with her long finger touching the base of her thumb. She wore a gold crown, a green sari and jewellery, as if she belonged in the Tirupati temple.

'Bhudevi,' a voice behind her boomed. 'Ayn Rand is the consort to Lord Venkateshwar here.'

Maximillian Reddy did not wear a mask, had a broad forehead and a clipped moustache that ended just below where his lips met. He could have been mistaken for a younger man had it not been for the wrinkles bracketing his narrow and wide-set eyes. His short, dark hair was functional and he wore a black velvet jacket that, at the bottom, revealed a bulky and glittery belt buckle dominated by a jewelled 'M'.

Alongside him was his fleshy wife, who had a kind face and long hair that was dyed auburn. Her husband introduced her and then himself, and then she disappeared.

'I'm here to ask a few questions about the deaths of the Reddys.'

'Quite,' Maximillian said. 'Rowdy Panja told me you were curious about our trip to China.'

This caught Mona off-guard for a moment. 'You went to China with Rowdy Panja?'

'Yes. He forgot to mention it.'

An attendant entered with a tall glass of a ruby red drink balanced on a pink tray. 'Rowdy Panja told me of your fondness for Rooh Afza,' Maximillian said.

Mona gulped it down. 'What other surprises do you have in store? Are you going to confess to killing the Reddys? And their HR manager?'

'No, of course not. Why would I want to kill them when we were about to get into a lucrative partnership for Chinese vaccines?'

Soon, Mona got to know that it had started a month back, when Sankatram Reddy had called him to his house and showed him a story in his newspaper.

'Well, the paper he used to own,' Maximillian said. 'He was sore about that. He was plotting ways of getting enough funds to wrest his newspaper back from Shrek Fund.'

The story was about China's silent long march to a vaccine against the coronavirus. The news was not splashed for the pages were dominated instead by Western pharma's race to bring out a vaccine. The Chinese, nonetheless, had more than one institution working on it. The state-run Sinovac was producing a vaccine it planned to call CoronaVac; it hoped to produce 600 million doses by the end of the year, half of which would be earmarked for developing countries.

'Just imagine. And Western pharma didn't know if it could finish trials and get governmental approval in Europe or America before the beginning of 2021. And our own Satyam Biotech? Ha! A state minister up north volunteered for it. Two weeks after the first dose, he came down with the virus. They switched to testing it on the Bhopal gas tragedy victims, without telling them it was a trial and by paying each guinea pig ₹750'

'We Indians are great at cutting corners.'

'Our state government took an interest in Satyam Biotech and watched it closely. It also took an interest in the local lab that was testing the Russian vaccine. CNT probably thinks that Pharma City is his government's baby, that the state needs to give it every boost available, that otherwise Hyderabad wouldn't be the vaccine capital of the world, as they keep promising again and again.'

'But you were keen on importing the Chinese vaccine and getting a head start with our population?'

'Yes. We also looked into Sinopharm and CanSino Biologics. Both Chinese firms. They were keen to sell. We figured out the pricing. The Western vaccines would cost about ₹2,800 and we'd get the early Chinese version for ₹10,000.'

'People will pay that much?'

'People are desperate,' Maximillian said, rubbing his hands in glee. 'There's a long queue. People who aren't in healthcare, or who aren't elderly, don't want to wait till August 2021, or even the year after, for their turn. People with money are desperate, people with businesses are desperate. The lower-middle class wants it. Employers will prefer vaccinated job seekers. We will fill a need. Demand and supply.'

'But will anyone trust the Chinese vaccine? After all, the mood in the country is anti-China after the Ladakh land grab and the death of our jawans. Made in China has anyway not stood for high quality.'

'That's what. DT was going to wage a newspaper campaign extolling the virtue of Chinese vaccines. Sankatram had the editor-in-chief sacked because the fellow was doubtful about writing pro-Chinese articles. His second-in-command, Canning Sairam, was amenable even though publicly he was totally anti-China. Sankatram said Canning's anti-China stand would have more credibility when he recommended the Chinese vaccine.'

Mona marvelled at this ruthless business acumen.

'Now you are going to be naive,' Maximillian said, reading her thoughts. 'We're trying to bring medicine for our countrymen, and you are thinking of us as arms dealers or drug traffickers. Or billionaires who terminate people's jobs during the pandemic while still earning billions more.'

'I do not judge businessmen conducting transactions. But there is an element of smuggling here.'

'The government has not banned the import of Chinese pharmaceuticals; it has only banned TikTok. No one can accuse us of smuggling.'

They were interrupted by a phone call. Maximillian stood up, went to the far corner of the room and spoke in Telugu. Mona stared at Ayn Rand as Bhudevi.

'Sorry, where were we?' Maximillian said after his call ended.

'Tell me about the China trip.'

'Yes, why not. We went about six weeks back ... in September. We went in my jet to Tianjin. Stopped in

Beijing, at the head office. Met the executives, who were forthcoming except when we offered them guinea pigs for trials. They said they had already tied up with companies in Brazil and South Africa. Not in Pakistan though. The SinoVac looked like our breakthrough thanks to our contact with a top executive. We were on the verge of making the payment towards the first consignment.'

'How?'

Maximillian looked at her. 'Are these details relevant?'

'Yes, but I won't put it on record. And I won't go after you on the commercial transactions.'

'Anyway Sankatram is dead. It doesn't matter that he was going to arrange the money he had kept abroad, far from the prying eyes of the banks to whom DT was indebted.'

Maximillian told Mona about how they had concocted an elaborate money trail whose essential elements were that he, Sankatram and Rowdy Panja were partners. Rowdy Panja was to provide the front company, Sankatram was to offer the seed money and Maximillian was to be the shield against enforcement or other 'difficulties'. They planned to split the profits, but then Sankatram died. The venture was doomed to fail even before it got off the ground.

'No one is sadder than me over Sankatram's death,' Maximillian said. 'I'm now thinking I'll fund the import myself. I could have done that at the beginning, but it was Sankatram's idea. I was happy to go along.'

'Perhaps it was convenient for you to have him out of the way.'

'Don't be silly. That's like saying Western Big Pharma conspired to kill him and his HR manager. Ludicrous.'

Maximillian was telling the truth. He looked at Ayn Rand's painting.

'What about the temple?' Mona asked.

'Oh, that was part of the cover. The registered address for the importing entity was part of Rompy Reddy's Waiting for Godown Pvt. Ltd. Sankatram said it would help him launder more of their stash abroad. We agreed that what India lacked was a temple to the greatest woman who ever walked the Earth. Ayn Rand. The state granted the land and the paperwork was to be done the very day that the Reddys died.'

'Seems so businesslike.'

'Perhaps. The BGP also showed interest in the temple. That was perhaps not to the state government's liking. I don't know where that matter is stuck. Perhaps the BGP is still interested.'

'They are,' Mona said. And then, on a hunch, she volunteered, 'Probably they will rope in Magnolia Reddy.'

Maximillian stared at her. 'What do you mean they will rope her in? This whole thing was her idea, not Sankatram's. It was her brainchild. She's the one who roped the rest of us in through her late husband.'

21

Pavani messaged Mona for lunch. They met in Ameerpet, at a Rayalseema eatery where Mona had a non-vegetarian thali whose spiciness cleared her head of all who-did-its. As she ate, she listened to the recording of Pavani's interview with Bharathi Rao. Pavani, meanwhile, listened to Mona's meeting with Maximillian Reddy.

Pavani had done a good job. She had the makings of a superb detective, but this only made it harder for Mona to fathom why she was reporting to CNT. Perhaps such compulsion grew in an inverse proportion to the city or town you served in.

Bharathi Rao's testimony was useful. It laid out the plan that had been put in place to obtain land in the heart of Pharma City for the construction of the Ayn Rand temple, which was also to serve as the hub for the import and distribution of the Chinese vaccine against COVID-19. He did not hesitate to inform the police that he had met Rompy Reddy briefly to show him the registration papers in the name of Waiting for Godown Pvt. Ltd and to apprise him of the construction schedule.

Rao had not, however, spoken of CNT's role in facilitating the land allotment, or registry, or the permit for the temple construction—even though these were processed far more rapidly than it would ordinarily. Pavani had not pressed him on this point either.

Mona looked at Pavani as she put a scoop of ragi, doused with ghee and mutton curry into her mouth, her concentration on Maximillian's sonorous voice.

The interesting part was how Bharathi Rao had managed to buy the land—by swapping another piece of land that the Reddys held in benami in another part of outer Hyderabad.

'They had lots of property around the state, in coastal Andhra and across the country,' Bharathi had told Pavani. 'What happens to all that now is worth seeing. If Magnolia Reddy begins claiming any of it—'

'Assuming she knows about any of the properties under fake titles and registries,' Pavani had quickly added.

'Exactly. Assuming she knows and begins to claim them, the banks will swoop down on her and snatch each property for realizing the Reddys' debts.'

'She needs someone smart to advise her and dispose of the properties should she need liquidity.'

'Exactly, Rao had said. 'That, however, is not me.'

'I don't believe you.'

Bharathi Rao had also said that Rompy Reddy did not look as if he was going to have a heart attack soon. What he had witnessed, however, was Rompy Reddy handing over an opened tin of paayasam to Sainath Rao, who had come to his room for a signature relating to a termination order.

'How do I know whose?' he had said in response to Pavani's query that was not captured in the recording.

'What was Rao's house like?' Mona asked after the recording ended.

'Tasteless as usual. Funny, he had a large painting in his living room. You'll never guess of who.'

'You're right. I'll never guess.'

'It was Ayn Rand.'

'I'm beginning to suspect that it was Ayn Rand's ghost that gave each of these men a cardiac arrest.'

'That's not all. You'll never guess what she was depicted as.'

'A goddess?'

'Yes, but which one?'

Mona put her hands up in surrender.

'As Padmavathi,' Pavani said. 'Dressed in gold and green. Emerging from a lotus.'

At that moment, Mona got a call from Dr Dharma.

'I went over the toxicology report and had the samples redone,' she said breathlessly. Apparently, the viscera sample was retained for a certain period of time after a suspicious death.

'You found anything?' Mona asked impatiently.

'There was a slightly high level of succinic acid and choline, both normal metabolites in the human body. Ordinarily, we would not give this a second thought. They were less than five per cent higher than they ought to have been, given the victim's age and weight.'

'Does it prove anything?'

'See, if they metabolized from a high dose of succinylcholine, a neuromuscular paralytic drug, then it definitely proves something. But the killer wouldn't need a large dose if the intended victim had already taken high levels of high-purity cocaine. A smaller dose would have done the job.'

'A quick shot.'

'Yes. The victim's heart muscles simply hardened ... while he was still alive. His last moments must have been awful. Terrifying. On top of it all, the sense of impending doom given his body's inability to function was probably heightened by the cocaine. He suffered.'

'This is a usable conjecture?'

'I am willing to testify in a court of law,' Dr Dharma said. 'But best will be if any succinylcholine went missing from an anaesthesiologist's cupboard, or if you found a missing vial of it somewhere. Or if someone confessed.'

Mona put the phone down just as Pavani, who was walking back from the wash basin, reached the table.

'Dr Kiran Mulukutla is ready to meet us,' she said. 'Not far from here, ma'am. What did Dr Dharma say?'

Mona got up from her seat. 'She was mentioning some technical stuff about the cocaine levels in Babloo Jubilee's blood.'

'Tragedy,' Pavani said.

Minutes later, they stopped their motorcycles in front of the residence and clinic of Dr Kiran Mulukutla. She had recently returned from her rounds at the hospital and was having a late lunch. She invited the police officials to join her.

'I'll just sit,' Mona said. 'I'm still feeling stuffed after that lunch.'

'Me too,' Pavani said.

'Exciting, isn't it?' Dr Kiran said. 'Four cardiac arrests in one swoop.'

'Must be exciting for a cardiologist,' Mona said.

'Yes, yes. If I didn't know better, I'd say that I did it,' Dr Kiran said and burst into peals of laughter.

'This isn't a laughing matter.'

'Sorry.'

'Why did you go to the DT office that morning?'

Dr Kiran looked at each of the police officers. 'To meet Magnolia,' she said. 'She's an old friend. Poor woman. She is completely shattered by her son's death.'

All three of them silently pondered over another woman's despair. Then, Dr Kiran continued. 'We have a charity function at the hospital, and I wanted to make a special request for a photo spread in her tabloid. Otherwise newspapers just put one staged photo with a wordy caption and dump us on a back page. Shabby. Till their editor or owner develops some heart disease.'

'You didn't interact with any of the victims?'

'I wish I had. I would have told them to stop eating so much paayasam.' Again, Dr Kiran burst into laughter.

'Whatever was in the pudding, so much sweet is never good for one's blood sugar.'

'But we Indians have a weakness for sweets.'

'We Indians allow ourselves an excess of everything under the cover of fatalism.'

'In your opinion, Dr Kiran, what could have caused this series of heart attacks?'

'Hubris.'

'I beg your pardon?'

'Hubris. Not in the technical sense or as a proximate cause. That would be some chemical imbalance or a hardening of each man's heart muscles, etc. I mean their lifestyle. Thinking they were kings, whereas ancient kings probably led better lives, riding horses and having sex with dozens of women.'

'That does sound better,' Mona said.

'I don't think the Reddys ever meditated, even though India is filled with all manners of meditation masters nowadays. If you're going to live a stress-filled life, you must meditate. Do you meditate?'

Both Mona and Pavani were caught off-guard. 'No,' they replied simultaneously.

'Take my advice and start, instead of working so hard. Has your hard work solved the case yet?'

'Not yet,' Mona admitted.

'Really?' Dr Kiran said. 'And this one has been on the scene from the start. She was at the office that day,' she said pointing to Pavani.

'What to do, Dr Ma'am,' Pavani said. 'ACP Ma'am was brought into the investigation after we first responders arrived on the scene.'

Dr Kiran grinned. 'Of course, of course, she's the outsider. Must be head-spinning, all this Telugu being spoken around you?'

'Most people speak Hindi too,' Mona said. 'Tell me, did Magnolia Reddy ever talk to you about the state of her marriage?'

'Not much, even though we are college mates. She's a tough cookie, you know. She looks non-glamorous, but underneath she's tough as nails. Our common friends said her husband was a philanderer, but such men usually are, especially businessmen. It's normal for them, an accepted transaction. I think she was slightly unhappy the nights he stayed out, but she never showed it or discussed it. Not with me, at least.'

'Not with your common friends either?'

'No. Many of our common friends are not in Hyderabad; they live abroad. Some in Chicago, some on the West Coast. In any case, she wouldn't tell me if she were planning to kill her husband.'

'Or her son.'

'How could she ever harm her son? Impossible.'

'Agreed.'

That seemed to be it. Mona and Pavani left. Dr Kiran forlornly saw them off as they headed back to the DT office.

At the office, Mona stopped at the reception. 'Is Manish Manaktala around?' she asked. 'Pavani, please get him and escort him to the fourth floor. I'll meet you there.'

Pavani went up the stairs, but Mona waited at the reception. She had a question for the receptionist.

Minutes later, after getting her answer, Mona went upstairs. As she stepped out of the lift, she saw Ravi. She asked him the same question she had asked the receptionist. She got the same answer.

She then went to Sankatram's room and waited for Pavani and Manaktala, who arrived moments later.

'Mr Manaktala, sorry to drag you down to Hyderabad, but you have some questions to answer,' Mona said.

'Shoot, please.'

'Shoot?'

'I meant, go ahead.'

'What were you doing in Hyderabad the day before the murder, and also on the morning that you flew back home?'

'Several things. I had come to check accounts, to check on the usual siphoning of revenue. Mostly, I had to arrange the deposit of TDS, tax deducted at source, with the income tax department. The Reddys deducted TDS from staff salaries but did not deposit it with the government. This was no doubt to lower the amount they had to scrounge up for salaries, etc. They hadn't deposited TDS for the past three years, so most staffers could not get their Form 16 and were unable to file income tax returns. The government penalized the staffers for no fault of their own. I was trying to arrange funds for at least two of those three years. I felt bad for the staff.'

'Nobody filed a case against the Reddys on this count?'

Manaktala shrugged.

'No other business?'

'I did have a talk with Babloo Jubilee Reddy.'

'You did? I thought the Reddys hated you?'

'I know. I was surprised,' Manaktala said. 'But he was the one who reached out to me a week ago. Look.'

He proceeded to show Mona his call record. Sure enough, Babloo Jubilee had called and spoken to him for about thirty-three minutes.

'Not a butt dial, it would seem,' Mona said. 'What did he reach out to you about?'

'He seemed genuinely interested in turning the paper around. That's what he said. He probably had sanction from his uncle, though he didn't say so.'

'Did you believe him?'

'Why not? If it's for the benefit of DT, then I am all ears. I will keep an open mind to all suggestions.'

'Did you meet his mother?'

Manaktala appeared surprised. 'Magnolia ji? No, I rarely met her. I saw her once in the beginning, when Shrek Fund decided to bid for the company during the bankruptcy process. Then I met her when I came down and was invited to dinner at Sankatram Reddy's house. But that was a long time ago. A different era almost.'

'Now you wouldn't get invited?'

'No chance,' Manaktala laughed.

'I have to ask you. Do you not stand to gain the most with the death of the Reddys?'

'Of course. They were clinging on to the company and refused to let go. They expected me to simply invest money and leave them to run it the way they liked, siphoning off revenue for their escapades and lavish lifestyle. We had a tug-of-war. I wouldn't hand over funds and they wouldn't hand over power. With them on the other side of the rope, we can now win the tug-of-war. Finally, we can get down to cleaning the Augean stables. Fix the newspaper, revitalize it and restore its glory.'

'What about that Ayn Rand temple?'

'You know about that? No problem. I met a priest, Swami Bonanand, on the day before the deaths. He was worried that once Shrek Fund took over, the temple would be forgotten. I told the priest I would not let him down. I was willing to help with the temple if it helped in facilitating the departure of the Reddys.'

'You're a fan of Ayn Rand?'

'That's a fad one outgrows in school,' Manaktala said. 'Unless you're from this neck of the woods. The thing is, the priest told me that a powerful minister was interested in the temple. I figured it wouldn't hurt to build bridges with this particular minister.'

'Did it?'

Manaktala paused before answering. 'Yes, it did. The evening before I left, after coming to an agreement with Swami Bonanand, I went and met the minister.'

'The same minister?'

'Yes, C.N.T. Rao.'

'And you two are pals now?'

'I don't know about pals, but we did come to an understanding.'

'This means that you can comfortably take over the office, now that the Reddys are conveniently out of the way.'

'I suppose.'

'When?'

'I was thinking tomorrow itself. I'll stay for the cremation and then start putting in my people. There is a vacancy, suddenly, for an HR manager.'

'That there is. This means you will begin to change the newspaper's editorial direction, once you're in charge?'

'All in good time. I don't want to shock the readers. But yes, I have to align the editorial direction with the country's current realities. Of course, while balancing it with the minister's requirements.'

'Why is that?'

'We're thinking of entering a cartel with other newspapers in different parts of the country, so that we can dictate to advertisers the rates if they want all-India coverage,' Manaktala said. 'For this, we need to align with them on editorial content. Otherwise we won't survive in the current climate, given how newspapers have taken a massive body blow during the pandemic.'

'But you couldn't have discussed any of this with Babloo Jubilee?'

'You're right about that. But I'll tell you one thing. Babloo Jubilee and I discussed our partnership for the newspaper in the future. Without his father and without his uncle.'

'Is that so?'

'Yes. I assumed that the father and uncle were thinking of stepping down and leaving the company to be run by the boy, though I've never seen a businessman retire. In hindsight, it could be that Babloo Jubilee was planning to rub out his relatives and take over, but I doubt that's true. They would have been alerted in that case.'

'By whom?'

'By Sainath Rao,' Manaktala said. 'He had walked in on us while we were discussing this. No doubt he overheard part of it. Who can be sure how much he heard? But Babloo Jubilee turned white when he saw Sai. He immediately changed the subject. Sent Sai out of the room.'

'And this happened when?'

'This happened when I visited. The day before they died.'

22

Mona sat alone in Sankatram's room, mulling over the tangle of meetings and motives. Pavani had left to write up the latest interviews that she would email, as usual, to Mona. It felt like the moment had come to bring it all together, to finally figure it out.

Her phone rang. It was ACP Sandesh Solvekar.

'I have the manifest from the flight you asked about,' he said. 'Four passengers beside the pilot, co-pilot and cabin steward. Their names are S.R. Reddy, M. Reddy, R.P. Naidu and one more.'

'Who?'

'Minister C.N.T. Rao.'

Mona no longer found this surprising. She became preoccupied with her thoughts, forgetting that Solvekar was still on the line.

'Hello? Ramteke?'

'Sir, is Venus Rodrigues still with the *News of India*?'

'She is,' Solvekar said. 'In Mumbai. I'm surprised that you aren't in touch with her after all these years.'

'Sir, she avoids me. She thinks that since you and I worked together, there was no need to maintain contact with both of us.'

It was Solvekar's turn to pause. 'It's true that she and I were friendly, and that I was more than just a source of news, but when I returned to Mumbai from Gadchiroli the first time, things had cooled down and we were just friends. I've been in touch with her even after I was posted here again.'

'Sir, I need you to do me another favour.'

'Go on.'

'Give Venus a story.'

'That is hardly a favour.'

'She needs to understand that this story cannot be done by a reporter here in Hyderabad, and that her newsdesk has to be sensitized about not leaking it online before it is published. What I am going to tell you will take a while. You'll have to take notes.'

Mona proceeded to tell him the story. As promised, it took a while.

'That's a lot of detail, but I'll pass it along,' Solvekar finally said. 'If she needs any clarification?'

'She can call me,' Mona said. 'But I can't be quoted.'

'Then I'll keep you out of it. I may call you about clarifications though.'

'Thank you, sir.'

'Best wishes, Ramteke.'

Mona mulled her next move. The bodies were being released that evening. The cremation was the next morning. For now, she would go through the daily motions.

She first met the ACP and told him of her conversations with Maximillian Reddy and Manish Manaktala. She did not, however, reveal every detail. She did the same with the DCP and the commissioner. Then she went to the minister's house.

'I hear you're close to cracking the case,' he said, beaming. He seemed to be in a good mood.

'Yes, sir,' Mona said, thinking of the Ayn Rand portrait she saw on her way in. 'Looks like Magnolia Reddy had plenty of motive to murder her husband. She had personal grievances due to marital unhappiness. She stood to gain from inheriting control of *Deccan Testament*. I'm just trying to figure out the sequence of events.'

'But she didn't murder her son, did she?'

'Unlikely, sir. That seems to be a case of a drug overdose. Rao was collateral damage.'

'You're on the verge of wrapping it up?'

'Tomorrow, sir.'

'Fast work. Kudos, ACP Ramteke. Maybe you should come on permanent deployment to the state government. I could use a sharp, smart officer like you. We politicians never run out of the need for a fast-acting troubleshooter.'

'That's kind of you, sir,' she said and then saluted before departing.

Mona then went to Sharmila's flat, where she offered a more detailed briefing on the case. 'A newspaper report will appear in a national daily tomorrow morning,' Mona said. 'I'll wrap the case up at the cremation.'

'Even I was thinking of attending the cremation,' Sharmila said. 'For a friend.'

Mona nodded and left.

She called Gurleen, who invited her over later in the evening. Mona then phoned Rocky.

'Finally,' he said. 'I've been losing my mind, sitting here in Hyderabad and doing nothing. I wish we could go to the Secunderabad Club for a drink, but it's still closed due to the pandemic.'

'I'll get a bottle and come to your place.'

Rocky lived adjacent to the cantonment, in Jyothi Colony, on the first floor of a grey house that was constructed in the 1970s. The ground-floor occupants did not emerge because, as Rocky explained, they were octogenarians terrified of their vulnerability thanks to the coronavirus. She climbed up the stairs by the side of the house to the first-floor verandah where Rocky had set out two chairs. He grabbed the bottle of whiskey from her and poured out two drinks. They clinked their glasses.

'Are you coming to the cremation tomorrow?' she asked.

'I don't know,' he said. 'I was terminated, so why express condolence or mourning? Though I could go and piss on the funeral pyre.'

'Please don't do that.'

'When can I return to Delhi?'

'Tomorrow, after the cremation. I'll wrap up the case.'

'Why not wrap it up right now?'

'I have to wait for a newspaper report to be published in the morning,' she said. 'Trying to smoke out the guilty party. Since the cremation is in the morning, I might as well wrap it up then. I expect that the culprit, or culprits, will be in attendance.'

'I guess that does not include me.'

'I'm afraid not. Also, I sense you're not going to blab tonight. Just to make sure, I'm going to watch you drink that entire bottle till you pass out.'

Rocky laughed and then abruptly went quiet. 'What newspaper story?'

'What do you care? You're not with any paper.'

Rocky pulled a sullen face. 'Still.'

Mona felt a pang of compassion for the former editor-in-chief. 'You can pass on the story to a national newspaper not based in Hyderabad, so long as your former DT colleagues don't come to hear about it and as long as my name is nowhere,' she said.

'The *Iyengar*?'

'Perfect. So long as the report is done in Chennai.'

'Their people here will remain clueless.'

Mona told Rocky the salient points of the story and watched as he called a senior newsroom manager of the *Iyengar* in Chennai. Rocky dictated the story. Mona was impressed as he whisked paragraphs out of the air without relying on notes and constructed a lucid narrative.

Rocky downed two more drinks before she stood up to leave. 'Mum's the word,' she said.

'See you at the cremation ground.'

Mona then left for Gurleen's house. There, they cuddled for a while, with Gurleen occasionally taking a break for some 'gleefreshing'.

'That always turns into doomscrolling,' Mona remarked.

'Not for me. Oh, look at this picture.'

'I want to ask you something.'

'Are you going to interrogate me again?'

'Maybe I'll handcuff you to the bed and give you the third degree.'

Gurleen smiled.

'Tell me,' Mona continued. 'When you visited Babloo Jubilee Reddy, did he offer you the cocaine, or did you ask him for some?'

'What? I don't know. I don't remember. I was a little coked-up, remember?'

Mona sat up. 'Tell me the truth. Which was it?'

Gurleen did not look up from her phone screen. 'Maybe I asked, I'm not sure.'

'You asked. Just like that?'

'I guess.'

'You weren't instructed to ask for it, were you?'

Gurleen finally looked up. Her eyes were filled with alarm.

'CNT asked you, didn't he?' Mona continued. 'He specifically asked you to go and see Babloo Jubilee and indulge in cocaine, didn't he?'

Gurleen looked back into her phone, not saying a word.

'If you tell me the truth, you will not be charged under the NDPS Act. If you do not cooperate with me, I will make a case.'

'How can you make a case for something that you say happened two days back?'

'I have a constable waiting to take your blood sample for examination at the forensic lab. Given the fact that you've been doing cocaine the past few nights, there should be no problem in finding traces of the drug. And then you will be charged. Also, I'll leak the news to Magnolia Reddy for her tabloid.'

'What about CNT? He's not going to sit still.'

'I will protect you,' Mona said. 'Nothing will happen to you. I'm a woman of my word.'

Mona grabbed her own phone and began recording. 'It is true,' Gurleen said. The minister had asked her to get Babloo Jubilee to share some cocaine with her. He had even given her a vial of cocaine in case Babloo Jubilee did not have any. Her cover story was to pick up the taser and generally throw charm at him.

'Why?' Mona asked.

Gurleen shrugged. 'He never said why. And I never asked. I just did what he asked, as always. After all, CNT is the minister.'

The recording was complete. Mona silently rose from the bed and began getting dressed. Midway, she had second thoughts and got undressed again, but this time only partially.

'I'm staying here tonight,' she said. 'To make sure you don't alert anyone. By the morning, it won't matter.'

Mona and Gurleen lay on separate edges of the bed, not speaking to each other. Mona felt as if she was back home. Gradually, past midnight, when she felt that the most dangerous stage of the investigation had passed, she allowed herself to fall asleep.

23

The doorbell rang impatiently. It was still early. Mona opened her crusty eyes and saw that Gurleen had already hopped out of bed. She sat up.

Gurleen popped her head around the door. 'Someone to see you,' she said.

It was Pavani. She held a copy of the *Iyengar* in her hand. Mona did not bother to ask the sub-inspector how the latter knew her whereabouts. *After all, what could be a secret if both Pavani and Gurleen were CNT's informants?*

'No copy of the *News of India*?' Mona asked.

'The Hyderabad staff alerted the minister about this story from Mumbai last night, and he was able to stop it. But this,' Pavani waved the paper in her hand, 'somehow flew under the radar.'

'I guess the *News of India* people must be pretty annoyed for missing the story,' Mona said. 'I wouldn't be surprised if it is up on their website this morning.'

Pavani said nothing. Gurleen, seated on her sofa, scrolled through her phone till she found it. 'Wow,' she said. 'Minister link to Reddy deaths under scanner.'

'Now it's out,' Mona said.

'But this is not what you briefed him last night,' Pavani said. Mona did not bother to ask how she knew. She had anticipated this.

'I know,' she said.

'You're in a lot of trouble,' Pavani said. 'The minister was nowhere near the DT office when the deaths happened. This is not only slander but also grounds for having you dismissed from service under Article 311 (b) of the Constitution of India.'

'Why? Does either story attribute anything to me?' Mona asked.

'Not this one,' Gurleen said promptly, still scrolling on her phone.

'And not that one either,' Mona said, gesturing towards the *Iyengar*. 'In any case, nobody is saying that he's the one who actually pulled the trigger. According to these reports, he only provided the weapon.'

Pavani said nothing. She threw down the newspaper, which Gurleen immediately picked up and began reading. 'CNT behind Reddy's Chinese vaccine conspiracy.'

'Provided the weapon to who?' Pavani asked flatly.

'To you. Isn't it, Pavani?'

Gurleen looked up from the *Iyengar* and stared at the sub-inspector.

'You are the one who went to the DT office and killed the Reddys with three different injections, isn't it?'

'This is the stupidest thing I've heard,' Pavani said. 'A fantasy. And besides, you have no proof to back up your fantastic theory.'

'I don't, but you do,' Mona said. 'In the interrogation reports, all of which you emailed me, Dr Kiran Mulukutla mentioned that she saw you at the office.'

'So?'

'How could that have been the case if she left the office, according to Sukhi Puri's and Magnolia Reddy's testimony, before the deaths happened? Before the police were called to the scene?'

'Sounds like they deflected the blame from the real culprit,' Pavani said. 'From Magnolia Reddy.'

'I asked the DT receptionist and office boy. Both confirmed that you had entered the office earlier in the morning, before the deaths.'

'For editorial purposes.'

'Except the only editorial people present that early in the day were Canning, Sairam and Magnolia Reddy, neither of whom you visited. I asked Ravi why he didn't include your name in the morning's visitors' list to me, but he said he did. He said that he told you when you drew up the list.'

'You believe him?'

'Ravi realized, when he was being questioned, that I had no idea you had visited in the morning. And that you would never tell me that you had been here in the morning. He was smart enough to put two and two together. That you hadn't included yourself on the list that you gave to me.'

'What nonsense!'

'Ravi was no doubt afraid that if he said anything, he would also end up like the Reddys and Sai, and that he would die. Of a heart attack.'

Pavani put her hand on her holster and swiftly pulled out her service revolver. 'Sorry, ma'am,' she said.

'You can't kill me,' Mona said. 'You'll have to kill this actor as well. It will just become a bigger mess. The press will ask more questions. They will link it to this morning's news. CNT will be in bigger trouble.'

'Better him than me,' Pavani said. 'This will look like a murder–suicide. By two unhappy lovers.'

It was then that Pavani was jolted by a shock of 25,000 volts at 3.6 milliamperes. Her body convulsed and she collapsed on the floor, unconscious. Gurleen finally stopped aiming her taser at the prostrate police officer.

'Am I in trouble?' she asked.

'Not if you hand me the taser and help me cuff this killer.'

Mona got out a zip tie-style restraint from her pants and secured Pavani's wrists tightly. Then she took an old dupatta from Gurleen's dresser and gagged her.

'What now?' Gurleen asked.

'A senior officer will be here any moment now,' Mona said. 'This particular officer will also be coming here on CNT's behalf. Help me drag Pavani into the bedroom.'

They waited. Mona read through the news reports, which sketched out a conspiracy by CNT to provide illegally smuggled Chinese vaccines to the population, and to smuggle Shrek Fund into the DT management.

The intercom buzzed. The building watchman announced the arrival of a police team.

'This is the other officer working for CNT in a personal capacity,' Mona said.

'Who do you suspect it is?'

'Probably the ACP. He's had it in for me from day one. I hope it doesn't get messy here.'

The doorbell rang. When Gurleen opened the door, Mona was in for a surprise. DCP Chittla Suresh Kumar stood there, flanked by two subordinates. As usual, he was smiling in a relaxed manner.

'ACP Ramteke, what nonsense have you been up to?' he asked.

24

'Where's Sub-Inspector Pavani?' DCP Chittla Suresh Kumar asked.

'Hasn't turned up yet,' Gurleen quickly said.

What a good actor, Mona mused.

'Shall we wait for her?' the DCP said. 'She should be here any second now.'

The three of them sat down on the sofas, while the two constables remained standing at attention. Mona wondered how long they could wait, and for who? Eventually, Pavani would regain consciousness and the game would be up.

It was at this moment that the watchman again buzzed to announce the arrival of more policemen.

A few moments later, the doorbell rang. One of the constables opened the door.

ACP Chittla Srinivas Kumar strode in with two sub-inspectors. 'Game's over,' he said to his twin brother.

He looked over at Mona. 'Good job, ACP Ramteke,' he said. 'I knew you would get to the bottom of this.'

Mona heaved a sigh of relief. 'You knew?'

'I figured it out this morning,' he said, 'when I saw the newspapers. Where's the sub-inspector? Disarmed, I presume?'

Mona gestured towards the bedroom.

25

The cremations were to be held at Vaikunta Mahaprasthanam, in Whisper Valley near Film Nagar.

'Only the three Reddys will make their final journey there. Sainath Rao will no doubt have to settle for the Bansilalpet crematorium,' Gurleen said.

The media was gathered just outside the architecturally grand entrance comprising two parallel walls in smooth grey granite. As soon as the herd saw Mona, it burst into a cacophony of questions.

'Have you people no shame?' she said. 'Wait till later.'

'But, ma'am, the police appear to be implicating CNT,' one reporter shouted. 'How can they do that? Is it not a BGP conspiracy?'

'We have not arrested anybody,' Mona answered.

'Aren't you afraid the state government will dismiss both the inquiry and the investigating officers?' another reporter shouted.

'No. I'm sure if that happens, the opposition parties will demand a CBI inquiry.'

'So, you expect the state BGP to make this demand?'

'Why? Even the state Congress can do the same.'

Mona and Gurleen hurried ahead, ignoring the never-ending avalanche of questions. They entered the crematorium where three regular pyres were set up for the Reddys. Three priests had already begun the prayers and lighting incense, pouring ghee and fiddling with flowers.

The three Mrs Reddys were there with sundry relatives. A delegation of employees was in attendance, led by the union's general secretary, Ghattu Katcha. Gopalaiah and Ravi assisted the priests with various chores. Manish Manaktala and Srilatha stood uncomfortably isolated. Maximillian Reddy, Bharathi Rao, Raghupathi Pullaiah, Rowdy Panja Naidu and Swami Bonanand were also present.

Sharmila was there with her retinue, talking to Akbaruddin, with Canning Sairam and Commissioner Chandravardhan hovering around them.

Mona waited till the pyres were lit. She then approached Magnolia Reddy, who was sobbing inconsolably, and Sukhi Puri, who was comforting her best friend.

'CNT was behind this?' Sukhi asked.

Mona nodded. 'And he tried his best to have the blame pinned on Mrs Reddy,' she said. 'At every stage, he tried to direct the suspicion towards her. Motive after motive was piled upon her, but essentially she was to be the woman who got rid of her husband.'

'How did the killings happen?'

Mona told the two women about the plan.

The minister was unhappy with the Reddys' diffident approach when it came to covering his party's policies and programmes, especially with the municipal elections around the corner. He feared that the BGP would do tremendously well, maybe not enough to capture power but enough to have a platform from which they could eventually wrest power in the next assembly election.

CNT was also part of the Chinese vaccine smuggling plot. He could see how lucrative it was and how it could bring immense goodwill to his party, particularly in the rural areas. The Reddys, however, were not keeping all their eggs in one basket. They had tied up with the SSS and the BGP for the construction of an Ayn Rand temple in Pharma City. This worried CNT because, as he saw it, the BGP would eventually muscle itself into the vaccine racket.

The evening before the deaths, he met Shrek Fund's Manish Manaktala. They came to an understanding that Shrek Fund would take over the management and receive the cricket board settlement money, but they would have to 'work' with the state government.

With this, a plan was rapidly put into effect. The lynchpin was Sub-Inspector Pavani Reddy.

Pavani had been lured into the minister's circle some time back. She had performed various favours, which instead of ensuring that he was obliged to her, made her more dependent on him. After all, he could blackmail her with the very illegal actions she did on his behalf. Now, it was time for the biggest deployment: for her to commit two murders on his behalf.

CNT had obtained a rare and exotic poison in Brunei, during a stopover while returning from China with Sankatram, Maximillian and Rowdy Panja Naidu. He had quietly purchased the poison when they had all visited the Gadong Night Market. Back home, he had kept it in a special freezer.

On the fateful morning, SI Pavani went to the DT office. She met Rompy Reddy on the pretext of carrying a message from the minister. Sankatram and Maximillian were already there. Maximillian might have recognized her later if it were not for the stroke of luck that he was interrogated by Mona alone. Pavani had pretended to sulk at not being taken along, just so Mona's suspicions were not roused. Had Mona not suggested they split up that day, Pavani would have done it one way or the other.

Sankatram took a liking to Pavani and invited her back to his room. He opened a tin of paayasam. Pavani prepared a syringe of the toxin and, when he went the bathroom, squirted it into the tin, expecting him to eat it and have a heart attack.

She then visited Rompy Reddy's room.

He was alone. Happy to see her, he stood up. Pavani went close to him and then twisted his arm around, holding his neck in such a tight grip that he could neither move nor make a sound. She jabbed the second syringe with the toxin into his underarm, waiting till his body stopped moving.

Pavani then returned to Sankatram's room, but he was still alive. His paayasam, however, was missing. She had an empty syringe that she was to use on Babloo Reddy, to incapacitate him, so she took it out and injected in as much air as she could. Then she found an excuse to get close to Sankatram Reddy. He showed her a burn mark he had sustained while setting off Diwali firecrackers with Richard Lessness a decade back. She jabbed him with the air-filled syringe, right into the burn mark. Though he was a huge man who struggled, he was no match for a strong and well-built woman like Pavani.

She pushed the plunger all the way in. His death throes were more convulsive than his brother's; in holding him still, Pavani's hair flew open. Finally, he gave up.

Pavani came out of Sankatram's room and found Ravi sitting on his seat near the elevator, chatting on his phone. She went to Babloo Jubilee's room, managing to avoid Gurleen who had just exited. Babloo Jubilee was 'high'. Pavani told him that CNT had sent her with a message.

Before he could ask what the message was, Pavani had taken the larger syringe and, as per CNT's directions, filled it with liquid from a vial that was procured from an anaesthesiologist at a nondescript hospital in the old city. She plunged it into Babloo Jubilee. He died almost immediately.

It was only later that she found that the tin of paayasam had reached Sainath Rao, who had died either from eating it or masturbating into it. Which one, she did not know. Why he masturbated, no one could fathom.

'Because it was a gift from me,' Magnolia said matter-of-factly.

Pavani was now under arrest and had confessed. The ACP had recorded the confession and taken custody of SI Pavani Reddy for the murder of the Reddys at the DT office. Mona, meanwhile, was at the cremation.

A cavalcade of cars pulled up at the entrance of the crematorium. There was a hubbub. Moments later, the chief minister walked in, trailed by a gaggle of reporters and photographers.

He first went to each of the funeral pyres and, with his eyes closed piously, bid a final namaskaram to each of the part-aflame, part-ashes Reddys. The news cameras clicked furiously.

Then the chief minister scanned the crowd and an aide whispered to him. He looked directly at Magnolia and approached her. He did namaste and spoke softly in Telugu. She smiled and nodded.

The chief minister then spotted Sharmila and summoned her over. He then turned to Mona and smiled at her, though not with his eyes. 'Thank you,' he said, with zero trace of gratitude in his voice.

He exited, but before that, at the granite gateway, he loudly announced to the media that CNT had submitted his resignation and would join the investigation into the murder of the Reddys. Sub-Inspector Pavani Reddy had already been arrested on this count, he added. ACP Chittla Srinivas Kumar was to take charge of the case.

The press gasped. 'Who will take CNT Sir place?' one reporter shouted.

'Sharmila will be sworn in tomorrow afternoon,' the chief minister said. 'She will handle his portfolios.'

He then got into his car and gestured for Sharmila to join him. They left, with the press still shouting questions.

Mona stood there, not knowing what to do. Her job was done.

She wondered if her training course was over. It didn't seem likely that the police academy would keep her around if the chief minister had so openly indicated his displeasure of her.

She found Akbaruddin next to her. 'Obviously, CNT will never be charged for this conspiracy, though it will be a millstone around his neck for years to come,' he said. 'It's just the beginning of a fight between him and his sister for political supremacy. A fight that will never end, even after their father exits the scene.'

'Naturally,' Mona said. 'I wonder if she foresaw this ending.'

'Who knows?' Akbaruddin said. 'She knew you would stay the course. She must have heard from her friend in Mumbai, that other politically powerful daughter of India. Tell me, who recommended you for the course at the police academy?'

Yes, Mona wondered. *Who indeed? Who put her in Hyderabad so that she would naturally be called upon when this murder took place?*

'There is nothing to indicate that Ms Suryawanshi had anything to do with my posting at the police academy at this moment in time,' she said out loud. 'It was a routine administrative matter.'

'For a deserving officer, I know,' Akbaruddin said. 'Still, a happy coincidence.'

Mona looked at the politician. *Could she believe a word of what he had said?*

'And do you know who else is Sharmila's friend?'

'Who?'

'Magnolia Reddy. They've been friends for quite a long time.'

Mona said nothing. It was not so surprising in this town called Hyderabad, a sprawling metropolis that comprised three cities but was still nothing more than a small town. But it was a striking coincidence in the context of this case.

'That doesn't mean the investigation was manipulated,' she said. 'Even if it was monitored by them.'

'True,' Akbaruddin said. 'But you have to wonder. Why in the first place did Sharmila want you to investigate the murders that eventually brought her brother down?'

About the Author

Aditya Sinha is an author and a journalist. His previous books include *Kashmir: The Vajpayee Years*, co-authored with former Research and Analysis Wing Chief A.S. Dulat, and *The Spy Chronicles: RAW, ISI and the Illusion of Peace*, co-authored with A.S. Dulat and former Inter-Services Intelligence Chief Asad Durrani. Aditya is currently the features editor (India) at Russia Today's website, rt.com.

30 Years *of*

HarperCollins *Publishers* India

At HarperCollins, we believe in telling the best stories and finding the widest possible readership for our books in every format possible. We started publishing 30 years ago; a great deal has changed since then, but what has remained constant is the passion with which our authors write their books, the love with which readers receive them, and the sheer joy and excitement that we as publishers feel in being a part of the publishing process.

Over the years, we've had the pleasure of publishing some of the finest writing from the subcontinent and around the world, and some of the biggest bestsellers in India's publishing history. Our books and authors have won a phenomenal range of awards, and we ourselves have been named Publisher of the Year the greatest number of times. But nothing has meant more to us than the fact that millions of people have read the books we published, and somewhere, a book of ours might have made a difference.

As we step into our fourth decade, we go back to that one word – a word which has been a driving force for us all these years.

Read.

Harper Collins
4th
HARPER PERENNIAL
HARPER BUSINESS
HARPER BLACK
हार्पर हिन्दी
HarperCollins *Children's Books*
HARPER DESIGN
HARPER VANTAGE
Harper Sport